TERMS OF WAR

LtCol. Mattson tried to explain the Rules of Engagement:

"We are to *deter* passage of hostile armed elements in order to permit the Lebanese Armed Forces to carry out their responsibilities in the city of Beirut. . . ."

A platoon sergeant from India Company asked, "Sir, what does 'deter' mean? I understand 'deny' or 'stop' or 'blow the fuckers away,' but how do we tell the troops to *deter* the bad guys?"

OUTRAGE
A Novel of Beirut by Dale Dye

". . . there is no escaping the fact that our government brutally abused the commitment, willing sacrifice, and admirable discipline of its frontline fighting force in Beirut."

—Dale Dye

Don't miss these other electrifying novels of men at war by Dale Dye

PLATOON
and
RUN BETWEEN THE RAINDROPS

Books by Dale Dye

RUN BETWEEN THE RAINDROPS
PLATOON
OUTRAGE

Outrage

DALE DYE

JOVE BOOKS, NEW YORK

This Jove book contains the complete
text of the original hardcover edition.
It has been completely reset in a typeface
designed for easy reading, and was printed
from new film.

OUTRAGE

A Jove Book / published by arrangement with
Little, Brown and Company, Inc.

PRINTING HISTORY
Little, Brown edition published in 1988
Published in Canada by Little, Brown & Company (Canada) Limited
Jove edition / January 1990

ISBN: 0-515-10206-7

Jove Books are published by The Berkley Publishing Group,
200 Madison Avenue, New York, New York 10016.
The name "JOVE" and the "J" logo
are trademarks belonging to Jove Publications, Inc.

PRINTED IN THE UNITED STATES OF AMERICA

10 9 8 7 6 5 4 3 2 1

When the 'arf-made recruity goes out to the East
'E acts like a babe an' 'e drinks like a beast,
an' 'e wonders because 'e is frequent deceased . . .

—RUDYARD KIPLING
  from "THE YOUNG BRITISH SOLDIER"
  in *Barrack-Room Ballads*

Contents

Author's Note

LIKE MOST PROVOCATIVE works of fiction, this book contains large dollops of fantasy woven around a solid core of fact. Most of the events described during the deployment of American Marines to Beirut did not occur *exactly* as I have written them, but there is no escaping the fact that our government brutally abused the commitment, willing sacrifice and admirable discipline of its frontline fighting force in Beirut.

A noxious admixture of political concerns and a vaguely stated military mission, a narrow-minded adherence to ludicrous Rules of Engagement in the face of an escalating threat, and a failure to back commitment with sufficient military might all led to the tragic death of 241 Marines, sailors and soldiers in the bombing on October 23, 1983, as well as others before and after that infamous day.

Although it's an easy exercise to match some of my fictional players with factual counterparts, readers should not presume actual identities for any of the characters in this book. They are all composites of people I've known, loved or hated during service in Beirut and elsewhere around the world. Veterans of The Root who insist on seeing themselves in one or more of the personalities I've introduced should remember that fiction is usually more interesting than fact.

Three Marine Amphibious Units (MAUs) of varying compositions served in Beirut during the American military commitment to Lebanon. I mention the 32d MAU and focus on the 24th MAU simply to avoid reader confusion with a constantly shifting cast of characters during regular rotation and redesignation of 32/24/22 MAUs in and out of Beirut. Also given short shrift or ignored in the telling of my story is the sacrifice and commitment of various French, Italian and British components of the Multi-national Peacekeeping Force. No offense is intended and I sincerely hope those nations will not reflect negatively on their experiences in Beirut the next time Western military solidarity is required.

To the families of the men who were killed or wounded in Beirut, my deepest sympathies. I was proud to have served with such heroes.

Outrage

Sword or
Shield?

CHEWING THOUGHTFULLY ON a full lower lip, the President's personal envoy to Lebanon watched squatty tugs maneuver rusty freighters and bulbous ferry platforms into position beside the long quay that kept the wild waters of the eastern Mediterranean at bay. Despite the fact that he was born in Lebanon and cut his diplomatic teeth on the chaotic menu of interlopers that had melted in and out of the country since 1948, Piere Hakim still had trouble accurately identifying many of the national colors that fluttered from the fantails of the hastily assembled evacuation fleet.

Gradually, over the next ten days or two weeks, the flotilla would steam in and out of Beirut's deep-water port and the Palestine Liberation Organization—including most of its allied and heavily armed factions—would recede from Lebanon to become a looming threat of continued violence from places like Jordan, Iraq, Syria and South Yemen.

Hakim understood—as only one steeped in the turbulent cauldron of Middle East intrigue can understand—that his arrangement to shoehorn the PLO out of Beirut before the Israelis stomped them into oblivion at a high cost in innocent lives was, at best, a compromise.

But then, he reminded himself with some small satisfaction, the entire art of diplomacy is compromise.

* * *

"Dat da dude?"

Corporal Steve Mallory turned his attention from the distinguished gentleman entering the Mercedes limousine and eyed the squatty Chicano standing next to him at the battered intersection leading to the port facilities. Lance Corporal Rojas had a way of making everything he said sound like background lyrics to a doo-wop song.

"Is that *what* dude, Rojas?"

"You know, man. Dat dude dat runs the ragheads round here . . . whatsisname?"

"You mean Arafat? Jesus H. Fucking Christ, Rojas! You got an IQ about three points lower than plant life. You know that?"

Armando Rojas stabbed his squad leader with an icy glare and then blinked away the threat in his eyes. Mallory didn't mean any insult. He let a grin crawl across his face to signal that none had been given.

Mallory watched the limo glide away from the intersection and rubbed idly at a hot spot under his steel helmet.

"That's Hakim, man. He's the guy who engineered this deal. He got the Hebes to haul-ass while talking Arafat into leaving with his troops."

Rojas hitched at his rifle and followed the NCO up the street toward the muster area for the rest of the squad.

"So dat's why we here, *verdad.*"

It was a statement rather than a question. Rojas had heard the background briefings aboard ship with all the rest of the Marines of 32d MAU.

"There it is, Rojas. We're supposed to keep 'em from blowin' each other away until the Lebs can take over."

The grin widened as Rojas thought of how easily his uncle and cousins recrossed into the U.S. every time the border patrol escorted them back to Mexico. "So, what

gonna keep dese dudes from comin' back anytime dey
want?"

"The Leb Army, man. What do you think?"

"I think dat's bullshit, man."

The tinny echo of his own voice over the satellite telephone
transmission was disconcerting and Hakim wished the
President had not chosen to put him on a speaker in the Oval
Office. There were certain subtleties in what he had to say
that could be misconstrued by the circle of high-level
advisors assembled to hear his status report.

He would be asked for his assessment of the future before
the call was terminated and Hakim wanted the President's
full and focused attention for that. Experience had taught
him that this chief executive had trouble focusing on
complex problems with staffers banging at his ears, each
espousing a different course of action. That, he supposed as
he waited for a response to his greeting, was why the
President tended to delegate rather than make decisions.

"Our best guess is that we have some fourteen thousand
PLO fighters to shuttle out of Beirut, Mr. President. The
evacuation began this morning."

Hakim recognized the voice of the chairman of the Joint
Chiefs of Staff asking the disposition of troops. Consulting
his notes, Hakim tried to make it brief.

"The Israelis are generally holding on the outskirts of the
city with the main concentrations of troops to the northeast
between Beirut and Tripoli, and to the south straddling the
coast road near Kaldeh. The IDF has also dispatched troops
to cover the withdrawal of the Syrian 85th Brigade and the
Palestine Liberation Army auxiliaries along the Beirut-
Damascus Highway.

"The Multinational Force is in place with the French in
the north around the ports, the Italians in the center sector
and the Americans in the south around the airport. Of

course, we've clumped all the uniforms together along the evacuation route for the purposes of press coverage."

From the rumblings on the other end of the line it was clear to Hakim that the military wanted a more precise explanation, but the President saved him the trouble.

"Can you give us a rundown on casualty figures, Piere?"

Hakim ran his finger over columns of figures in his notes. "You should understand, Mr. President, that these figures are incomplete . . . and really guesswork when it comes to the PLO and the Syrians . . . but here's what we figure.

"The Israelis lost about three hundred killed in action and about twenty-five hundred wounded in Operation Peace for Galilee. The Syrians probably suffered slightly more than a thousand killed and triple that in wounded. The PLO . . . call it fifteen hundred dead and an unknown number of wounded. Lebanese civilian casualties are devilishly hard to estimate, but the Red Cross seems ready to settle for four to five thousand killed and up to twenty thousand wounded . . ."

There was eerie silence on the line for a moment. Hakim got some small satisfaction from the shocked reaction to his words. The rain of blood had been torrential in Lebanon and there was no guarantee that it had ended. That was the point he intended to make.

The President abruptly changed the subject to ask about the upcoming Lebanese elections.

"A faint ray of sunshine, sir." Hakim felt himself coming onto firmer ground. "Elections are scheduled in the next few days. I think the people's choice will definitely be Bashir Gemayel. He's viewed as the great conciliatory hope for Lebanon.

"The future really lies in his ability to reform the tradi- tional coalition government and get the country back in business. If he can control all the people who want to keep stirring the pot, he's got a chance."

The Secretary of State cleared his throat and posed the question Hakim had been waiting for all along.

"What's your assessment of his chances, Piere?"

"It's an uphill battle, Mr. Secretary. Gemayel faces some tough opposition from Sunni and Shi'ite Moslems that resent his connection with the Christian Militia. Naturally, the Christian Phalangists want to stay in the catbird seat.

"Meanwhile, the Druze are pushing for a stronger voice in government, there are still several thousand Mourabitoun gunmen in Beirut and there is a growing threat from ultraradical groups like the Hezbollah, which is backed by Iran."

"Bottom line, Piere?"

Hakim took a deep breath and let it out slowly before answering. "I think Bashir Gemayel can do it if anyone can, gentlemen. For the most part the people of Lebanon— Christian and Moslem alike—are sick to death of fighting and killing. Our best bet is to keep the dogs at bay and let them get on with their lives."

"And all those dogs are now at bay . . . right, Piere?" The President sounded as if he wanted to get off the line and put this unpleasantness behind him.

"Relatively speaking—and for the moment—Mr. President . . . the dogs are at bay."

Piere Hakim hung up after the appropriate pleasantries had been exchanged. As he left the American Embassy, he couldn't help wondering if the superpower policymakers understood just how much nature deplores a vacuum of the dark, ominous sort that was settling over Beirut.

Watching the two camouflage-clad American Marines turn the corner and stride up the street past the refugee camp that had been his home for the past month, Wafic al Kadima wondered how long it would be before he had such men in his rifle sights.

Men? He spat into the dust of the Sabra Camp and squinted against the glare of sunlight. They look like boys playing at war. Such silly trappings.

A steel helmet in a place where the sun threatened to bake a man's brain. Mottled green camouflage uniforms in a monochrome world of dun-colored sand. And armored vests! A sign of weakness in a soldier.

Wafic believed commitment and courage were the only protection a holy warrior needed. Those things—coupled with the training and modern weapons provided by the Popular Front for the Liberation of Palestine—had been all he required to kill Zionists in battles from the Golan Heights to Damour in the 1976 war. Nothing but a thin cotton shirt had protected him when the Zionists attacked Beaufort Castle, and his faith in Allah had brought him through the brutal fighting in the streets of Beirut.

A smile creased Wafic's face as he noticed the two Americans pause on the other side of the street. They were watching PFLP fighters boarding trucks for the trip down to the docks. The taller of the two men seemed to be pointing at a sign bearing the likeness of Chairman Arafat. Wafic's men had prepared these placards to demonstrate their continued commitment to the struggle for a Palestinian homeland.

He glanced away from the Americans and frowned at the men arranging their meager possessions on the Lebanese Army trucks. Such long faces. They should understand the evacuation from Beirut was only a delay in the inevitable triumph over Zionist oppression, but it was hard when most of the men were leaving families behind in the squalid refugee camps of West Beirut. Wafic knew what was needed to shatter such a somber mood.

He eyed the unsuspecting Americans again and casually

lifted the AK-47 assault rifle from his shoulder. Raising both hands in praise to his God, Wafic triggered all thirty rounds in the weapon's curved magazine into the muggy air over Beirut.

"*Allah Akhbar!* Victory is ours!"

Truckloads of PFLP fighters took up the cry and began firing their weapons into the air. Wafic grinned as he watched the two Americans scramble for cover. Nervous as sheep, he thought. Such men die easily.

When they were sure the burst had not been fired at them, Mallory and Rojas peeked over a low stone wall and tried to determine who had opened fire. It was impossible to tell. Practically all of the wild-eyed fanatics crammed into the back of the trucks lined up across the street were burning rounds in different directions. Mallory thought it looked like a scene from some old Western movie, with the bad guys terrorizing a town, rearing their horses in the middle of the main drag and firing their pistols in the air.

Rojas pointed at his squad leader's helmet, which had fallen off when they scrambled for cover.

"Better get your piss pot, Corporal. Dese *locos* might decide to lower sights."

Mallory gingerly reached out and snatched it off the sidewalk. He wiped the sweat from his brow but decided not to put the helmet back on his head. The damn thing cramped his neck muscles and the webbing made his hair look like someone had run through it with a dull lawn-mower. Most Marines avoided the problem by keeping their hair clipped bristle-short. Mallory avoided that affectation. Coupled with the corporal's chevrons he'd picked up about six months ahead of his contemporaries, he thought it made him look too much like a Lifer.

"Wish I knew what the fuck that was all about."

Rojas grinned and stood to watch as the trucks began to

snort and stagger their way into formation for the trip down to the Beirut docks.

"Mebbe dey pissed off 'cause you point at de picture of da honcho."

To show Rojas the difference between the man they'd seen down near the docks and Yasir Arafat, Mallory had pointed at the poster and mentioned that the PLO Chairman "looked like he had a bucket of ugly poured over his face and someone burned it off with a flamethrower." No way anyone but Rojas could have heard him say that. Not with all the pissing and moaning that was going on over at the refugee camp.

"Nah. These fuckers are just stone-assed nuts, Rojas. No fire discipline. No nothin'. Your granny could fuck 'em up with nothin' more than a reinforced fireteam. They're just tryin' to show off."

A familiar roar suddenly cut through the snarl of diesel engines and practically every other sound in the noisy streets of Beirut.

"Corporal Mallory! I best see your ass double-timin' up that street! And get that helmet on your gourd before I cram it up your ass!"

Rojas stifled a giggle and beat feet away from the threatening spectre of Gunnery Sergeant Harlan Barlow, the man who was bearing down on them, flapping his tattooed arms like some hammerheaded gargoyle fueled by fifty gallons of high-octane kick-ass.

Mallory turned to follow but Barlow's whiskey-raw growl tripped him in midstride.

"Freeze in place, ass-bag! You wanna tell me what the fuck a rifle squad leader is doin' away from his rifle squad when every dune coon in the goddamn world is runnin' around this AO like a scalded-ass ape?"

Struggling to suppress a grin, Mallory popped his helmet back on his head and wondered for the hundredth time where this lanky buzz saw from someplace in southeast Missouri got such a colorful vocabulary. Given the guy's military history, revealed in a gaudy display of decorations and service ribbons on the rare occasion when he was ordered out of combat dress, it could have been Vietnam, Korea, Japan, Africa or any combination of exotic duty stations in both peace and war.

He'd nearly pissed himself trying not to laugh at sea when the Gunny tore into his squad over some infraction. With Gunny Barlow a word to the wise was always insufficient and an ass-chewing was a work of art to be lovingly crafted from creative profanity. The Gunny seemed to have marked him for special attention ever since the day he'd been promoted out of a skate job as driver for the Commanding Officer of 32 MAU.

Barlow moved into bayonet range and slashed Mallory from head to toe with a withering glance. The fading tattoos on his wiry arms rippled as he jammed fists onto hips, precisely at a forty-five-degree angle, thumbs hooked over the edge of his cartridge belt.

"Spit it out, Mallory. Colonel's makin' his rounds and I ain't got all day to be screwin' the pooch."

"Gunny, Colonel Skaggs pulled me and Rojas away from our post. He come around in a jeep and told us to stand by near the docks as security for that guy Hakim."

Barlow's Adam's apple bobbed as he digested that information. A raucous burst of gunfire seemed to distract him momentarily and then he was locked back into Mallory's eyes.

"I see one of yer shit-eatin' grins formin', Mallory. Stifle it and lissen up. I got two things to say to you. One: Until we get out of this Ethiopian jug-fuck, I don't want to see you any more than six feet away from them maggots in your squad. Two: That sugar-tit the Old Man had you on has dried up. Colonel Skaggs and me been around the grinder together more than once. Don't be playin' him off me. Is that clear?"

Barlow didn't wait for a response. He turned to charge up the rubble-strewn streets of Beirut as though he was back on the drill field at Parris Island.

It figures, Mallory mused, removing his helmet to massage a sore spot on his scalp. Wherever the Gunny goes, might as well be Parris Island.

Before Mallory could leave his position, Barlow did a neat about-turn and took three strides to plant himself back in position for another ass-eating session. He was staring at the helmet in Mallory's hands. Slapping the steel pot back on his head with a painful thump, Mallory tried a feeble smile.

Surprisingly, it worked. The corners of Barlow's pale blue eyes crinkled as he shook his head in mock disgust.

"When you gonna learn, son? Didn't nobody ever teach you what goes up must come down? All that lead these clowns are poppin' up into the air has got to fall and the unlucky agent that's standin' in the wrong spot when that happens is gonna find out about terminal ballistics the hard way."

Mallory was too shocked to respond. Son? As well as he could recall, it was the first time the Gunny had ever put two words together without one of them being profane.

"Knew a dude like you in Vietnam, Mallory. He never had much shit together either."

There was laughter in Barlow's eyes. Mallory let the long-suppressed grin spread over his features. It seemed like something he could get away with this time.

He was right. Barlow shook his head once more, spun on his boot heel and sauntered up the street.

Mallory wondered what to make of the Gunny's concern for his health and welfare. Finally, he laughed out loud and borrowed one of Barlow's favorite expressions.

"I don't know whether to shit or wind my watch!"

* * *

It was nearly time for Wafic to leave Beirut and the camp that had served as his headquarters during the most recent Zionist campaign to eradicate the Palestinian people. Over the past week he had pumped his men up with assurances of their ability to continue the struggle, told them not to worry about their families and packed them off for shipment out of Lebanon.

Fortunately, they were allowed to take their personal weapons along, which made their recent survival against an overpowering enemy somewhat easier to pass off as an interim victory. As an old soldier, Wafic deeply regretted having to leave the antiaircraft guns, tanks, mortars and rockets provided by the Iranians, Syrians and other Arab brothers, but there were more and better weapons to be had elsewhere. The Zionists, he thought, had managed to wiggle off a high-explosive hook in Beirut but they would not escape the ultimate fate of those who desecrate the homelands and challenge the might of Islam.

Like the *sura* of the Koran, he thought. You repeated such things until they took on a reality beyond human reason. You repeated what you *should* believe until it became the only truth in your life. This is faith, he supposed, and faith is the food of the holy warrior. Wafic smiled as he picked up his rifle and shouldered the Soviet backpack that contained personal items packed by his fat wife.

She waited for him at the end of the street where the last trucks from Sabra were idling. He could see her dumpy form as she clutched his two sons to her side. She wore the traditional *hijab* and covered her face with the *niqab*. Just as well, Wafic thought.

The woman had been weakened by twelve years of struggle. He did not wish such softness exposed to contaminate others. His sons would have to become hard men to survive the constant threat of extermination by the Zionists.

Wafic accepted a paper parcel of food from his wife and grimaced at the tears that flowed from her dark eyes to form an irregular line of moisture along the edge of her veil. The wife of a PFLP officer should have more courage. Wafic thought to reprimand her, but women are only women and women are weak. *Ins'allah*. It was irritating, but it was what God intended.

He knelt to kiss his sons on both cheeks. At least the boys had smiles for their father. Wafic reluctantly broke the hug he was sharing with his sons when his wife sobbed aloud. He stood and stared intently into her brimming eyes.

"Hush, woman! Listen to me. There is a plot to weaken us by forcing Palestinian children to live with the Jews. You have one duty while I am gone. No matter what happens, you will see that my sons do not fall into Zionist hands."

His wife nodded dutifully and Wafic watched the *niqab* cling to her mouth as she took a deep breath. She was trying to be strong, but there was weakness in her vacant stare. He glanced over his shoulder to see the last trucks preparing to leave Sabra for the docks. The woman would need courage and there was no time for lectures.

He unsnapped the holster at his hip and drew out the chunky Makarov pistol he had been issued in Damascus. With an angry motion, he jacked a round into the chamber of the weapon and handed it to his wife. She stared at it only momentarily before tucking it into the folds of her dress. No further words were necessary. With the gun resting on her belly, Wafic's fat wife would do whatever must be done.

He turned to leave and did not look back at his family.

From the rubble-strewn rooftop of a battered four-story building overlooking the refugee camp, the convoy of trucks looked like a wounded snake crawling away from tormentors.

A deeply tanned man in dusty, nondescript military uniform refocused his binoculars and remembered the serpents that had crawled out of the ruins of Beaufort Castle following a week of desperate fighting between entrenched terrorists and the Golani Brigade. After the PLO had been driven off that historic redoubt, Israeli soldiers stood in weary clumps throwing rocks at the stunned desert adders that slithered away seeking shelter from the relentless sun.

The soldiers had been active witnesses to brutal death and destruction for a full week. Yet, even in victory, they could not stop killing. It was as though the terrified serpents were Palestinians and the men of the Golani Brigade considered them deadly until they were fully and finally destroyed.

Watching the trucks full of shouting, shooting Palestinian fighters roll toward their departure from Beirut, the observer decided the head of this virulent snake had been lopped off, but the fangs were still very dangerous. He wondered what the final outcome would be as he picked up a radio handset and glanced at his partner.

"That's the last convoy from Sabra. I'll radio in the report."

The second sun-scorched man on the rooftop did not seem to hear. He swept his field glasses away from the trucks and focused on the wall of wailing refugee families left behind in Sabra.

"Just look at that," he finally commented, "all that Palestinian scum in such a confined area. A couple of good air strikes and we'd rest assured all those little urchins would never grow up into big terrorists . . ."

The first observer paused with the radio handset halfway to his ear. He ground his teeth and searched for sympathy.

"David . . . revenge is not the answer. We must . . ."

Without breaking concentration, the second observer cut him off in midsentence.

"Come to me with that argument after one of these little

bastards has tossed a bomb into your living room. Until then, don't preach!"

"My God, David. You talk like a fucking Nazi!"

There was no anger in David's eyes when he finally turned them toward his partner. Emotion had been burned out of him by the bomb that killed his wife and daughter along a highway near Jerusalem. He smiled serenely.

"And you talk like a man with a serious death wish."

Since Corporal Mallory and Doc Grouse commenced horse-trading with the lunatic legionnaire from *2eme Regiment Etrangère de Parachutiste*, some of the other squad members had wandered away from the intersection they were assigned to control. A temporary trade impasse had been reached in both language and terms, so Mallory let the lanky Navy hospital corpsman negotiate in high-school French while he rounded up the troops.

The Frog had a weird light in a set of very strange eyes and Mallory didn't mind getting away from it for a while. Something about that stare—and the way the guy fondled the FAMAS assault rifle slung across his chest—seemed to indicate he'd be most pleased to blow away any and all living things that wandered into his assigned field of fire.

The shrunken green beret crushed over his buzz-cut scalp gave the man a gnomish, slightly retarded look but there was nothing backward about his bargaining ability. Mallory signaled Doc Grouse to up the ante for the pair of winged dagger beret badges currently on the auction block and left them to haggle. Fucking Frenchies, man. They'd seen this sort of "colonial problem" before. Give the Foreign Legion its head and they'd snap all the cheap shit out of Beirut in something less than a hot second.

Rojas seemed to be on the stick today. He'd completed his own bargain for the insignia of the San Marco Battalion and walked away from an Italian NCO to study the growing crowd of Lebanese and refugee civilians forming along the broad avenue.

From past experience, Mallory knew what to expect. A truck convoy carrying PLO fighters down to the docks would be through his sector shortly. The Pals would be firing in the air and raising hell like they had something to celebrate about getting booted out of Beirut. The Lebs would be bidding good riddance to what they considered bad rubbish and the refugees would be crying the poor-ass about being left behind in Lebanon.

Walking up the avenue in search of the only two men not in his immediate view, Mallory tucked at the checkered scarf he'd taken to wearing around his neck. It was the black and white pattern of the Palestinian *kefiyeh,* or head scarf. Arafat wore one just like it wrapped around his gourd in every picture you saw. Did it mark guys who wore it as pro-Palestinian?

Mallory had found it in a bombed-out building near the airport one day and decided it added dash; a certain flair to mark him as a salty veteran, like the nonregulation North Vietnamese Army belt buckle that Gunny Barlow wore. It suited him to stand out slightly from the shapeless mass of conformity the Marine Corps forced on people. Until he landed in Beirut, getting away with alterations to standard uniform items had been a main source of amusement.

Mallory spotted his two errant Marines pointing cameras at the shattered hulk of Beirut's once-palatial Holiday Inn. A Lebanese liaison officer had told them the logo on the facade of the familiar landmark had been used by Israeli self-propelled artillery gunners in an attempt to get the hotel's unregistered Palestinian guests to check out early.

Damn good shooting for cannon-cockers. The sign now read "H lid y nn." Give a guy enough ammo and he'll find a way to waste it.

Over the babble of the growing crowd, Mallory heard the

crackle of gunfire and the snarl of truck engines. It was time to get back to playing traffic cop. He shouted at the two Marines and led them back to the intersection. If they could keep the trucks rolling today, it would be on to ordnance-clearing down at the airport tomorrow. Scuttlebutt had it they would depart for a postponed period of liberty in Naples when that job was done.

Colonel Tom Skaggs hunched his meaty shoulders as he stepped out of the jeep, rolled his eyes and shook his head in a broad imitation of Richard Nixon facing the press after the Watergate hearings. He put a nervous tremble in his right hand as he returned the parade-ground salute fired at him by Gunnery Sergeant Harlan Barlow.

"Ah am neither a crook . . . nor a colonel."

Despite an inability to cover his North Carolina accent with a Nixonian growl, Skaggs knew he'd scored on the Gunny from the smile that creased the man's weathered face. He rolled his eyes back toward the confused young Marine at the wheel of his command jeep and decided the kid deserved a break. It's tough to know how to act when you've never seen a field-grade officer as anything but a sour sonofabitch with a swab handle up his ass.

He straightened into a more dignified posture and walked over to clap Barlow on the shoulder. "You didn't learn a damn thing in Nam, did you, Gunny? You keep tossin' me high balls like that and I'm gonna wind up sniper bait."

Barlow held the smile for his Commanding Officer, but the suggestion of the Old Man being hit at this point in a distinguished career made him angry. He'd volunteered his way out of a cushy job at Division G-2 to follow Skaggs into the Med, just as he'd followed the officer into the Belgian Cóngo and jungles of Vietnam. The first cock-sucker to take a sight picture on Colonel Tom Skaggs would find his shot blocked while Harlan Barlow unscrewed his head and shit right directly into his shoulders.

"Colonel, you and me been to three county fairs and a goat-fuckin' contest and I ain't seen you hit by nothin' heavier than shrapnel . . . and I still believe that was from your own grenade."

Skaggs checked his watch and decided there was no time to renew a running argument about the source of the wound that had prompted Barlow to carry him out of an ambush and onto a helicopter so many years ago. By his own reckoning, the incident marked the day that young Lance Corporal Barlow went from fat-mouthed maggot in a mortar squad to leader of Marines. From a hospital bed in Danang, Captain Skaggs had personally endorsed the recommendation for a Silver Star that Barlow won for turning the tide in that disastrous situation.

Both veterans flinched instinctively as a four-barreled antiaircraft weapon manned by a departing PLO crew spat streams of tracers into the air. Skaggs shook his head in disgust at the display of bravado.

"Damndest thing I ever saw, Harlan. You'd think these clowns won a war instead of getting their asses kicked off the battlefield."

"Don't mean shit, Colonel. Take a look at The Nam. It ain't the noise you make or the number of rounds you fire. It's the hits that count. These camel jockeys woulda fired half of what they're burnin' up in this evacuation at the Israelis and it might have been a different story."

"Let 'em get their kicks. Sooner we get 'em out of Beirut, the sooner we can get on with this cruise."

"That still include liberty in Naples, sir?"

Skaggs bashed Barlow's shoulder and grinned. "Sure as hell does, Guns. Last fling for me. I'm slidin' out slow and easy when we get back Stateside."

Barlow tried to hide the disappointment on his face as he

followed Skaggs back toward the command jeep. "That'll be the day, Colonel."

"That'll be the day the missus meets me at dockside with the retirement papers ready to sign. She's gettin' a mite pushy about that log cabin I promised her thirty years ago."

Skaggs hoisted a stumpy leg into the idling jeep and paused. "How's young Mallory doing, Harlan? My former driver packin' the gear down in a rifle squad?"

"Still got shit-bird tendencies, Colonel. I got to fire him up every once in a while but Mallory . . . well, I'll take care of him, sir."

Skaggs wedged himself into the front seat of the command jeep and flashed a final smile at his old shipmate. "Gonna mold him in your own image, Harlan?"

Barlow snapped his hand to the rim of his helmet and returned the smile. "Nah, sir. Even Mallory don't deserve that."

"Tell me she don't look exactly like Sophia Loren, Doc."

Doc Grouse followed Mallory's gaze to the olive-skinned woman across the crowded street from their post. He guessed she did look like a coarse, unpolished version of the actress; the Earth Mother type that made you want to hide your face between her sturdy thighs. She was struggling with a six- or seven-year-old brat and every time the kid jerked on her arm, a pair of voluptuous breasts bobbed around under her blouse like two bobcats battling it out inside a burlap bag.

"Shit like that proves what I been sayin' all along, Steve. When God made the world he had two of His fairies linger over Lebanon. The nose fairy and the tit fairy."

The rattle of gunfire broke his reverie and Mallory signaled for the corpsman to take his post. The last convoy from Sabra Camp was on the way and Doc might have some real work to do if the crowd got out of hand. There was a last glimpse of the woman and her unruly charge before the lead truck swung around the corner and blocked the view across the street.

The first truck was slightly ahead of the convoy, full of shouting, shooting Pals. As it passed, Mallory watched two exuberant assholes squabbling over a dusty red beret. Neither man managed to get a grip on the hat as it sailed over the tailgate, floating on a current of hot exhaust gas like an errant Frisbee.

A scream pierced the babble around him and Mallory caught sight of the buxom young woman trying to fight her way through a solid crowd. The bratty kid had broken away, ducked through several pairs of legs and run into the street to claim the lost beret.

The high-pressure hiss of air brakes and the howl of a diesel horn spurred Mallory into action. The kid stood screaming, terrified by the sight of the truck bearing down on him. Get the fuck out! Bolting for the center of the intersection, Mallory swept the boy up in his arms and flashed a glance at the truck over his left shoulder. All he could see was a bug-splattered grill. No time to make it clean! He rolled right, keeping himself between the kid and the skidding, screeching vehicle. The bumper caught him on the flak jacket and sent him sprawling to the other side of the street.

His neck hurt and his shoulder felt like someone had slapped it with a sledgehammer, but there was no significant damage. From the screams the kid was spewing into his face, it was clear he'd also survived. Mallory struggled onto shaky pins and set the boy on the ground. The gabbling crowd cleared to make room for Doc Grouse and his medical kit.

"Damn, Mallory! You're gonna get yer dick knocked stiff doin' shit like that."

He started to formulate a response but his attention was

riveted on the woman as she broke through the crowd to kneel beside the boy.

She really is a fucking fox.

The Lebanese truck driver had halted his vehicle in the middle of the intersection to loudly disclaim any fault in the incident. Horns blared long and loud and Mallory noticed some nervous faces peering over the rail of the truck. Shit was getting a bit tense.

"Get these goddamn vehicles moving! Show's over! Move 'em out!"

Rojas escorted the panicky driver back to the cab of his truck while the other Marines began to push the crowd back and clear the roadway. In less than a minute the convoy was rolling again and the incident had been forgotten by everyone but the three people clustered around the squalling boy. When you've seen a lot of death, a close call doesn't even make good gossip.

Jesus, that kid can bellow. Makes my head ring like a ten-penny nail beat with a greasy ballpeen hammer. What the fuck is his problem? Kids get hurt worse than that in the States every day.

"Probably just scared shitless. Only damage I can see is a coupla skinned knees." Doc Grouse applied ointment and bandages to the angry red scrapes on the boy's legs.

The woman stood but maintained a firm grasp on the child. She stared into Mallory's eyes, seemed to be sizing him up for a moment, and then she spoke.

"He does not cry from the pain. He cries because he did not get the soldier's hat."

She cut her glance back and forth between the amazed expressions on both American faces. The beginning of a smile played on her somber features.

"English is not such a hard language. Before the fighting I was a student . . . at the American University."

Before either man could respond, the snuffling youngster

managed to refocus attention on himself. Mallory reamed his ear with a little finger and then reached into the cargo pocket of his trousers. He slapped a camouflage Marine Corps cover out of its folds and plopped the hat down on the boy's head.

Tears dried immediately as the boy reached up cautiously to touch the brim of his prize. Before Doc could finish bandaging his legs, he tore away to prance before a clutch of friends who had been watching the encounter from a distance.

Mallory shook his head and grinned. In the States you give 'em a lollipop for being brave. In Beirut you buy it with a piece of military gear. Same tune; different instruments.

Doc Grouse was packing away his medical equipment. When he stood, he towered over the woman. "He'll be fine, lady. But I'd damn sure keep my kid out of the streets if I was you."

She started painfully when he spoke, as though someone had discovered her doing something evil or embarrassing. She began to back away from the Americans. Her features seemed to be fighting each other as she struggled to hide fear behind the traces of a grateful smile.

"He is not my child . . . only someone I care for. I . . . I must go now."

Christ, we can't be that intimidating. Couple of yahoos from the States. Shit, these rifles ain't even loaded. Bitch has got no class. Plenty of the stuff that makes a man's dick hard, but no class.

"Where I come from, we generally say thank you when someone gives us a hand."

The woman dropped her head for a moment. She seemed to be struggling for the right words. When she looked up into Mallory's eyes, he detected a spark; the same sort of look you get from a strange woman when she's willing to give you a shot.

"Of course . . . *marhaba* . . . thank you."

Still backing up, dammit! Mallory flashed his best let's-crawl-in-the-backseat-and-get-nekkid smile. The spark still glowed but this woman was clearly not going to fulfill his fondest wish by dragging him into a doorway and dropping her drawers out of sheer gratitude.

"You bet, lady. Anything us foreign devils can do, you just call."

"If you will give me your name, I will tell the boy who saved his life."

Couldn't hurt. "Mallory. Steve Mallory."

She nodded and turned to worm her way through the thinning crowd. Doc Grouse admired the sway of her hips under the coarse fabric of a long skirt for a moment and then shook his head.

"I ain't never seen anybody so fucking paranoid. These people really been fucked over."

"And speaking of fucking, Doc . . . I'd like to break her down like a twelve-gauge shotgun and get her with my number-nine gut wrench."

When the truck came along to pick up first squad just before sundown that evening, Gunny Barlow jumped down from the cab and pinned Mallory with a withering glance. There was no time to hide the checkered scarf or do anything much more than prepare for a tirade.

"I heard about yer fuckin' escapade this afternoon, Mallory. I hope that kid wasn't no more than six feet away from your squad position."

"Damn, Gunny . . . I was just tryin' to . . ."

Barlow jammed a finger under Mallory's nose and slowly raised his hand until their eyes were locked.

"That's your trouble, boy. You're always tryin' and never

succeedin'. Don't be makin' eyes at these local cunts, young agent. You been told to stay away from Moslems and they sure as hell been told to stay away from you!"

What kind of shit is this? You save a little kid from getting killed and all he's worried about is whether or not I'm gonna nail some Arab's old lady.

"Cut me a little slack, willya, Gunny? We been out here all day."

"Check the dictionary, Mallory. You'll find slack somewhere between shit and syphilis. Get rid of that fuckin' rag around your neck and mount the truck."

Before Mallory could get up over the rear tire of the deuce-and-a-half, Barlow yelled for him again and he started to climb back to the ground.

"Go on, young agent. Get up there. I just wanted to let you know I approved a recommendation for the Navy and Marine Corps Medal with your name on it. They're sendin' me out to see the shrink tomorrow."

Jesus. Go figure the fucking Gunny.

Colonel Skaggs sat quietly in his jeep, parked near the docks, and watched the diminutive figure of PLO Chairman Yasir Arafat climb the gangplank of the Greek ferry *Atlantis*. The man who single-handedly made Arab nationalism synonymous with terrorism was clearly enjoying his day at the center of worldwide attention.

The majority of his noisy, ecstatic supporters thronged to the right of the gangplank but Arafat played his victorious departure stage-left to a clutch of TV and still cameramen.

Skaggs shook his head and wondered what gave such an ugly little fart that powerful charisma. Crawled out from under a camel turd one day and the next thing you know he's got people willing to kill women and kids and blow up the whole fucking world for him. Someday they'll be studying that little no-neck maggot in the War College. Just like Hitler.

Find a nation of people who've been handed the shitty end of the stick, pump them into a nationalist frenzy with rhetoric, convince them that might makes right, focus the hate on a target and stand by for a torpedo amidships. You got yourself a Holy War. God Himself, personally, will tear you a new asshole if you lose or give up before you die fighting.

Skaggs spotted Piere Hakim walking his way trailing a bevy of American Embassy officials in his wake. Everyone seemed to be in high spirits, anticipating the gala round of self-congratulation that would mark the end of a successful evacuation. Hard to imagine a guy like Hakim really believes there's a light at the end of *this* tunnel.

They'd had dinner together last night and Skaggs figured the Lebanese-born diplomat for a straight-shooter. When Hakim walked over to offer his congratulations on the conduct of the Marines, Skaggs pulled him aside.

"Mr. Hakim, let me ask you an impertinent question. When the President sent you out here, did he give you any idea how he wanted us to control the Syrians, Iranians and all the rest of the radical elements that want to keep things stirred up in Beirut?"

Hakim glanced nervously over his shoulder and indicated he would join the Embassy party momentarily. When he faced Skaggs again, his eyes were hooded above a confident smile.

"It's not our business to control those people, Tom. Bashir Gemayel will have to do that. I believe when he wins the election next week, this country will be on the road to forging its own destiny. I've got to go. Please pass my thanks along to all involved in this . . . this . . . terrific effort."

Before Skaggs could respond, Hakim breezed toward his

limousine. Skaggs was unconsciously shaking his head over Hakim's comments when Lieutenant Colonel Jack Mattson, commander of the MAU's Battalion Landing Team, spit tobacco juice on the rear tire and demanded attention.

"Trucks're haulin' the troops back to the airport now, Colonel. EOD and Engineers are set to start sweeping the perimeter for unexploded ordnance tomorrow at first light. You got anything else for me?"

Skaggs smiled at the rawboned officer. The epitome of a Marine grunt. Fuck, fight or get the hell out of the way. Mattson would make a good Foreign Legionnaire. Maybe an exchange program with the French before the unit leaves Beirut? Nah. The troops love Jack and he loves the troops. Couldn't ask for a better arrangement in similar circumstances.

"No, that's it for now, Jack. Tell your people 'well done' . . . and make sure you tell the Engineers to be careful tomorrow. I'd like to get out of this Chinese fire drill without taking casualties."

Mattson offered his version of a salute and then brought his hand down to catch the glob of Copenhagen leaking down his chin.

"Aye, aye, sir. They been briefed."

Skaggs climbed into his jeep and thought painfully back on all the high-blown rhetoric he'd been subjected to over the past two weeks by bureaucrats of every ilk and persuasion, in and out of uniform.

"Yeah, Jack. We've all been briefed."

"Engineers up! Pass the word!"

Mallory raised his left fist in the air to hold his squad of riflemen in place. It wasn't really necessary. They knew the drill after a solid week of walking around the airport perimeter escorting the sweepers assigned to clear the aftermath of battle in West Beirut.

For the first few days, the Marine Combat Engineers and Explosives Ordnance Disposal technicians had been extremely cautious. There was high-explosive crap lying around all over the place. Everything from pre-World War II pack howitzer rounds to modern multiple-warhead munitions fired by God knows who at God knows what.

At this point the sweepers were getting salty. Not really careless, just cocky; anxious to take full advantage of their time in the spotlight and lord it over the grunts who normally got all the attention from a Beirut press corps rapidly running out of stories now that the PLO was gone.

Most of the deadly stuff, the ammo that lay in the sun sweating nitro or rounds rigged with particularly dodgy fuses, had been blown in place or carted off to remote dump sites. Everyone assigned to the perimeter sweeps knew that but it didn't make the long, hot walks in the blistering sun any more inviting.

The stuff still around was less obvious; the sort of thing you accidentally kick or sit down on and it blows your asshole somewhere over the left-field fence. It made Mallory nervous and, despite a rash of bitching, he'd ordered his people to stay on their feet rather than crapping out along the perimeter road when the Engineers were called forward to check something suspicious.

He turned to make sure the order was being carried out and saw a jeep with two engineers rolling up the road. Guy in the front seat was the motor-mouth of the whole operation. Done a whole hell of a lot more interviews than ordnance-clearing over the past week. Always wanting to deliver a lecture rather than getting on with the program. Figures he'd be on duty.

The jeep halted next to Mallory and the engineer nodded toward the front of the formation. "What's he got up there?"

"How the fuck should I know? Go on up there and check it out."

The man didn't seem inclined to do that anytime soon. Mallory shucked off his helmet and wiped at his face with his neckerchief. The engineer nudged his buddy behind the wheel and raised his voice to be heard by the grunts.

"Prob'ly another one of them Soviet four-deuce mortar rounds. Most of 'em they fired was incomplete detonations. Assholes cleared the old ammo lots out of their warehouses and shipped it all over here. Bet that's what it is."

The driver glanced at Mallory and rolled his eyes up toward the rim of his helmet. Mallory grinned silently back at him and nodded.

There it is, man. I don't give a fuck what it is either. Let's just get the bastard out of the road and get on with this shit.

The jeep trundled forward as Mallory lit a cigarette and waited. He stared over his left shoulder, through the chain-link fence that marked the airport perimeter, at the ramshackle Moslem ville on the other side. Fucking place.

Tourists step off the airplane and look right, they see what's left of a modern metropolis—Switzerland of the Middle East. Crank your head around the other way and you got something that looks like a high-rise goat pen. Is she out there somewhere in that ville? Jesus. Do people still find time to fuck with all this other stuff going down?

Mallory tossed his cigarette butt into a mud puddle when the engineers called him forward. He signaled for the other Marines to stay put and walked ahead to see what they'd found at the feet of his point man.

Probing the ground with a bayonet, the talkative engineer licked his lips and smiled.

"Looks like I was wrong, Corporal. Lucky your boy stopped when he did."

Mallory stared down toward the tip of the bayonet. Something that looked like a black golf ball was barely visible, mostly buried in the mud. He glanced up at his point man and shrugged.

"That's one of them fuckin' butterfly deals, ain't it?"

The engineer saved Mallory the trouble of saying he had no goddamn idea what it was.

"Yep. It's from a CBU . . . Cluster Bomb Unit. It's U.S. gear we give to the Israelis. Looks and works just about like a regular aerial bomb but it goes off before it hits the deck. When that happens, it sprinkles all these little butterfly-lookin' things around. Inside them is little black golf balls like this here. And that fucker's full of HE. Don't step on 'em, don't kick 'em and don't fuck around with 'em . . . unless you want to rotate out of here in a body bag."

During the lecture, Mallory's point man had backed up considerably and broken a sweat that had nothing to do with heat.

"So what are you gonna do with it? You want us to hang around or what?"

The engineer was watching the point man retreat. He grinned and wiggled the bayonet in the ground very close to the bomblet. Mallory took another step backward and thought about exercising the prerogative of his rank. The engineer was wearing the single chevron of a Private First Class.

"Don't be fuckin' around with that thing, man."

"Jesus, you grunts are gettin' skittish all of a sudden. Go on, Corporal. Take yer people on up the road. We'll get this puppy up out of the deck. Just leave it to the Engineers."

Mallory was most happy to act on that suggestion. If you guys want to play John Wayne, have at it. Ain't worth the sweat off my balls to jerk you around about it.

He motioned his Marines forward and fell in behind the last man as they cleared the area. Everyone took a close look at the spot in the road where the engineer probed, failed to see anything obviously life-threatening and then fell into the standard swivel-headed shuffle of the grunt on patrol.

Ain't my MOS, man. Do what you gotta do.

When the infantry squad had moved some fifty meters down the road, the engineer grinned up at his buddy and deftly popped the little black golf ball out of the mud. He resheathed his bayonet and held the bomblet up on a flattened palm.

"Ain't no use takin' the edge off 'em, is there? These damn things mostly turn out to be duds. If they don't go off when they hit the deck, they prob'ly ain't gonna go off at all."

He rolled the bomblet around in a hand, savoring the rush of danger. You never knew with these little things, man. What if? What if?

The engineer grinned at his buddy, already reseated at the wheel of the jeep, and tossed the bomblet into the air with a casual flick of his wrist.

It exploded with a deafening crack when it landed back in his outstretched palm.

There was nothing Doc Grouse could do to repair the damage to his shattered stomach and chest cavity. Shrapnel from the explosive device had pierced the man's sinuses and he couldn't get a good seal for mouth-to-mouth resuscitation. He cursed loudly, causing Mallory to look away from the radio on which he was calling a medevac chopper.

"Ain't no way, man. Bird won't help. He's gone."

Mallory walked over and looked at the pulpy form of the engineer. The man's blood was pooling beneath his body, swirling like oil into a nearby mud puddle.

One down hard and nobody even fired a shot. How you gonna fight shit like that? Fuck a bunch of campaign ribbons. Let's get out of here.

* * *

Mallory flipped his cigarette butt into the muggy breeze blowing across the fantail of the USS *Lenier County* and squinted at the receding skyline of Beirut.

Spiky city skeletons rattling against the layered terraces of the Chouf foothills and the majestic alpine sweep of the Anti-Lebanon mountains. Along the curving seaside corniche, anchored at the north end by the hump of a Ferris wheel that was once the hub of a lively amusement park, people stood and stared at the narrowing silhouettes of the American flotilla.

Mallory stared back and tried to find something in his experience that would match the scene; something to explain why he felt uneasy about leaving. Like changing a tire and rolling off down the road, only to jam on the brakes because you couldn't remember whether or not you'd tightened the lug nuts. Unsettling.

Yet the people gathered around small bonfires along the Mediterranean shore didn't seem worried. Kind of like the early crowd at a rock concert, using the warm-up group to psyche themselves for the heavy shit to come. Yeah. Well. Who the fuck knows?

They got themselves a new President and he's supposed to be some kind of Superstar. Maybe he can find the harmony. News reports calling Bashir Gemayel the Lebanese JFK. Handsome sucker with a great sense of timing; preaching unity and a greater destiny for his country. Like Kennedy, he'll have to overcome the burden of religion if he wants to create Camelot out of chaos.

Mallory grunted away the reverie and thought about going below to watch the shipboard closed-circuit TV broadcast with the rest of the Marines. Sailors had video-taped a number of news reports featuring the American effort in Beirut. Those, and plans for a memorable liberty run in Naples, seemed to be the primary preoccupations now that Beirut was fading into the distance.

One killed and a couple wounded. A footnote in the scheme of things. No more than one or two sentences in the history books. No reason to get your bowels in an uproar.

"Ain't you supposed to be belowdecks, Mallory?" Gunny Barlow stood at the rail with an unlit cigarette dangling from his lips.

Flicking his Zippo under the end of the smoke, Mallory wondered what switch was tripped in Barlow's brain this time. Was he in a talkative mood? Or was this prelude to getting his ass handed to him on a platter?

"Don't take an NCO to teach Marines how to scrub Navy shitters, Gunny."

"You got an attitude problem, Corporal Mallory."

"No I ain't, Gunny. No shit. My attitude is—and always has been—*Semper Fi* . . . do or die."

It took him a while, but Barlow gradually let the angry set of his jaw sag to match the easy smile on Mallory's face.

"Roger that. Eat the apple and fuck the Corps. Right, Mallory?"

"Naw, Gunny. I ain't got no major bitch with the Marine Corps. Except for the fact that a certain Gunnery Sergeant is constantly on my case."

Barlow blew a plume of smoke into the wind, which was freshening now that the amphibious task force had taken steaming positions off the Lebanese coast.

"Knew a Marine like you one time, Mallory. In Vietnam . . ."

"Yeah, you told me that before. He got killed, right? Because he was such a shit-bird."

"Negative, smart-ass. Matter of fact, he shipped over in the Corps."

Mallory eyed the wolfish grin on Barlow's face. This guy has got more stories than an unemployed hooker. Just when you think you're reading him right, he snaps in that O. Henry twist.

"So? Who was this guy?"

"Don't matter, Mallory. He finally got his poop in a group. That's all that counts."

End of discussion on that topic. Barlow's got something else on his military mind.

"So what are you gonna do when you get ashore in Naples, Gunny?"

Barlow lit a fresh smoke and held the pack out to Mallory. "Same thing I always do when I go on liberty. Get stewed, screwed and tattooed."

Mallory eyed the fading display of artwork on Barlow's sinewy arms. There were more under the camouflage combat uniform. Barlow had once regaled an entire squad in the field, standing under a shower point and describing time, place and personal disposition when he'd had the pictures etched into his anatomy. Kind of like a diary, he'd said. Easier than trying to set memories down on paper.

"You sure you got room for another tattoo?"

"Always room for one more. It's smart for Marines to have tattoos. Helps 'em identify the body when you get blown away."

"Don't it hurt? I heard it hurts like hell when they hit you with that needle."

"Pain is relative, Mallory. You take a guy who's had his balls bashed in a Browning breechblock and he don't feel a thing after that. No matter what the fuck happens."

There was a dull glow in Barlow's eyes. The sun had nearly set on the western horizon and the pale phosphorescence of the rippling Mediterranean flashed on his face. He was thinking about something besides skin art. It seemed like a good time to change the subject.

"Scuttlebutt's goin' around that they declared this a

combat campaign. Most of the guys are talkin' about joinin' the VFW when they get home."

Barlow snorted, straightened and tossed his cigarette over the rail. "I'd hold off on that if I was you."

"How come?"

Barlow took some time responding. He craned over the rail and stared for a long moment at the twinkling lights that marked the last view of Beirut in the wake of their ship.

"There's at least two places in the world that got a lot in common with a Hoover vacuum cleaner, Mallory. They just keep suckin' you in, you know? One was Southeast Asia. The other . . . well, you ain't seen the last of Beirut yet."

Barlow disappeared into the bowels of the ship with the last rays of the sun. Mallory sucked cool night air into his lungs and wondered what Vietnam had in common with Lebanon. Not a fucking thing as far as he could see.

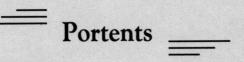

Portents

DESPITE THE DISCOMFORT of the coarse Lebanese Forces uniform cloth against his skin and a stiff new pair of combat boots, Henri Gilard felt a sense of elation as he trotted up the steps of Christian Phalange Party headquarters in East Beirut. He'd been flattered by salutes at the gate of the heavily guarded compound, but the real source of pleasure was a phone conversation just before leaving for the command council meeting.

His chief accountant had called with a preliminary report indicating somewhere near a hundred thousand pounds in deposits would remain unclaimed by customers that were killed or missing in the recent spate of fighting. He would have significant liquid capital to invest in the rebuilding efforts ordered by his cousin Bashir Gemayel. If they could just maintain a grip, the business of Lebanon would once again become business.

There was the refugee problem yet to be addressed but that was a minor matter. Decisions made in the room he was approaching should take care of it. Henri nodded absently at the slack-jawed Arab janitor and stepped around the pile of dust the man was brooming toward the end of the long marble hall.

A good man for menial tasks. Knew his place. What was his name? Fahdi? Yes, Fahdi Salim. From the south someplace. Always punctual; always at work. The sort of Arab that had a future in the new Lebanon. Good man despite his handicap.

Henri swept into the crowded conference room and greeted his fellow council members. As a full-time banker and chief fiscal officer of the paramilitary Lebanese Forces, he commanded a seat near the head of the table. He sat but did not bother with notes or ledgers. There would be no call for accounting at this meeting.

The subject was a teeming, potentially dangerous and disruptive population of refugees that occupied valuable space in and around the city. As the party chairman stood to speak, Henri glanced over his shoulder at the two military men who were seated beneath the LF flag. He found the juxtaposition distasteful; like a smudge on the white field that backed the Cedar of Lebanon inside a red circle.

They'll be gone soon enough, he supposed. Like the Americans, French and Italians so recently departed from Beirut. Henri turned his attention to the matter at hand.

Fahdi Salim leaned on his broom and spit into the dust pile swirling in the wake of the Christian officer's passage. For the first time in the workday, he allowed himself to smile. The change of expression brought a lance of pain to his jaw muscles. He regretted the simpleminded posture he'd used to insure selection for the janitorial post at Lebanese Forces headquarters more than a year ago.

It was a painful, humiliating pose for a man of his technical skill and political background. Still, Fahdi understood the necessity of such things. He was no longer regarded by the Christian officers and their sentries as anything more than a familiar fixture in the building. That gave him power and a status within the Syrian National Party that would pay huge dividends. Soon. Very soon.

Parking his janitorial cart at the foot of the marble stairs, where it would rattle if someone moved it to gain access to the second-floor offices, he picked up a metal tray that appeared to contain boxes of scouring powder and other cleaning supplies. Fahdi carried the tray up the stairs and turned left toward the vacant office directly over the small auditorium where Lebanon's powerful Christian elitists gathered for public forums.

Locking the door behind him, Fahdi moved to the center of the room and swept aside a large throw rug. Using a screwdriver specially bent and shaped for the task, he pried up a loosened floorboard and set to work. Out of a soap-powder box came four half-kilo blocks of trimethylene trinitramine. At the Army Engineer School outside Damascus, his instructors had simply referred to the explosive as RDX, but Fahdi prided himself on knowing the proper chemical name.

Loose ends of the detonating cord were right where he'd left them the previous day. He took a turn of the linear explosive around each block of RDX and calculated the status of the charge. Over the past week, he'd managed to place seventy-five kilos of Hexogen and RDX at strategic locations beneath the floor of the office. Like a cratering charge, the tamped blast would force a deadly rain of steel and concrete downward, obliterating the auditorium and anyone gathered there.

Fahdi did a quick mental calculation of the effect of such a charge detonating at a velocity of 25,000 feet per second and decided it was sufficient for his purpose. As he left the office to resume janitorial duties, he allowed himself the second smile of the day.

A shame, he thought, that so many delectable young women of the Lebanese Christian Youth Organization would have to perish in the blast. It would be more satisfying if he could humiliate them first. Use them.

Violate the pink, bouncy flesh they shamelessly displayed. Show them his power in a different form.

But there was a more important target. Fahdi sighed and resumed the gaping visage of a harmless idiot.

"This proposal is like holding a match near a powder keg. One false move . . ."

Henri sputtered and shifted his gaze from face to face around the long, polished table. Placid stares. No sign that anyone in the command council understood the gravity of the plan being discussed.

At the head of the table, the Lebanese Forces chief of staff motioned for Henri to take his seat. He picked up a well-worn briar pipe and pointed the stem like an accusing finger.

"You are a banker, Henri; used to a structured system of checks and balances. Ledgers and account books, eh? You want us to leave it up to the Red Cresent and the missionary organizations? That would be too expensive and too time-consuming."

Henri was nearly on his feet again, but Julian, the fire-eater who commanded the Phalangist Tactical Squads, beat him to the floor. "More importantly, it would not be the answer to our problem!"

The chief of staff rapped his pipe on the table and glared at Julian. When the younger man truculently slumped back into his seat, the militia leader turned a placating expression on Henri.

"You worry too much, my friend. We are simply proposing that we remove the Palestinians from Sabra and Chatilla camps . . . not stand them up in front of a wall and shoot them."

Henri flashed a look across the table. The murderous gleam in the operative's eye had not dimmed.

"Tell that to Julian . . ."

Muscles knotted tightly in the man's jaws and he leaned forward on his elbows. The response was aimed at Henri but it was not lost on the other members of the council.

"Don't mock me, Henri! You have not lost an entire family to the Moslem bastards . . . yet."

Henri breathed deeply in the silence that followed Julian's words. He did not know much about military tactics but he'd wielded enough power in his time to understand its addictive nature. The men gathered around this table were less interested in solving the refugee problem than they were in asserting their status as a force to be reckoned with in Lebanon.

That required a dramatic, decisive step. And they would take that step—no matter the potential for disaster—rather than allow themselves to be neutered by a coalition that granted equal status to shiftless people. The Arabs could be controlled. Had they all been at war so long they'd forgotten the *economics* of power? It is—and always has been—a simple matter of the powerful haves versus the powerless have-nots. Why this cry for a useless display of might?

Before he could pose the question aloud, a voice from the back of the room broke the uneasy silence. One of the men seated beneath the Phalange Party flag rose to his feet and shrugged as if easing a burden from his shoulders.

"You have said there are homeless Lebanese living in the camps. Fine. So weed them out. Help the ones who deserve your assistance. Don't waste time on the others. Get rid of them. Support your President. You know he intends to sign a nonaggression treaty soon. Do you think the Arabs in this country will take kindly to that?"

"Druze, Amal, Hezbollah, PLO, Syrian, Shi'ite, Sunni . . . what difference does it make? They all wish to upset traditional Christian control in Lebanon. Unless you wish to become citizens of yet another Arab nation in the

Middle East, you'll have to do something about it. Now or later."

Henri gazed at the faces around the conference table and found them all nodding agreement with the stranger's words.

His scraped knees long since forgotten, the boy in the oversized Marine Corps cap splashed through a mud puddle and gleefully mowed down his playmate. From a prone position across the street where he'd fallen, the victim grabbed for a pistol and cranked off four desperate rounds at his attacker.

Clutching the bill of his most cherished possession, the boy triggered a final burst into the air, groaned and fell into an agonized death convulsion.

Masra looked up from the book she was reading and gritted her teeth. Couldn't they find something else to play? Why had the guttural sounds little boys make to simulate gunfire replaced the shouting and laughter that used to accompany neighborhood soccer games?

She shouted at the boy and his playmate but they simply turned their stick rifles on her and made enough maddening sounds to fill her full of bloody holes. What would the future hold for such children? How soon before they traded the sticks for real weapons?

Not long, she supposed. The fourteen-year-old who lived next door swaggered around Hay es Sallom at night with a Kalashnikov. More guns and more strangers were appearing on suburban streets. And it was only a few days since the foreigners left Beirut.

As she walked up onto the sagging porch of the damp, windowless, one-room house to prepare a meal for the boy and his friend, Masra sent a prayer of thanks to Allah for His mercy in getting them out of the Sabra Camp. There had been so much sickness. No good water. And the mean-eyed ones who lived on hate . . . they were the real plague.

As a practical matter, Masra supposed she should be praying for her cousin Ibrahim. He had taken her out of Sabra and provided a small amount of money so that she could housekeep for him.

On the other hand, she thought as she fanned a charcoal fire, Ibrahim represented all the things she had come to hate about her fellow Shi'ite Moslems. He was a zealot for whom death had become a sacrament. Leader of a Party of God cell in Beirut, her cousin was a virulent anti-Zionist and devoted follower of Iran's Ayatollah Khomeni.

The boy howled in pain and Masra rushed into the muddy street, expecting to see him impaled on some makeshift implement of torture. Instead, she found her cousin Ibrahim pinching the boy's scrawny neck in his horny hand. She covered her mouth to stifle an impulsive shout. It would only cause Ibrahim to squeeze harder. He did not take kindly to comments of any sort from women.

When the boy agreed to stop his unmanly crying and do as he was told, Ibrahim released his grip. The child spurted forward, lunging for Masra's skirts. A cautionary word from Ibrahim brought him up short. He hunched his thin shoulders, ready to ward off a blow, and removed the American cap from his head.

Masra saw the tears, silent this time, stream from his eyes as he marched up to the house and reluctantly placed the hat on the charcoal fire. He watched as the flames licked through the cloth, carefully controlling sobs that threatened to shake his shoulders, and then escaped into the house.

"You must discipline him, Masra . . . or I will. No one with Moslem blood in his body should wear such symbols of American imperialism. Would you have him forget his heritage?"

She certainly would. She would have him forget everything that had happened in the seven pitiful years since the day he was born. And she would have Ibrahim—and all the others like him—out of their lives. She said nothing and merely lowered her eyes.

It was the reaction the Hezbollah leader expected. He swept past her and strode into the house. When she entered in his wake, Ibrahim seated himself on the only available chair and crossed his arms. He would wait there, saying nothing—eyeing her body with undisguised lust as he always did—until she brought him the sweet tea he favored.

Masra bent to place a steaming cup on the ammunition crate that served as her table and waited for what she knew was coming. Ibrahim put one hand on the teacup and the other on her right breast. He slid his hand underneath the firm mound and bobbled her in his palm like a merchant evaluating a melon.

He had never gone beyond this point, but there was no telling with Ibrahim. She closed her eyes and prayed for mercy. She did not move or straighten from her stooped position until Ibrahim felt the desire for tea again and removed his hand.

"How are you spending the money I give you, Masra?"

"Only to buy food for myself and the boy. There is nothing else. All the shops are still closed."

Ibrahim slurped tea and snorted through his long, thin nose. "That pig Gemayel will soon have them open. He thinks only of money. This nation will decay under him. We must have Moslem rule in an Arab state."

Masra said nothing. There was nothing to say. Ibrahim sometimes practiced his speeches on her. He did not expect critique.

"You have spent money on nothing else? None on books . . . like the one I saw lying on the porch outside?"

"It is only a book I had at the university . . . before the fighting."

Ibrahim rose and grasped her chin painfully. She stared up into his eyes and tried to mask the defiance she knew he would find somewhere in her gaze.

"I argued with your father about the university! Did his job there save him from death under the Zionist bombs? On the day a good Moslem takes you into his house, you will have the foreign ideas whipped out of you!"

He squeezed her chin harder for a moment and she stared in fascination at his eyes. They seemed to glow from a hot spot somewhere deep inside his skull. Had Ibrahim been smoking hashish? No. Impossible. He scorned the old men who sat in the streets sucking on the hubbly-bubblys.

She sensed a tremor in Ibrahim's fierce concentration. The fire in his eyes banked slightly and he relaxed his grip. A breath wheezed through his nose and she saw the long, coarse nostril hairs flare out to mesh with his thick mustache.

Deliverance. Ibrahim would go now, leaving a tense, scratchy atmosphere in his wake; the same palpable fear he inspired wherever he walked. People breathed a collective sigh when he passed them peaceably on the street. Most spent time thanking Allah they were spared.

At the door, he paused and reached inside a trouser pocket. Ibrahim handed Masra a sheaf of Lebanese pound notes with a disdainful motion, as though he were discarding something dirty.

"Use this to keep yourself in good health, Masra. There will be work for you soon. I have important visitors coming to see me."

His parting smirk told her all she needed to know, which was absolutely nothing.

The man from Damascus knew nothing of explosives, so Fahdi restrained his impulse to discuss the plan in technical details and concentrated on the blueprints. He moved an overflowing ashtray and tapped the document with a nicotine-stained fingertip.

"The dais will be here. Yesterday afternoon I cleaned the room and positioned all the chairs."

Removing a pair of light-sensitive glasses that had darkened in the harsh glare of an unshaded lamp, the Syrian Army intelligence officer craned his neck over the table. He was trying to see another dimension through the paper.

"It seems a long distance between the charge and the target, Fahdi. Why not put your explosives in the room with him?"

Asshole! When I become a national hero you will find yourself sweeping sand. Fahdi sighed, lit a cigarette and decided it was unwise to challenge the man at this point. Tomorrow—when they were on the road to Damascus and a victory celebration—would be another matter entirely.

"Colonel, was I not trained and specifically chosen for this mission? You must understand. I have calculated everything very carefully. There is no chance of error . . ."

Fahdi paused and glanced over the table at the man's unshielded eyes. The message was clear. An error would mean his immediate death. When one joined the operational arm of the Syrian National Party—committed to reestablish the unity and dominance of a greater Persia in the Moslem Middle East—one understood mistakes would not be tolerated.

"Security guards will sweep the room very carefully, Colonel. Any explosive device placed there would be immediately detected. The charge is in the floor of the room above . . . the same as placing it in the ceiling just above his head."

Fahdi extinguished his smoke and jabbed at the blueprint. "See these cross-members and this structural concrete?

Several tons at least. We will be halfway to Damascus before they are able to reach his dead body."

The Syrian officer replaced his dark glasses and pursed his lips. All seemed in order. He could spot no gaping holes in the plan. Tomorrow, all this work in Lebanon, all the time and money spent planting agents and operatives, would pay dividends. He reached for a small satchel under the table and carefully placed the contents under the light.

Fahdi expertly examined a small radio receiver rigged to trigger blasting caps and a transmitter set on a corresponding frequency. He extended the collapsible antenna on the transmitter and noted that Damascus had thought to include batteries. Such minor necessities were difficult to acquire in Beirut these days.

"Do you know the range?"

"The man who delivered it said half a kilometer. How much do you need?"

Fahdi pulled a Beirut city map from under the building plans and pointed to a spot near the Phalange Party headquarters.

"It will be enough, Colonel. I will leave through this gate at lunchtime. The sentries have seen me do it every day now for a year. You will be parked here . . . near the park. Bring the transmitter but do not touch any of the controls or switches."

Picking up the small device, the Syrian intelligence officer turned it over in his hand. Fahdi could see the gears turning in the man's mind. Did the fool think he was genuinely feebleminded?

"It would not work, Colonel. I will reset the frequency tomorrow morning. The device is ready to work when I am safely in your truck . . . not before. The time selected is one-fifteen P.M."

Fahdi Salim returned the reassuring smile and noted the

deferential nod as the Syrian officer replaced the transmitter and stood to leave.

"Until tomorrow then, Fahdi. We have great confidence in you."

As well you should, he thought, watching his control officer walk silently from the room. There have been no mistakes in this campaign. Every car bomb went off as scheduled. Every troublesome Lebanese nationalist was hit as ordered. Why should tomorrow be any different? The hallmark of a professional is consistency.

President Bashir Gemayel reluctantly shifted his gaze from the pudgy thighs of the short-skirted woman in the front row and glanced at his notes. The speech was going well. His prepared text—tailored for this audience of wives, daughters and female friends of influential Lebanese Christians— was full of reassurances and glowing promises of a bright future. He avoided any mention of the recently signed peace treaty with Israel and shied away from detailing his plans for an increased Moslem voice in the new Parliament.

These women feigned an interest in political matters but they really wanted answers to much more mundane questions. These were the yuppies of Lebanese society; concerned with national reform primarily as it affected life-style.

Sipping from a glass of water placed on the podium, Bashir Gemayel raised his eyes to sweep the room. Many of the women in his audience wore glazed expressions; a slight pout of the lips that he presumed to mark flights of sexual fancy. He'd noted the effect of his appearance during campaign speeches and worried that it might trivialize his political power.

His closest advisors smiled when he voiced such concerns and spoke of charisma. They pointed to Kennedy and Reagan of the United States . . . even to—God help us—Khaddafy of Libya. A magnetic, handsome, eloquent leader brought confidence and a sense of well-being to a nation.

So be it. If charisma was required to heal his nation, Bashir Gemayel would serve as object of any fantasy his people could devise. He glanced again at the nylon-sheathed legs of the woman in the front row and smiled as she recrossed her dimpled knees. It was not such a great sacrifice.

At the nod from his aide, positioned at the rear of the room, Bashir Gemayel checked his watch and noted the time: 1:14 P.M. Only fifteen minutes for questions from the audience but that should be sufficient. There would be nothing too complex. Were trade ties with Paris, New York and Tokyo still intact? How soon could they expect restored commerce through the airport and the deep-water ports? When would the police begin to deal with Moslem squatters? When would the shops reopen?

The President of Lebanon stepped out from behind the podium bearing the seal of his nation to accept questions from his adoring audience. It was a calculated move; designed to bring him closer to his people. It was also fatal.

At precisely that moment, an electronic pulse reached a receiver above his head and sent a tiny spark into a blasting cap. As predicted, the resulting horrendous explosion above dropped tons of steel and concrete into the auditorium below. Newly elected Lebanese President Bashir Gemayel was killed instantly.

Also crushed in the blast—according to veteran Middle East analysts commenting on the news that evening—were chances for a peaceful, prosperous coalition in post-PLO Lebanon.

While Gunny Barlow hassled alternately with the local squids and new platoon sergeants, Mallory sidled away from his detail. Rojas and the Doc could keep the new squad members busy putting tac marks on mount-out boxes. Unless they had been brain-damaged in transit from Camp Lejeune to Naples, the new guys should be able to paint out 32 MAU and stencil on 24 MAU, the Mediterranean Amphibious Ready Group's new designation.

Most of the Beirut vets had gone home to join the VFW or otherwise bask in the envy of other Marines. When the replacement troops arrived, Mallory heard an incoming staff officer tell Gunny Barlow that for the first time in his memory there had been more volunteers than slots for an outbound Med cruise.

Mulling over that information on the mess decks one evening shortly after their arrival in Naples, Mallory, Rojas and Doc Grouse stumbled onto the realization that they had somehow acquired a special status among nominal peers in the 2nd Marine Division. Each man knew from experience how quickly that sheen would be dulled by jealous officers and NCOs back in North Carolina venting their frustrations on the Beirut veterans. The next morning they met at the S-1 office to "double-pump," or volunteer, for duty with the new MAU in the Med.

There had never been a question about Gunny Barlow's intentions. Colonel Skaggs would command the new MAU and where the colonel planted his flag, the Gunny would be there to keep it flying. Home for a guy like Barlow was the ground beneath his combat boots and his property line was marked by how far he could piss while executing an about-face.

Mallory sucked on a cold Coke served up by the sailor manning the dockside geedunk stand and wondered if the distracted expression he'd adopted lately looked battle-weary.

"You with that outfit just come in from Beirut?" The

sailor said he'd made a mint selling soda and pogy bait to the crowd that showed up on the dock to greet the MAU.

"Yeah. New MAU now, but some of us stayed for the liberty here in Naples."

"There it is, man. Pussy here is finest kind. One step outside them gates and you're pole-vaultin' all over the area."

Mallory nodded, scratched at an itchy deltoid and felt the embroidered American flag sewn on the shoulder of his utilities.

"That's some hot shit, man. We seen you guys ashore over there on TV. That fuckin' flag looked great! Bet that kept them ragheads off your ass."

Ordering a second soda, Mallory remembered how the beautiful woman in the streets of West Beirut had stared at the flag on his shoulder. Distinct difference between respect and fear. She looked like she was staring into the open mouth of a poisonous snake. What the fuck? Most respect is based on fear anyway. Just ask the Drill Instructors at PI or Dago.

On his way back to join the working party, Mallory saluted a passing jeep automatically. Only when the vehicle had passed did he notice it was Colonel Skaggs headed somewhere in a hurry. He began to swivel his head, searching for the Gunny.

Barlow would be wearing the American flag on his shoulder also, but he would not be happy about it. Said the Corps discontinued unit patches on uniform shoulders after World War II, when they found out one Marine was as good as another Marine. Eagle, globe and anchor was the only unit designation a good man needed, by God, and any sumbitch that couldn't tell an American Marine by that symbol deserved to have his ass kicked up around his shoulder blades by an unknown entity.

Colonel Skaggs's jeep skidded to a halt near the forward

mooring line of the USS *Mount Pleasant*, the antenna-encrusted amphibious command and control vessel that served as his floating headquarters. Mallory noted the tide of camera-bearing humanity that swept toward the officer and decided he had time to eavesdrop on a press briefing.

The colonel was shined and starched but he looked tired. There were bags under his pale blue eyes. Mallory had been his driver long enough to know what that meant. Too many convoluted briefings and not enough exercise. Skaggs was a vigorous, physical man; a field Marine who struggled gamely—but not always successfully—with the political machinations of staff duties.

The Old Man spotted and winked at Mallory, ran a hand through a thatch of white hair and turned his attention to the clamoring reporters.

"Colonel, what's your assessment of the situation in Beirut?"

"Well, we were all shocked and saddened to hear of the death of President Bashir Gemayel. I think it's a sign of stability and cohesiveness that Amin Gemayel was immediately appointed to succeed his brother. I hope he can carry on and get the nation back on its feet."

A woman in an oversized safari jacket shouldered through the crowd and thrust a miniature tape recorder at Skaggs. "Colonel, you command a combat outfit. Did you have any trouble handling a political mission in Beirut?"

The Old Man riveted her with an icy glare above a plastic smile. "Politics is the province of politicians, ma'am. I'm a soldier. Next question, please."

She shouted over her companions and Colonel Skaggs widened his smile, showing polite deference to an aggressive female.

"Peacekeeping is an unusual mandate for Marines. How did you handle it?"

"Well, you don't find peacekeeping tactics spelled out in

the manuals. We did what had to be done according to what we understood the mission to be. I think it's important for all of you to understand that this sort of thing is not all that unusual for Marines. Look at your history. Congress put Marines aboard sailing vessels to control potentially mutinous sailors back during the American Revolution. If that's not peacekeeping, I don't know what is. It was also the start of some traditional bad blood between sailors and Marines."

Zingo! Shot her ass right out of the saddle! Mallory chuckled along with the reporters. The Old Man ain't gonna take any cheap shit today.

"What's in store for these Marines, Colonel Skaggs?"

"Well, the troops are going to get a week of well-earned rest here in Naples and then it's back to business as usual."

Mallory pondered that response as he walked away from the briefing. Business as usual for a MAU in the Med included endless rounds of lockstep landing exercises and preprogrammed training with NATO allies. Nothing new; nothing exciting.

Nothing to match the pulse-pounding rush; the cotton-mouthed case of the Mojaves when he stepped into the unknown in Beirut. He began to wonder about the wisdom of a double-pump.

As he led the twenty-five-man tactical squad east from Shamun Road toward Sabra Refugee Camp in West Beirut, Julian began to hear morning sounds. In another fifteen minutes they would leave this quiet residential neighborhood. He shivered with anticipation, like a dog watching its master prepare a meal.

If I had a tail, he thought with a tight-lipped grin, it would be wagging hard enough to make my ass ache. He signaled a halt and motioned for the man carrying his field radio.

"Call the team at Chatilla. Find out their status and tell them we are fifteen minutes away from Sabra."

The young radioman hesitated, toying with the handset. "Do you think they will resist, Julian?"

The tactical squad leader shrugged and looked back at his unit. "Who knows what will happen? Make the report and then tell the men to check their weapons."

Julian heard the oily snick of assault-rifle bolts and felt fairly sure he knew exactly what would happen in the next hour or so. It was inevitable.

This confrontation had been inevitable from the day the Moslems burned his family's farmlands in South Lebanon. Julian's family had worked that land and made a good living for at least four generations. And then one day the lunatics arrived with high-sounding words and fast-firing weapons for the family's Moslem field hands.

That marked the end of life as Julian had always known it. In the uprising he lost his family and found the militant Christian Phalange. Most of the men scattered to his rear in loose formation had similar stories. The necessary trigger would be easy to trip.

Julian raised his hand and gave the signal to move.

In all his twelve years, Hasan had never seen his grandfather so angry. Not when the Zionists had ordered them off their pastures. Not when his uncle had been shot by the policeman at the other camp near Kaldeh. Not when the strangers had come to load them in trucks and take them to this camp. Not even when the festering facial boils had completely closed Grandfather's right eye.

Now these other strangers in green uniforms were pointing guns at his neighbors and Grandfather seemed about to explode like a dead goat lying in the sun. Hasan went slowly to the old man's side, his eyes widening as he watched the muzzle of a rifle follow him.

The stranger standing closest to Grandfather spoke Arabic but there was no warmth in his tone. "Gather all the Palestinians immediately, old man. Bring them here. Trucks are on the way."

"We have no idea who is Palestinian and who is Lebanese here! We were stuffed into these camps by your own government. Where would you have us go? Have the Jew bastards finally left our land?"

The stranger raised his rifle and Hasan grabbed for his grandfather's hand. He was too late. The old man—half blind from the boils and the rage in his belly—raised his walking stick and swung it in a vicious arc.

Hasan heard the shot and watched his grandfather blown backward by the force of the bullet. He rushed forward and struck at the stranger, aiming for that spot between the legs where he knew from experience in scuffles with his playmates that the slightest blow could bring intense pain.

It was a moment before Hasan realized the high-pitched scream he heard was his own voice. It was just a moment later when he felt the crushing blow on the side of his head and fell across his grandfather's twitching body.

Wafic's fat wife fought desperately against panic. Who were these men? Why were they here, shouting, shoving and asking everyone for identity papers?

As a wedge of angry soldiers swept down her street, breathing in angry snorts through flared nostrils, she saw the boy who tended the vegetable garden knocked to his knees. Bright red blood gushed from a wound in his scalp. She saw the fifteen-year-old daughter of her neighbor grabbed and pulled screaming into a house. A familiar lust was in the soldier's eyes. The girl would not emerge intact.

Wafic's wife had heard only the single gunshot that caused her to run into the street, but she knew the killing would begin in earnest soon. She clutched her two confused sons to her side and waddled for the goat shed, where she had hidden the pistol.

Hasan knew his grandfather was dead as soon as he was able to open his eyes against the throbbing pain in his head. The old man was stiff and cold. His skin had a strange pallor, like the bellies of the fish Hasan used to catch in streams before they moved to the city. His uncle turned the same color after the policeman shot him.

A terrible rage grew in Hasan as he struggled to his feet. He wanted to scream and cry out in his frustration, but such displays were acceptable only from infants. Grandfather told him he would have to do a man's work when they came to this place. The time for play was over. Now it was time for work.

Hasan reached under his shirt for the slingshot he used to kill pigeons for his mother's stew pot and bent to grab a handful of rocks from the roadbed near his grandfather's body. As he had done on a hundred previous hunting adventures, he climbed the gnarled olive tree at the end of the street, slithered onto a thatched roof and began to stalk his target.

He traversed five rooftops and then spotted the stranger who had killed his grandfather. The man was talking with two other strangers. None of the men below his perch bothered to look up as they shoved and prodded people with their guns. It would be an easy shot.

Hasan examined his ammunition and selected the smoothest, roundest rock. The stone was too heavy for pigeons but it should do nicely for a man. He lifted the missile to his lips for luck and then fitted it into the sling. His vision was clear and his hand steady as he stretched strip of inner tube to its limits and brought the Y of his weapon onto the stranger's left ear.

When the stranger fell to his knees with blood gushing

from his temple, Hasan stood and screamed as he'd seen his grandfather do the day he saved the sheep by killing a wild dog.

"*Allah Akhbar!*"

The floodgates finally gave way when Julian's radioman blew the boy off the roof with a vicious burst from his AK-47. The angry, roiling tide crashed through the streets of Sabra Camp sucking everyone along with it. The power of that torrent was awesome and unstoppable from the moment the boy's bloody corpse crashed to the muddy street.

The incident sent a signal to the Phalangist squad sweeping through the camp. Someone had fired and very likely someone had died. Perhaps an order to begin shooting the Palestinians had been given. Perhaps not. It made no difference.

A crowd of screaming refugees plugged one of Sabra's main arteries in a desperate attempt to escape the line of fire. They simply compressed themselves into the center of the target. The soldiers fired long, scything bursts into the crowd, not bothering to select individual targets.

When the survivors turned down a muddy alley to escape the bullets, Phalangist troopers ambushed them from windows and doorways, killing most cleanly as they ran into hasty sight pictures.

A Moslem woman burst through the throng clutching her baby to her breast. She held the infant up before her face, hoping to find a sympathetic father among the killers. A wicked burst of AK fire tore through the baby and into her chest.

A Phalangist NCO grabbed an old man hobbling by on a crutch and forced him to his knees in the street. He drew a pistol, shot the man through the back of the head and then emptied the magazine at a clutch of wailing relatives who watched in horror.

From one of the more presentable hovels along the street, a pretty teenaged girl emerged waving a packet of papers above her head. She screamed at the soldiers.

"Liban! Liban!"

Nationality made no difference if any of the men even heard her over the screams, shouts and shots that blended and roared through the camp like the agonized howl of a wounded beast.

Enraged at the wanton killing, an old man in a greatcoat and a checkered *kefiyeh* tried to strike one of the killers with his cane. The soldier deftly ducked the blow and poked the muzzle of his rifle under the old man's whiskered chin. One bullet completely decapitated his victim but the soldier did not bother to watch the headless corpse collapse to the ground. He had another target.

Ushered by their screaming mother, twin girls ran into the street and faced the soldier with their hands raised in surrender. He swept his rounds through the children's bodies and up into the chest of their mother without taking his finger off the trigger.

Julian's radioman caught only a glimpse of the fat Moslem woman hunkered in a corner of the goat shed. He thought there were more of them inside but he couldn't be sure. The snap of the round she fired past his ear drove him outside, where he nearly collided with the tactical squad leader.

Julian's contorted features were streaked with dried blood. He pushed angrily at his radioman and aimed a kick at the rickety door of the shed.

"What the hell are you waiting for? Get in there and take care of her!"

"She's got a gun . . . and I thought I saw more of them in there with her."

"Asshole! You have no stomach for a fight!"

The confused radioman watched Julian burst into the goat shed and then followed, blinking to see in the gloom.

There were three of them squatting in a corner nearly covered by animal fodder and mud. A woman and two cringing boys. The woman aimed her pistol straight forward, at a spot somewhere between the two soldiers who covered her with their own weapons.

Julian slowly raised his rifle, savoring the moment; sure that the woman did not know how to aim. In that moment of standoff, she did the most unfathomable thing. Before their disbelieving eyes, the woman whipped the pistol across her body, snapping one round into each of the boy's heads.

As her martyred sons slumped away from her forever. Wafic's fat wife spun the pistol in her hand, clamped the muzzle between her teeth and pulled the trigger a third time.

Julian turned slowly to his radioman. The fire in his eyes was gone. He spoke quietly; nearly mumbled as he walked away from the grisly scene in the goat shed.

"Get on the radio. Contact all units and tell everyone we are leaving. Tell them to get out now. We are leaving."

Events at Beirut's other major refugee camp were similarly brief and bloody. Just one short hour after it began at Sabra and Chatilla, the killing ended.

Lieutenant Colonel Black Jack Mattson was having a hard time juggling the china mug full of wardroom coffee and a notebook containing the bets he'd made with his officers on the week's pro football games. He slopped a little of the hot liquid into the guts of a humming teletype machine and grabbed for a handkerchief to mop at the spill.

A Navy chief radioman with arduous experience at following the BLT commander around the comm center sponging tobacco juice, coffee or cigar ashes out of his delicate equipment rushed from his cubicle.

"Anything I can help you with, Colonel?"

"Nah thanks, Chief. I'm just waitin' for the Stateside scores. Got all my liberty money bet on the games."

The chief was in the middle of volunteering to bring the football report to the wardroom, when an electronic signal erupted from the machine. Mattson jumped at the abrupt noise in the quiet comm center and slopped more coffee on the copy paper beginning to belch out of the teletype.

"We call that the Bad News Beacon, Colonel. Every fuckin' time it goes off, there's a disaster somewhere and we wind up havin' to jerk the hook . . ."

Mattson wasn't listening. His eyes were fixed on the lines of print chattering out of the machine. He shoved his coffee cup at the chief, ripped off about two feet of paper and headed for the hatch.

"Chief, put someone on that machine full-time. Bring everything that comes across about Beirut directly to Colonel Skaggs's office. Keep it coming and don't let word of this get anywhere out of these spaces until I tell you otherwise."

Leaving a bewildered shipboard communications crew in his wake, Mattson ducked through the hatch and bulled his way down the passageway toward spaces aboard the *Mount Pleasant* occupied by the MAU staff. He rapped hard on Colonel Skaggs's office door but did not wait for permission to enter.

The senior officer was seated at his desk scribbling on a stack of documents. He glanced up over the rim of his reading glasses and studied the agitated scowl on Mattson's dark features. With Black Jack, this sort of visit could be caused by anything from a clap epidemic to the commencement of World War III. The MAU's ground combat commander was a man of many passions.

"Good morning, Jack. You look like someone just shit in your mess kit."

Mattson slid the teletype papers across the desk and slumped into a chair. "Worse than that, Colonel. Read that fuckin' story. The defecation has hit the oscillation."

While Skaggs readjusted his glasses and studied the story, Mattson grabbed a half-full coffee cup off the desk and squirted tobacco juice in it. He put the cup down, and then picked it up again to take a drink. It was a peculiar penchant of his that made every coffee-drinker in Black Jack's CP check carefully before sipping from any cup that had been out of their sight.

"Jesus Christ, Colonel. They're sayin' three hundred killed at Sabra and Chatilla and the Red Cross is still countin' bodies. See what they're sayin' there? The fuckin' Christian Phalange did the shooting!"

Skaggs finished reading, put the story aside and thumped his shined boots up onto the desk. He stretched, rolled his shoulders and then put his hands over his eyes. Mattson took another swig of the sludge in the coffee cup.

"So what do you think it means?"

Colonel Skaggs lowered his hands and turned red-rimmed eyes on his subordinate commander. Mattson had never seen the Old Man look this way: sad, haunted, hunted, strange.

"It means a lot of things, Jack. It tells me why the urgent meeting up at COMNAVFORMED was called for this evening. It explains why the CINC is flying in from Frankfurt to attend that meeting. And on a more personal level, Jack, it very likely means you and I are going to have to drag this lash-up back into Beirut."

Mattson slapped his hands on his knees and heaved himself out of the chair.

"Up jumped the devil!"

Skaggs did not respond. He was staring at two framed

photos on his desk: his wife in an evening gown, taken during the celebration of the past Marine Corps birthday, and his son in the dress uniform of a second lieutenant, taken the previous year when he was commissioned at Quantico.

"You know what else it means, Jack? It means my peaceful retirement will have to wait awhile. Jesus . . . after Korea, the Congo, Vietnam . . . I never thought it would end this way."

When Colonel Skaggs finally looked up, Mattson painted on his patented shit-eating grin, guaranteed to inspire confidence and/or fear in friend and enemy alike.

"It ain't endin', Colonel. Advance to the Forward Edge of the Battle Area! Pointy end of the bayonet! Hell, we'll kick this one in the ass Big Time . . . and have the troops home for Christmas."

Hard to hold a blue funk with Black Jack Mattson anywhere in your AO. Got to get him an exchange tour with the Legion. Got to do it. He'll blow their socks off.

Skaggs grinned and then chuckled. He slammed his boots to the deck and pointed a crooked finger at the hatch.

"Let's get a jump on this thing, Jack. Crank up the machine. Muster the officers right after noon chow and start recalling the troops from liberty. Drunk, sober or indifferent, I want them all back aboard by midnight."

Most of the bodies at Sabra had bloated into grotesque postures under the boiling sun. In shady areas where trapped gas did not have the element of heat to cause such rapid expansion, red-eyed rats gnawed at the flaccid flesh of corpses and demonstrated to the shocked visitors that they were—as always—the only survivors to prosper.

A television cameraman whose stomach had hardened to cast iron after two years of covering violence in Beirut carefully maneuvered to get a shot of rats scurrying across the bloody corpses of twin girls. He knew the network censors would never allow it on the air, but he felt someone should record the image anyway. It spoke volumes to refute the notion that the human animal was less deadly than any of his predecessors.

Signaling for his defense attaché to corral the cameraman, U.S. Ambassador to Lebanon Carlton Sanders tightened the strings holding the surgical mask over his mouth and nose. He swallowed the bile that surged into his throat following a whiff of putrid air and glanced around to insure none of the photographers were pointing a camera at him.

Not a chance. Such ghoulish concentration. Snapping, whirring and clicking around the bodies being carted away by helmeted Red Crescent workers. Most assuredly a black eye for the Embassy. Most assuredly. The Phalange must be insane! This sort of thing can only serve to weaken their claim of control in Beirut and keep the Israelis hanging around forever. Why no hint; no warning?

Colonel Jason Cameron spoke softly to the TV cameraman about the need for propriety and when the photographer told him to fuck off, did so. It looked as if the ambassador needed a shoulder to cry on and his was available.

"I don't know, Mr. Ambassador. It beats the shit right out of me. We've always had a good line on the Phalange in the past. Christ, if our sources didn't know about this, the Israelis must have . . . and they would have told us. Unless . . ."

"Jason! That's a can of worms that needs to stay tightly sealed just now."

Colonel Cameron glanced at the ambassador's watery eyes over the sweat-soaked rim of the surgical mask. What a wimp! He's scared shitless over the wire he sent to Washington last week. Wouldn't listen when we suggested the fucking thing might be premature. Tell the State

Department the worst is over in a place like Beirut and you're bound to get burned.

"Regardless of the circumstances, Mr. Ambassador, this is one unholy mess. I haven't seen anything like this since Vietnam."

Sanders waved for his limousine and longed for the air-conditioned interior.

"You have that advantage on me, Colonel. I have *never* seen anything like this. And it's a damned shame . . . not only from a humanitarian standpoint. This is just the sort of thing that supports the Israeli contention that the situation in Lebanon is too volatile for them to go home. We'll have the devil's own time convincing them otherwise."

Colonel Cameron fell into step with his boss and trudged toward the waiting Embassy car.

"I don't know, sir. The Marines have been ordered back into Beirut and they should be able . . ."

Diving into the limousine, the ambassador motioned the defense attaché inside with hurried hand motions. "I keep telling you this is *not* a military campaign, Jason. The Israelis tried that and where did it get them? Now the Phalange. And the Marines? My God, they'll start another war!"

Colonel Cameron stared out the window of the limousine for a last look at Sabra. There. The same dark shadow; like a low-hanging cloud. Noticed it at Chatilla this morning. It's flies, by God! Rats win; flies are runners-up. You betcha, Mr. Ambassador. Keep the goddamn jarheads out of Beirut. We sure as hell wouldn't want another war. But what is it we've already got here?

On a jutting finger of high ground overlooking the rocky shoreline south of Kaldeh, Ibrahim motioned for his assistant to connect the heavy battery to the infrared-light projector. The Zionist patrol boat had disappeared over the misty horizon, chasing a fishing vessel he hired to cruise this sector just before moonrise. It was safe to send the signal.

Despite the dark, Mohammed rapidly made the connection with the deft fingers of a man finely tuned to technical tasks. Any fumbling or delay would be an embarrassment to Hezbollah's foremost explosives and sabotage expert.

When Ibrahim tapped him on the shoulder, Mohammed flipped a switch and felt the casing of the projector warm to his touch. Somewhere out in the Mediterranean off this shore, the liaison officer from Tehran would spot a glowing point of light through his IR-sensitive goggles and rev the silenced motor of a small rubber boat. In thirty minutes or so—long before the thorough Zionist sailors had finished tearing apart the decoy vessel—the man called Wafic would be ashore and headed for Beirut.

"Why do they send an officer of the Popular Front, Ibrahim? Won't he be spotted by spies and informants?"

Mohammed saw his commander's teeth flash briefly in the gloom. "You worry too much about spies, my friend. It is up to us to insure he is not spotted. Wafic has a very special mission in Beirut."

"You mean the new explosives?"

"Anyone could have arranged for delivery of the explosives, but this man is special . . . a true holy warrior."

Mohammed waited silently for the rest. The Hezbollah leader was formulating a speech. He would deliver it when he was ready.

"Recall the concept of *badal*, Mohammed. The right of revenge is a pillar of our faith. When we strike at the Zionists or the Americans who give them power we seek *badal* for the people of Palestine . . . for all Moslems. Do we not? Are we not sworn to revenge the harm done to our families?"

Mohammed scratched at an ant crawling somewhere

beneath his belt and stared out to sea. Such questions are rhetorical when posed by Ibrahim. He does not require or expect an answer. And he has provided none.

"What does *badal* have to do with this man Wafic?"

Ibrahim smothered his strange, high-pitched laugh and began to gather his weapons for the trip down to the beach.

"Wafic's wife and children died in the slaughter at Sabra, Mohammed. He asked for permission to extract revenge . . . and the Ayatollah entrusted him with a very special mission. He will have his *badal* . . . and we will focus the eye of the world on us and our struggle."

Mohammed gave the infrared projector a final check and wondered why Ibrahim insisted on being so mysterious. The man spoke in riddles half the time. As he followed the Hezbollah leader down the slope toward the surf line, Mohammed decided Ibrahim struggled on two levels.

There was the practical war against the Zionists and their supporters . . . and there was the fanciful war that Ibrahim fought in his mind. If only he can keep the two from becoming confused.

Mallory motioned for two more bottles of the coarse red wine and watched the Gunny try to screw a shotglass over the engorged nipple of the hooker at his side. The experiment was costing Barlow fifty lire extra, but money was no object when he was engaged in scientific pursuit.

The chubby hooker and her thoroughly sloshed girlfriend roared with laughter when Barlow finally managed the feat.

"Looka there, Mallory! I told you that sumbitch would stay put. Didn't I? Huh? Didn't I tell you this gal had tits like twin forty-four mounts on a tin can and nipples like a couple of Bing cherries?"

Pouring wine for the party, Mallory jabbed the woman at his side with an elbow and pointed at her brimming glass.

She turned an unfocused glare on him and drooled down her chin.

"Shit, Gunny. This one you fixed me up with is so shit-faced she can't find her ass with a ten-man working party."

Barlow belched, lit a cigarette and squinted through the smoke. "What fuckin' difference does that make? You gonna take her to a tea party at the base library or get laid? Dago women don't have to be sober to fuck yer brains out of yer skull."

Mallory stared into the soupy red wine in his glass and felt the woman's head flop onto his shoulder.

Out like a goddamn light. That's what we get for drinkin' before dinner. Fuck it. Plenty of time. Get myself another hooker. Plenty of 'em around here. Like to find one looks like Sophia Loren.

The image set Mallory's mind wandering and he scratched idly under the bandage on his left forearm. Gunny was wrong about tattoos. Hurt like hell. Should have known that greasy Wop was into pain. Any pencil-necked geek that wears an earring and a rhinestone stud through his fuckin' nose is a kinky cocksucker.

"Leave that goddamn thing alone, Mallory! You'll tear the scab off and it'll wind up lookin' like shit."

Barlow rose, grabbed the woman at his side and sprawled into a darkened booth near the rear of the dingy bar. His thick legs were spread and an evil grin was forming on his face. It wasn't hard to see why.

Another fifty-lira note had persuaded the hooker with the pendulous tits to reach under the checkered tablecloth and administer a hand-job. Amazing dexterity and concentration. Her right hand jerked up and down with piston-like precision while she lifted a brimming wineglass with the left and carried on an unrelated conversation with the bored bartender. Barlow took it all in with undisguised glee until proximity to Nirvana caused him to close his eyes.

Mallory laughed, shook his head and wondered how in the hell he wound up sitting in a box seat at a circle-jerk, his head full of wine and his mind on an unreachable raghead woman somewhere in Beirut.

Dad would shit if he could see me now. Probably lay right the fuck down and die of envy. And Mom? Jesus H. Christ! She'll shit when she sees this fuckin' tattoo.

Peeling away the bandage, Mallory examined his new birthmark. Despite the scab, the blue design with lurid red highlights was quite clear. Plenty of unique patterns available on the walls of the parlor, but it took only a few minutes for Mallory to select an old Marine Corps standard. Grinning skull with a commando dagger piercing it top to bottom. Blood dripping off the point of the knife formed a background for the inscription: USMC—DEATH BEFORE DIS-HONOR.

The Gunny seemed slightly pissed when Mallory showed him the tattoo. Strange look in his eyes . . . as though Mallory had overstepped some unseen boundary. And then the invitation to "wet that goddamn thing down properly" had led to the bar.

When Mallory glanced over his shoulder, he saw Barlow smile and lift his glass. Mission accomplished. The hooker was wadding a stack of napkins into a neat ball and shuffling out of the booth, headed for the washroom in the back of the bar. Mallory picked up his glass, slid out from under his comatose companion and walked over to sit next to Barlow.

"Gunny, I know you ain't still got a hard-on at this point. How about tellin' me about that guy in Vietnam?"

"Lotsa guys in The Nam, Mallory. Which one you askin' about?"

"You know . . . the guy you're always sayin' I remind you of."

Barlow lit a cigarette and exhaled gouts of smoke from his nose. "Later, Mallory. When you got a need to know."

"C'mon, Gunny . . ."

"C'mon's ass, boy. There's only one thing you need to know about Vietnam." Barlow reached under the tablecloth and tugged at his zipper. "It started small . . . the way it should have stayed . . . with only the pros from Dover playin' the game. Then it got way out of hand. Every jack-off who ever read a book was tellin' us how to fight. That was, is and always will be bullshit. You want to prove somethin' by fightin', by God, you better shoot the politicians and let the soldiers get on it."

"What the fuck does all that mean?"

"It means if you want to run with the big dogs, Mallory, you got to learn to piss on the tall trees. Now let's get back to the ship. I need to resupply my money if we're gonna eat Dago chow tonight."

Not since the *carabinieri* swept Via Venedetti looking for gunrunners and Red Brigade terrorists had the tavernkeepers, merchants and pimps seen anything like the pandemonium in the streets. Questions were passed up the sidewalks in the wake of the Navy loudspeaker trucks, but no one had any answers.

"Attention! Attention all Navy and Marine Corps members of Task Force 76. This is an emergency recall. All Navy and Marine Corps members of Task Force 76 are to report to their ships immediately. This is an emergency recall."

Jeeps and trucks swept cash customers from their midst. Many big bills were left unpaid. There was all the fresh food that would go uneaten. The women would not make enough to pay for the rooms they had rented when the ships came into port.

A ripple of panic swept Via Venedetti until the Sicilian who sold security in the neighborhood arrived with reassurance. We have seen this sort of thing before, haven't we? It is usually some sort of drill and the customers always return, don't they?

Have faith, the Sicilian urged his clients. Have faith in human nature. Be patient until the authorities at the base are satisfied. The Americans will return with more money and larger appetites.

Gunny Barlow was all business as he flagged down a jeepload of MAU staff NCOs and hopped aboard. He pointed a finger at Mallory and roared over the blare of the loudspeakers.

"You know where your troops are?"

"Doc stayed aboard to make a phone call. Rojas has got the duty. The four new guys came ashore same time I did."

"Find 'em and be sure they get on one of those trucks!" The jeep bearing Barlow and the other senior NCOs bounded off in one direction as Mallory shoved off in another.

Easy to determine a direction of march. New guys came ashore following a Blue Steel Throbber on that Texas kid. Whatsisname? Dale? Yeah. Deeter Dale. Always looks like four pounds of shit in a one-pound sack. They'd head for the Kit Kat Klub.

Mallory figured he'd hit paydirt when he spotted the commotion outside the notorious dockside hooker haven. A Marine Corps five-ton was parked in front of the club bearing a full complement of cheering Marines. Whatever they were supporting was locked in the middle of a gang of white-helmeted shore patrolmen.

On the approach Mallory spotted three of the four. Lance

Corporal Leon Justice, the black kid from St. Louis who was always hoarding batteries for a ghetto blaster that cranked out enough amps to warp the bulkheads aboard ship. PFC Stone, the burly high-school jock from Upstate New York who thought boot camp was a breeze and PT was some sort of religious rite. Private Stankey from someplace in Colorado. Joined the Marines just to piss off his old man, who was an Air Force Lifer.

As he'd begun to suspect when he failed to find PFC Dale in the back of the truck, the scrawny Texan was in the center of the circled SPs. Dale had a pair of woman's bikini skivvies stretched over his head and snapped beneath his formidable ears. Despite profanity and some painful prodding from SP nightsticks, he hung on to a stout, half-naked hooker with sloppy makeup and hairy legs. Neither the woman nor the scrappy little peckerhead in her arms could be considered a prize, but they clung to each other doggedly.

"What's the problem?"

A First Class Quartermaster spun on Mallory and cocked an eyebrow. "Who're you?"

"His squad leader."

"Well, you tell that little piss-ant to mount the truck and stop fuckin' around."

Mallory pushed past the SP and confronted the errant M-60 machine gunner. Dale's eyes were wide with righteous indignation. It was hard to hear over the screams of the hooker.

"What's your problem, Dale?"

"Look here, Corporal Mallory. These squids is fuckin' with me. Ah paid for this woman but ah never got no pussy."

"It's a recall, Dale."

"Wouldn't take more'n a few minutes, Corporal. Ah

figured to whack me off a piece on the ride back to the ship."

"Get in the truck, Dale."

"Fuck!"

"In the truck."

Mallory helped the lovers disengage and then followed PFC Dale up over the tailgate. The driver ground gears and they rolled off with Dale suffering the abuse of his drunken buddies.

Lance Corporal Justice shoved his way back next to Mallory and shouted over the noise. "What's this recall about?"

Mallory shrugged and squinted at the dockside sailors singling up the lines which moored the amphibious task force to Naples.

"How the fuck should I know? Probably found out Dale's got a case of the blue-ball clap and called us all back for penicillin shots."

Quagmire

NOTING THE WAY the visitor from Tehran admired Masra's movements around the low table, Ibrahim sat silently and let the woman complete her task. When the coffee had been poured and a bowl of fresh fruit placed in easy reach, he opened the meeting.

"We welcome our brother Wafic and humbly accept the gifts he has brought to us from Tehran."

Wafic replaced his coffee cup and eyed the lean faces around the table. Ibrahim and the explosives man he knew from the beach. The youngest of the Hezbollah brain trust in Beirut had been introduced as Eladar, a cabdriver who ran the cell's intelligence network.

"I bring you greetings from the Ayatollah himself. He asked for Allah's blessing on our efforts in Beirut."

Each of the devout men around the table bowed his head momentarily and Wafic paused respectfully. When they looked up again, Wafic signaled for the woman to refill his cup and continued.

"A large shipment of explosives has been moved into the Bekaa Valley, primarily for use against the Americans . . ."

Mohammed interrupted the visitor by holding his hand out in front of him suspended over the table. He stared at Masra until she finished pouring the coffee and left the room. "Excuse me, brother . . . but it is best to talk in private."

Ibrahim drew an angry breath. The interruption was an embarrassment. Wafic would think he was lax in security procedures. Best to make light of it.

"You grow old too soon, Mohammed. The woman is my cousin. She is no spy!"

"She studied at the American University. Who knows what ideas have been put into her head?"

Wafic intervened before the discussion could expand into an argument. "Brothers, time is short. We must turn our attention to the matters at hand. Our revolutionary comrades of the Red Brigade report the Americans have left Italy bound for Beirut."

Eladar spoke in a quiet voice, consulting a sheaf of handwritten notes. "Also bound for Beirut are units from the French and Italians. They have been ordered to support the Gemayel regime in Lebanon."

Ibrahim flashed his smile around the table and raised his cup in silent salute to the picture of Ayatollah Khomeni that dominated one wall of the apartment. "Allah sends us three targets instead of just one."

Wafic returned the smile but his cold eyes sent a more serious message to the Hezbollah leader. "Do not become confused, brother. The Ayatollah was very specific in his orders. The Americans are the primary target. The mission is to drive the Americans from Lebanon."

"Swear to Christ, man! It's just like back at Pendleton. We land at San Onofre and the fuckin' civilians have a picnic on the beach while they watch the show."

Private Stankey waved merrily at a car full of civilians passing along the coast road that paralleled the Marine landing beach. He'd have done more unofficial greeting, but Lance Corporal Rojas cut him short.

"Ain't no fuckin' Pendleton, man! Move your ass!" Rojas shoved the replacements out of the path of an oncoming amphibian tractor and shouted over the clatter of helicopter rotors.

"Beirut . . . *verdad?*" He jabbed a finger downward at the sparkling white sand of what was ironically dubbed Black Beach and then pointed at a noisy crowd of Lebanese spectators gathered to watch the second coming of the U.S. Marines. "And them? Ragheads . . . *comprende?*"

Stankey didn't look like he comprehended very much at all. None of Mallory's new squad members seemed to understand the circus atmosphere on the beach. The squad leader caught sight of them trying not to look confused or overly concerned about their destiny as he walked down the sand, fresh from a hasty meeting of platoon NCOs.

They keep looking back out to sea for a sense of balance. Easy to identify with the conga line of haze gray ships vomiting landing craft into the water and spewing helicopters into the sky. The world as we know it. But this business on the beach? Shit! How many Marines have actually *seen* a monkey fuck a football?

Mallory pointed at Rojas and then tapped himself on the helmet. His number two said something to Doc Grouse and then trotted off to meet the squad leader.

"Keep 'em in one spot and out of the way for fifteen minutes or so. We got the airport again. Amtracs are gonna go on into the perimeter. I gotta go up the beach and meet the trucks, then I'll be back to pick you up."

Rojas watched Mallory trudge up the strand, stepping around snorting jeeps and frenetic Navy Beachmasters like a toreador. The image made him smile as it had when he'd conceived it out aboard ship while listening to an officer talk about why they had to come back to Lebanon.

Beirut full of *toros malos,* man. You keep wavin' de cape and callin' in *piccadores* and . . . well, you got to stay in de middle of de ring, man. Don't get your back up against no wall. Damn good thing I got two gringos . . . no, not just gringos, man . . . buddies. *Verdad. Estan muy importantes.*

Rojas walked back toward the squad. A couple of them were wrestling with each other on the sand as he wrestled with his own demons.

So many heavy changes dese days, man. *Mañana? Yo no se.* Not feelin' so . . . so *Mejicano* anymore, man. Hard to be a beaner with all these ragheads around. You know? *Ay, esta loco. Verdad, hombre! Yo no se.*

"OK, knock off de grab-ass! We wait here. Corporal Mallory goin' after de trucks. Don' get lost and don' get run over."

Rojas strolled toward the spot where Doc Grouse had found some shade. Maybe there would be time to teach him Spanish. He asked. And he's a buddy. Buddies don't bullshit, man.

Private First Class Deeter Dale closed his eyes momentarily and felt the card rattle into the appropriate slot inside his brain. It always worked that way. Didn't matter where he was.

Waco High School, Daddy's feed store, Parris Island, Swamp Lagoon, Beirut, don't matter none. Hear some sumbitch mouth off, close your eyes . . . click, rattle, thunk. Got the bastard pegged.

Now you take this here fuckin' Meskin right here. *Lance Corporal* Rojas. Ain't nothin' but your basic beaner. Nothin' at all. But you give him a set of crossed rifles under that stripe of his and you got . . . well, you got a wise-ass is what you got. Acts like he invented this fuckin' Beirut or somethin'. They's lotsa places I ain't never been before and I'm the first one to say so. I believe that Mex has got me confused with somebody that gives a big rat's ass about his rank.

Now you take me, by God. Them officers can say what they want about peacekeepin' and muscle-flexin' and image-makin' and all that other horseshit. I ain't takin' no crap from nobody and the first sand nigger that gets over onto the fightin' side of me is gonna find out about that . . .

"Hey, Dale! Gimme one of your smokes, man." Click, rattle, thunk. Bill Stone, pretty fair old boy for somebody born and raised in New York. Funny way of thinkin', though. Runs PT like an Aggie chasin' poontang, preaches all about stayin' in fightin' trim . . . and then bums smokes all day long. Sumbitch like that . . . well, you got to shade him a mite out there in centerfield.

"Dale, man . . . we just got ashore! You can't go around shittin' on the beach, man. You smell that? Jesus Christ! Dale took a shit over behind this rock!"

Rattle, thunk. Stankey. Lookit him climbin' around that gawdamn rock. Like a fuckin' dawg sniffin' a stump. He'll lift his leg in a minute. Best part of that little fart ran down the leg of them high-water Air Force trousers his daddy wears. What the hell's he found back there?

Behind the man-sized rock jutting up from the sand of Black Beach, a combination of coral fans and urban sewage formed a small breakwater. What floated there was undisturbed by the surge of landing craft screws and the grind of armored amphibian tracks. What floated there was beyond disturbance by anything anymore, except the crabs that nipped and the gulls that nibbled.

Doc Grouse shouldered his way through the semicircle of Marines staring at the bloated corpse in morbid fascination. He held his breath against the cloying cloud of stench that rose from the mouldering body and noticed that the others were doing the same.

The dead man floated faceup with his arms spread like a crucified Christ figure, but the resemblance ended there. No nail holes in his bloated, outstretched palms; the crabs had ground his fingers to ragged nubs. No agonized expression of suffering or supreme sacrifice on his face. The gulls had pecked out his eyes, stripped away his lips and deformed his nose. No wound mark in the side. No mark of violence at all—save the fact that the once-young man was dead before his time.

Doc Grouse began shoving people away from the hypnotic sideshow. "Just some poor asshole that zigged when he shoulda zagged. Dead body's the worst disease carrier in the world. Get the fuck away from it."

Most of them did. They returned to the activity on the beach and revised secret visions of sunning and swimming in the balmy Mediterranean while they kept the peace in Beirut. The azure sea that carried them to adventure in the mysterious Middle East was now another color in their minds. It no longer seemed odd to name this pristine stretch of sand Black Beach.

Private First Class Deeter Dale lingered at water's edge until he was sure everyone else had disappeared around the other side of the rock. And then he quietly puked his prelanding breakfast of steak and eggs into the surf.

Through the shimmering curtain of heat waves that rose from the coast road, Mallory could see the long line of empty trucks parked some five hundred meters up the beach. Probably waiting for the traffic to die down a bit, he thought as he watched Lebanese military policemen windmill their arms and curse in an insane cadence of Arabic and French. Anything to roust the rubberneckers and clear the road for the military vehicles that must cross to reach the airport perimeter.

Mallory noted with a grin that Murphy's Law was valid in

the Middle East. Find the worst possible point of congestion and that's where your car will always malfunction. Just ahead—where the road curved slightly and traffic slowed to a crawl—a gray Mercedes sedan sat off the side of the road, its hood gaping and two swarthy Arabs digging around the engine compartment.

Another snarl was being unknotted at the surf line. Mallory caught sight of Gunny Barlow, waist-deep in the churning waves and cursing mightily in hopes of scaring a swamped jeep up onto the beach. Four Marines and two sailors were also in the swim, straining to move the stranded vehicle while the driver sat, waves pouring over his lap, laughing at the Gunny's imprecations.

"You beady-eyed, slab-sided sonofabitch! Get up on that goddamned beach! Get up there or I'll stomp a mud hole in your sorry ass and walk it dry! Goddamn you, you heathen piece of shit!"

Most of the working party were laughing too hard to push, but the jeep apparently knew when to suspend mechanical crankiness in favor of survival. A watery belch, an insincere snort, and then the engine roared to life. The chuckling driver jammed the vehicle into four-wheel double-nuts and careened onto the sand.

Mallory watched the jeep skid to a stop at the beach road crossing point and then turned his attention to the stranded motorists. One of them was shrugging helplessly, holding a frayed coil wire in his hand. A nearby Leb MP was apparently unimpressed with the evidence.

He lit a smoke and wondered if any of the high-toned rich bastards who owned Mercedeses back home ever suffered from frayed coil wire.

Not very likely. Still . . . there's something reassuring about shit like that. We're all tied to machines: mechanical machines, electrical machines, money machines, communication machines or Big Green Machines. Don't make any fuckin' difference. They break down and we're all up Shit Creek without benefit of a paddling machine.

Mallory waved his kinship and understanding at the embarrassed owners of the Mercedes sedan and trudged up the beach. Don't feel like the Lone Fucking Ranger, he told them. Bigger than shit them trucks up there won't start either.

"Move it! Move along. This is not a garage!"

The military policeman was certainly full of his own importance. Given his attitude, Ibrahim marked the man as a nonbeliever and hoped he would be killed. If he continued to stand next to the car, that would surely happen.

As rehearsed, Mohammed reached under the carburetor for the frayed coil wire they had placed there and held it up to show the soldier. He shrugged helplessly and offered a placating smile.

"Here is the problem, brother. Good parts are hard to find these days . . ."

A combination of heat and frustration prompted the MP to aim a kick at the fender of the Mercedes. Ibrahim tried to hide a flinch. There were ten kilos of plastic explosive in the trunk of the vehicle and he knew the heat would be causing some instability. He nudged Mohammed and began walking up the road.

"Where are you going? You must move this car!"

Ibrahim offered an eloquent shrug and pointed north toward the shimmering image of Beirut. "We will get a new wire and return very quickly, brother."

Before he could do anything more than shout another protest, the policeman was distracted by blaring horns and grinding gears. It was as Ibrahim had known it would be. He walked easily, silently beside Mohammed until they had rounded the curve in the beach road.

With only a quick glance over his shoulder, he smiled and

nodded at his companion. Mohammed reached inside his jacket pocket, extended a telescoping antenna and delicately pressed a button with his thumb.

"Two minutes . . ."

The Hezbollah welcoming committee picked up the pace and waved at the vehicle waiting to take them home from a pleasant day at the beach.

As a natural result of being left-handed, Mallory jogged toward the sea rather than nearer the beach road as he moved to avoid a passing tank. Reflecting on the incident later, he decided it was the first time in a right-handed world that his opposite orientation had brought him anything but grief.

The helmeted commander in the cupola of the roaring M-60AI was a guy Mallory had double-dated with back at Lejeune. Mechanical genius. Always had a car that ran and a tank full of gas. A grin showed beneath his goggles and the TC held up his hands to let Mallory know he had no idea what the fuck was happening either.

It was the last image Mallory saw before his eyelids were slammed shut. When he forced them open again he saw a flaming shish kebob with legs.

The Lebanese MP he'd seen standing next to the gray Mercedes up on the beach road was on fire, pummelling himself in a masochistic frenzy as he ran toward the spot where Mallory lay gasping in the Mediterranean surf.

Help the poor bastard! Jesus Christ! His face is melting! What the fuck happened? What happened, man? Was it incoming? Did somebody shoot at the tank? Christ, I see everything twice. Lemme get a little water on my face.

Mallory tried to dunk his head into the roiling surf but something was pulling him up and away from the water. He shook his head until his vision cleared and tried to get his legs set into the shifting sand.

Tank's OK. Buttoned up tight and traversing the turret toward the airport access road. Buncha guys hunkered down behind it. Amtracs racing across the road. Where the hell is the Mercedes? Can't be that scorched spot on the roadside. Can it? Jesus, all that's left is a chunk of the engine block.

Mallory felt water cascade over his head followed by the familiar jolt of his helmet settling into place. He staggered momentarily under pressure on the shoulders of his flak jacket. He found himself facing Gunny Barlow and felt the welcome support of the man's arm as he was led out of the booming surf.

"C'mon, boy, walk. Walk it off. You ain't hurt. Just had your bell rung is all."

Like a rubber-legged fighter and his solicitous corner man, Mallory and Barlow walked up onto Black Beach. A clutch of Navy hospital corpsmen were hustling the badly burned Lebanese MP toward an ambulance. Idling engines were being revved back to operational levels. Officers and NCOs were trying to get confused Marines to ignore the incident and move out smartly.

For once Mallory was glad the Gunny had time for him. He felt abused, violated and wronged, like a man who was sucker-punched. He gestured up the road and shook his head.

"What the fuck . . . that Mercedes? Was it mortars or incoming arty or what? Why the hell would they shoot at a car with all this other stuff . . .?"

Barlow retrieved Mallory's M-16, shook the sand loose and handed it back. Mallory expected him to be highly pissed; leading a bayonet charge after the bastards who dared to fire on his beloved Marines. But Barlow was quiet; philosophical after an initial surge of adrenaline.

"No incomin' to it, Mallory, unless you count the fact that a coupla assholes drove that Mercedes down here. They call it a 'Beirut Salute' . . . kind of a Middle East version of Welcome Aboard or Have a Nice Day from some geeks who'd just as soon we turned around and went home. They pack a bunch of HE in the trunk, park the car next to a target and then set it off by remote control or time-delay mechanism."

Mallory stared down at the rifle he'd been taught was one half of the world's finest fighting machine. Supposedly, he was the other half. Clean off the sand, put all the rounds in the world in this plastic sonofabitch and you still can't shoot a car bomb out of action. Despite the military hardware and weaponry rolling past him into the Marine perimeter at Beirut International Airport, Mallory felt naked and vulnerable.

"How you gonna defend against something like a car bomb, Gunny?"

Barlow chewed on the inside of his cheek and took awhile to answer. He pondered the seaborne armada for a long moment and then stared at the sand. When he faced Mallory, his green eyes were hooded.

"Beats the shit right outa me, boy. I guess you just keep damn tight control of your parking lot." Barlow punctuated his opinion with a deep sigh. The man breathed so deeply that Mallory thought for a moment he was in pain.

"Haul ass, Corporal Mallory. Trucks're waitin' and so are your troops. World don't stop spinnin' just 'cause some people ain't got no respect for a fine automobile."

Eladar pulled his taxi into a reserved slot at the north end of the seaside corniche across from the American Embassy and carefully placed the off-duty sign on the windshield. The Palestinian in the seat next to him indicated no desire for lunch, so Eladar left him to stew and walked slightly south toward Pigeon Rock. A friend sold falafel near the landmark and Eladar was hungry.

The Palestinian would have no trouble with security

forces on this brilliant, sunny day. The corniche was packed with strolling lovers and lunchtime dawdlers. Nearly everyone had a camera. Those who had sufficiently photographed the huge black rock that rose from the sea below the corniche to serve as rendezvous for city pigeons and seaside gulls turned their lenses toward the picturesque buildings on the inland side of the broad promenade. Wafic would attract no more notice than any other tourist after a souvenir shot of the attractive American Embassy.

Security was not the problem in the taxi where Wafic sat sweating profusely in the airless, polyester oven of a Western-style suit. It was the damned camera. Weren't the Japanese always talking about the beauty of simplicity? How could they design such a complicated instrument and let it stand as a symbol of their culture throughout the world?

Wafic mashed his thumb on yet another button and was rewarded by the click of the shutter. He put the camera to his eye, twisted the focusing ring and zoomed the lens back and forth. When he pulled backward, the entire facade of the four-story building rushed into view.

A corner location with a sweeping driveway that allowed access from two directions. A heavy portico that shaded the drive directly in front of the entrance. A nest of antennae and aerials on the roof. Steel bars on many of the windows. A double-doored entryway with the seal of the United States on one side.

Wafic pushed slightly forward on the lens and narrowed his view to the guards who stood on either side of the entryway. Local men carrying outdated carbines. Moslems or Christians? Difficult to tell . . . except for the one on the left. Is that a *masbahah* in his hand? Yes, the prayer beads. At least one of the guards is a believer. No sign of American guards. They would be inside . . . controlling access to the interior offices. Not a problem.

"*Badal*," Wafic reminded himself as he unloaded the camera and slipped the exposed roll of film into his pocket. He savored the word, filling his mouth with it; feeding his soul and ignoring the rumblings in his stomach.

In a briefing room on the second floor of the Embassy, Colonel Tom Skaggs contemplated a scuff on the toe of a spit-shined combat boot. It was hard to keep resentment and impatience from showing through his expression. Apparently Ambassador Sanders and the chairborne Doggie that served as DAO in Beirut thought Marine officers couldn't pour piss out of a boot with the directions written on the heel. He tried to relax his facial muscles and glanced up at the map of Beirut which covered one wall of the air-conditioned room.

"You should understand some things from the start, Colonel . . ." The ambassador unbent his lanky frame and began to pace in front of the wall map. ". . . I don't consider this military presence the optimum solution. You'll pardon the civilian perspective, but I've never believed soldiers solve anything. We are characterizing the American, French and Italian presence here as a Multinational Peacekeeping Force. Emphasis on the word 'peace-keeping,' Colonel Skaggs. This is not a combat mission and I don't want it turning into one. I hope I make myself clear on that point."

Skaggs recrossed his knees, folded his arms and wished once again he hadn't quit smoking. If the ambassador noticed the Marine officer's discomfort, he chose to ignore it. He twirled toward the map and rapped the linear representation of Beirut International Airport with a bony knuckle.

"This is the key to the mission. BIA is the heart of the Lebanese corpus. These people are descended from Phoenician traders. They tend to gauge the strength or weakness of their government by the commerce that passes through the airport. Translated to your situation, that means we can't allow any element in this country to interrupt traffic. Normal business must continue and that means we can't afford to build some sort of Fortress America down by the terminal buildings. We don't want to send any false signals to indicate the U.S. is digging in for the long haul."

Skaggs took a deep breath and reached into his map case for the piece of paper that crossed his desk in the predawn hours before the landing force was sent ashore.

"I understand all that perfectly, Mr. Ambassador. What I *don't* understand is this message that was generated by the State Department and somehow pumped into my military chain of command. Apparently I am ordered to have nothing to do with the Israeli Defense Forces here in Lebanon. Can you explain that to me?"

"Of course I can, Colonel Skaggs, but I should think it hardly needs amplification. The United States is *not* condoning the Israeli incursion into Lebanon. We officially consider them as unwelcome here as Syrians, Iranians or Palestinians. America's position is—and always has been—Lebanon for the Lebanese. Our forces are *neutral* here. If you climb into bed with the Israelis, you violate that neutrality."

"Ignoring the incident on the beach this morning, Mr. Ambassador . . ." Skaggs cocked an eyebrow to let the diplomat know he was most assuredly *not* ignoring it. ". . . I'm sure you understand the security complications this order represents. The IDF has armor and infantry units literally on my flanks. No commander in his right mind is going to occupy a position with an ally on his flank and not coordinate operations with that ally. It's asking for dangerous accidents to happen."

Ambassador Sanders seated himself and crossed his own arms over a blue tie embroidered with tiny American flags.

His experience in difficult negotiations had taught him how to play trump.

"Well, Colonel . . . regardless of such considerations, you are going to obey your orders. Are you not?"

Skaggs felt the angry flush building up along his neck and underneath his ears. He did not react well to threats. Never had; never would.

"I consider this order invalid and improper, sir. My chain of command would never endorse such restrictions on a commander in the field!"

Ambassador Sanders lifted his bushy eyebrows and tilted his head to cue his defense attaché. Colonel Jason Cameron straightened in his chair and spun the legal pad he'd been doodling on so Skaggs could read it. He swept a ballpoint pen over the tangle of boxes, triangles, squares, squiggles and dotted lines.

"It's like this, Tom. As chief executive, the President makes his desires known to State. That's this channel. As commander in chief, he talks through JCS on this line over here. That comes together through the Embassy chain which meshes with Unified Theater Command. So . . . we get EUCOM and State on the same channel. Because you're Marines, it passes through CINCUSNAVEUR in Stuttgart for European operations. They shake hands with the diplomats over here . . . just so we're all singing from the same sheet of music. Then it filters over to PhibGroup out of Naples. The admiral passes it down to the commodore with an action copy to us for comment. Then it comes to you. Naturally, Headquarters Marine Corps, the commandant and Second MarDiv get a chance to chop on it through the back channel . . ."

Colonel Skaggs struggled to keep his eyes from crossing. He breathed deeply but the influx of air-conditioned oxygen did no good.

"Just who in the hell am I supposed to be taking orders

from here? Huh? That's not a chain of command! It's a goddamed Chinese crossword puzzle!"

Nodding absently at the greeting shouted by a four-man working party moving field desks into his new command post, Lieutenant Colonel Black Jack Mattson backed off, turned slowly and tried again. It didn't help. For the past hour, while his troops set up housekeeping, he'd tried every angle and rationale at his disposal and he still couldn't get comfortable with his position at Beirut International Airport.

The Lebanese aviation official who showed him the four-story building with the huge open atrium at its center had waved away Mattson's questions about structural stability. His guide had proudly pointed out that the concrete and steel structure had once housed the Lebanese Ministry of Transportation. It had been on the periphery of devastating Israeli air and artillery strikes during the summer and withstood all the high-explosive quakes, the guide said. Why worry?

Because—Mattson answered hours later when he'd finished his personal inspection of the area—the whole position is like a jet engine: It sucks and blows!

Violates every goddamn tenet of infantry operations there ever was. A fucking fireteam leader in the rear rank with a rusty rifle will tell you not to bunch up. One round will get you all. Been singin' that song since the first infantry unit in the world formed up and moved out. In spite of that, we stick two hundred warm bodies in one hole. Gotta do something about spreadin' these people out . . . soon as I solve a few other problems.

Mattson turned about and pondered his tactical dispositions. To the west, near the end of the active runway where India Company's position intersected the coastline, was another problem. Got our backs to the sea with potential enemies all around. Dunkirk. Evacuation under fire? Fuck that!

And what kind of silly sonofabitch with the first day of military training defends a strategic location by occupying only the low ground? You take the fucking high ground around the location and defend that! But nooooo! We got some kind of Druze Moslems up there and they get to sit on the high ground while the Marines sit down here in the middle of big-ass Dog target. Hotel Company and Weapons are right under their muzzles.

That don't even take into consideration the principle of consolidating your defensive perimeter. I got a whole shit pot full of ragheads out there in . . . what's the name of that place? Fuck it, call it Hooterville. There they sit between me and Golf Company out near Sidon Road. Easy to cut 'em off. Too easy. And we got an artillery battery holding down the left flank! Christ, if we were gonna be here any longer than a coupla weeks, I'd have a fuckin' coronary.

Mattson shrugged at the questioning look on the grizzled countenance of his sergeant major and led the way inside the noisy CP. It was time for Officers' Call and yet another unpleasant examination of the Rules of Engagement.

"Don't say it, Sarn't Major. I know. This position sucks Big Time. But I don't want to hear another fuckin' word about Dunkirk, Dien Bien Phu or Khe Sanh!"

The white-haired sergeant major—who had landed with the Marines in Lebanon back in 1958—grimaced his way toward a smile. "Aye aye, sir . . ."

There was nothing more to say. He'd served under Marine officers for more than thirty years; long enough to tell the wheat from the chaff. Skaggs and Mattson were good Marines. They'd bitch long and loud to the right people when the troops weren't around to hear it.

Morale was the sergeant major's main concern and he

understood it could not be maintained if you went around
pissing and moaning about the stupidity of your superiors.

Barlow and the other Battalion Landing Team NCOs were
invited to Officers' Call since the subject was Rules of
Engagement. On the first pass over these simple stipula-
tions, the officers interpreted the intent and passed it along
to the NCOs, who interpreted the practical meaning. They
passed it along to the young Marines, who shrugged,
scratched their asses and didn't understand a word.

There were more questions than answers, so the NCOs
were brought to the source. The idea was to avoid misin-
terpretation of a code that could mean life or death among
highly disciplined and literal-minded Marines. Barlow
could tell it wasn't going to work as soon as LtCol. Mattson
opened his mouth.

"From our security posts at major intersections on the
south and southeast sides of the city, we are to *deter* passage
of hostile armed elements in order to provide an environ-
ment which will permit the Lebanese Armed Forces to carry
out their responsibilities in the city of Beirut . . ."

A platoon sergeant from India Company took the well-
chewed pencil out of his mouth long enough to interrupt the
colonel's roll.

"Sir, what does 'deter' mean? I understand 'deny' or
'stop' or 'blow the fuckers away,' but how do we tell the
troops to *deter* the bad guys?"

Mattson blinked twice and glanced down at his notes for
a pat answer. It wasn't there. Barlow saw grins, grimaces
and glances begin to spread around the room. He crossed
his arms, stared at the ceiling and chuckled silently. Here
we go again; headed downhill in a handcart. Black Jack
Mattson cleared his throat with a rattling roar.

"Well, Staff Sergeant Grey . . . 'deter' in this case
means to . . . well, it means to sort of play the bad-ass

and make 'em think twice before they try to come through our sector."

Grey wasn't buying any cheap answers to expensive questions. "Yessir . . . but what if they only think *once?* What if they decide they're gonna come through anyway? Does 'deter' mean we blow 'em away? Or does 'deter' mean we let 'em go?"

Snickers became audible and Barlow saw a Gunny from Amtracs pull his utility cover over his face to keep from laughing out loud. The colonel removed his wad of Copenhagen and worked a finger around between lip and gum to clear errant tobacco particles. He finally removed the finger and pointed it at his subordinates.

"It means *deter*, goddammit! Now let's get on with this. Rule One: In every possible case, local civil or military authority will be used . . . "

Golf Company Commander Captain Ron Jennings raised his hand to catch LtCol. Mattson's attention. Barlow silently cheered his CO's temerity in the face of the battalion commander's growing heat. Here it comes. The CO's gonna shit in his mess kit.

"Sir, I have a question that relates to my situation out at the University of Science and Technology. All the 'civil or military authority' in my AO is related to the Moslem population of Hay es Sallom. I don't think they'll be wanting to hassle Cousin Omar even if he's trying to come through my area carrying an RPG. What do I do if the Lebs won't respond?"

Mattson reloaded his lip and wiped at a bead of sweat hanging from the tip of his nose. "If the Lebs don't respond, Captain Jennings, we refer to Rule Two: Marines will use only the degree of military force necessary to accomplish the mission or reduce the threat."

Barlow watched the Amtrac Gunny cautiously lift his

cover and try to disguise his voice. "Does 'military force' include beating the shit out of them?"

Mallory's voice was clearly recognizable above the chuckles that were sweeping through the audience.

"Sir, when you 'reduce the threat,' does the threat wind up dead . . . or just wounded?"

The kid broke 'em up. Even Black Jack is laughing his ass off. One major mistake: Never try to bullshit a bullshitter.

"Let's secure this crap and get back to work, people. You been around long enough to know you can't make chicken salad out of chicken shit."

Doc Grouse pawed through his Unit One medical kit in search of throat lozenges for the smiling, caramel-colored Marine squatted next to him. He'd enjoyed the clear, sweet falsetto Lance Corporal Justice brought to the Soul Brothers' jam last night and Grouse didn't want to see the guy damage valuable vocal cords.

He finally found an aluminum package of Cepacol tabs and handed them over after a quick check for pus nodules in Justice's throat. "Just some redness, irritation. You got to take care of them pipes, man. You blew my ass away on 'Tracks of My Tears.' No shit."

Justice slapped the corpsman's outstretched palm and popped a lozenge into his mouth. "Be all right soon's the weather clears up, Doc. What the hell happened to the sun, man? Three weeks ago I was worried about gettin' my black ass burned."

PFC Dale drew the sleeve of his utility blouse under a snotty nose and offered his assessment of the situation. "It's The Root, man. Ain't like Texas, where the sun shines all the fuckin' time!"

"Ain't nothin' shines in Texas 'cept a rhinestone in a horse's ass . . ." Private Stankey's opinion nearly killed everyone in the squad room with the exception of Justice, who had just discovered PFC Stone sweating all over his poncho liner.

"Stone, get the fuck off my rack, man! Sweatin' all your bullshit on my poncho liner, man! What kinda shit is that?"

Stone rose from the rack and began stripping off his smelly PT gear. "Watch your voice, Justice. This is honest sweat, man. I shit you not. You dudes ain't gonna believe this, but I just got shot at. No shit! I was runnin' out on the perimeter road and some asshole took a shot at me."

Justice stripped his poncho liner, tied it to the frame of a broken window and shoved it outside into the air for drying. "Bullshit, Stone. You probably got upwind of one of the sentries and he tried to kill you to keep from suffocatin'."

Stone stood naked in the center of the room and shook his head. "Say what you want, man. Couple of other guys heard the shot . . . and I seen the fuckin' mud splash where the round hit."

PFC Dale finished tying the tiny Texas flag on the stanchion that held the mosquito netting over his rack. "Anybody shoot back?"

Stone picked up his girlfriend's high-school graduation picture and studied it for a moment. "Fuck no, they never shot back. Dude standin' watch down around Hotel Company said he saw the muzzle flash. He called the COC but they never gave the word to lock and load."

Doc Grouse repacked his gear and went to look for Mallory. The squad leaders were trying to get something done about the shitty chow the Navy was sending ashore. Most of it looked and tasted like it sat on deck in the rain for several hours before the helos arrived to pick it up for delivery.

BLT corpsmen were upset over the situation also. Not only was it embarrassing to them as Navy men stationed with the Marines, but their patients needed extra nourishment now that the weather in Beirut had turned cold and damp.

Mallory had a theory that the quality of chow was directly related to morale. Doc Grouse wanted to tell him there was nothing to worry about in their squad. He paused at the door and looked back at his patients.

"Now you assholes remember something, willya? Doc don't make house calls, so abide by Number Five of the Rules of Engagement . . ." The Marines chorused the popular chant in unison.

"Hunker in the Bunker and Don't Make Waves!"

As soon as the CH-46 Sea Knight helicopter staggered into a landing on the rolling deck of the amphib carrier, Gunny Barlow hefted his laundry bag and moved to the rear exit ramp. A deck crewman in yellow jersey, helmet and goggles waved toward a yawning hatch in the big ship's flight control island.

Barlow ducked in out of the rotor wash and headed for the Chief Petty Officers' mess. In just over three minutes he had a steaming porcelain cup of Stateside drip-grind coffee in hand and his target in sight.

Willis Bagwell, master chief stew burner aboard *Inchon*. Thirty-year squid with a dick-skinner in every scam afloat. Sumbitch raped my ass in Sardinia. Poncho liners, K-bars and cash to boot for steaks and beer. Fuckin' beach party got rained out anyway. Bubblebutt anchor-clanker ain't had a good word to say about Marines since World War Twice. And them assholes ashore wonderin' why the chow's fucked up.

Barlow straddled a seat across from the master chief and set his coffee cup on the green felt tablecloth. Bagwell stripped a pair of reading glasses off his roseate nose and squinted at the smiling Marine. Such encounters dictated a certain decorum.

"Hey, Barlow. You out here for a little R&R?"

"Shit, Bags. You know there ain't no Marine R&R on one of these haze gray hotels. I come to see if you're interested in doin' a little business."

"What kind of business?"

"Look here, Bags. You know things been heatin' up ashore. Snipers around the perimeter. Coupla stray tank rounds. Shit like that. Now I got word the Old Man is gonna cancel the Navy's sight-seein' tours of Beirut."

"Maybe now I can get some work done around here."

"And maybe you can make a lot of money toward that sailboat you wanna buy down in Key West . . ."

"Howzzat?"

"Figger it this way, Bags. If the sailors can't get ashore to take pictures, they're all gonna want some other kind of souvenir, right? Something to take home and show they been in Beirut?"

Barlow hefted his laundry bag and set it on the tablecloth. He upended the bag and watched Chief Bagwell's eyes scan the display: red PFLP armbands bearing the hammer and sickle; esoteric Arabic pins and badges; AK-47 bayonets that fitted into the scabbards to form effective wire cutters; ragged pieces of shrapnel bearing Cyrillic characters; and two artillery shells that could easily be cut down into ashtrays in the ship's metal shop.

"Now this shit's layin' around all over the place, just waitin' for a couple of smart guys to pick it up . . ."

"What's the split?"

"Fifty-fifty, Bags. I ain't lookin' to rip nobody off. I been aboard enough of these scumbuckets to know what it's like drillin' holes in the ocean, man. Your boys deserve a break for all the support they been givin' us."

Mallory sat at the wheel of Barlow's jeep and watched the Gunny pace up and down the beach. He looked like a football coach with a critical play in the offing and a substitute calling signals.

Barlow paused to wave as the Navy coxswain maneuvered the Mike boat through the surf. He could just make out the chief staring over the gunwales.

First act curtain. Mallory checked his pockets for the items Barlow issued and then depressed the clutch pedal to start the jeep. The vehicle groaned slightly as Barlow and the fat chief climbed aboard.

"Where to, boss?" Deliver the lines as rehearsed. Don't ad-lib.

"Take us up by the mosque, Mallory. I want to get back in that bunker over behind the antiaircraft guns." Mallory popped the clutch and swung the jeep in a northeasterly direction. In the backseat, Barlow was setting the hook.

"This place where we're goin' has got enough shit layin' around to buy you that sailboat outright, Bags. We gotta be a mite careful, though. Syrians was in the position up next to the mosque, see? And they put in a mine field. What with all this rain, some of them bastards probably shifted. So we got to step lightly . . ."

Mallory fought to control his expression and stole a glance at the rearview mirror. As predicted, Bagwell was sweating pure bullets. On cue, the distant boom of artillery echoed from up in the Chouf foothills. Walid Jumblatt's territorial imperative. Set your watch by it. Cue driver.

"Don't let that bother you, Chief. They ain't been able to hit nothin' yet. Sometimes the Druze get antsy when they see a vehicle approaching the mosque."

There were huge half-moons of perspiration staining Bagwell's khaki shirt when Mallory parked the jeep next to the muddy field that was graveyard for four S-60 57mm AA guns abandoned by the PLA. The man had not budged from the backseat. Act Two.

"You didn't say nothin' about no mines, Barlow . . ."

"Bags, stop talkin' like a man with a paper asshole, willya? See them strips of white tape out there? Me and Corporal Mallory put 'em there this morning. That's a safe path through the mines."

Mallory reached under the jeep seat and handed Bagwell an empty sandbag. "Just follow the Gunny, Chief. Mud's pretty deep, so watch your shoes. I'll be right behind you."

Act Three. We got him. Walkin' like a man with a screwdriver shoved up his ass, but he's walkin'. Final check. Clicker in hand; dummy mine in pocket. Do it, Gunny.

"Bags, these here mines we're talkin' about are what we call pressure-release type. They don't activate until you take pressure *off* the firing device, see? So if you step on something and hear a click . . . just freeze in place."

We'll never pull this shit off! He's gonna pass out before we get another three steps. Who's gonna hump his fat ass outta this field when he keels over and dies of a heart attack? Goddamn Gunny always preachin' about usin' the chain of command. Oughta practice what he preaches. Everybody been bitchin' about the chow. Let the colonel and the commodore get it unfucked. This is stupid. Potentially very funny . . . but dumb.

Mallory caught his cue when the Gunny reached up to scratch something under the high collar of his flak jacket. He moved a pace closer to the wobbly-legged Chief Petty Officer and pressed firmly on the cricket in his left hand. The metallic click sounded like a rifle shot and had just about the same effect on Bagwell.

The burly sailor froze instantly, hunched his meaty shoulders until his neck completely disappeared and fought hard against a palsy that seemed to pass up one side of his body and down the other.

"Barlow! Jesus Christ! I stepped on one of them mines!"
Barlow backtracked cautiously and knelt beside the

trembling chief's rigid right leg. "By God, Bags, I believe you did just that. Sure as hell sounded like it. Corporal Mallory, come on up and help me scrape away some of this mud."

Mine-planting time. Act Four. Scrape out some of the mud under his foot and then plant the dummy mine where he'll see it when we gallantly save his ass. Where's the cameras, man? Barlow's bound to win an Academy Award.

"Bad news, Bags. It's a Bouncing Betty. No use shittin' a man in your position. It don't look good. We better get some help. Let's go, Mallory."

"Jesus, Barlow! You can't leave me out here! You know about this shit. Disarm it. Do something!"

Gunny on his knees again, shakin' his head like a doctor wishin' he had better news for a terminal patient. How long's he gonna drag it out? Chief's already pissed himself twice.

"Bags, you're askin' an awful lot of me and Corporal Mallory here. These fuckers are *sensitive*, man. We make the wrong move and we go up too . . ."

"Look, Barlow . . . I know you can do this shit. You ain't no amateur. Let's make a deal, OK? You get me offa this thing and chow gets better for you guys startin' tomorrow. Laundry too! No shit. Hot chow delivered to the beach and laundry in plastic bags. It's all I got to offer, man!"

"That just might swing her, Bags. But I wouldn't want to think you'd try to con me. If I thought for one minute you wasn't gonna deliver, Bagwell . . ."

"Swear to God on my mother's grave, Barlow! Just get me off this thing and back out to the ship."

"Don't move a muscle."

Act Five. Fuck around in the mud for a minute or two while Bagwell sweats and plans menus. Ad-lib time?

Mallory grinned at Barlow through the chief's trembling legs. Sometimes you just gotta wing it.

"OK, Chief. Real easy now. We got a temporary pin in it . . ."

Mallory stood quietly, put his finger to his lips and his shoulder near the small of the chief's back. When Barlow did not visibly object, he shoved hard and launched Master Chief Bagwell toward a nearby mud puddle.

While Bagwell wiped away a combination of sweat, tears and mud, Mallory stooped to retrieve the dummy mine. He examined it critically and whistled between his teeth.

"Lucky thing, Chief. These bastards bounce up out of the deck and go off about crotch level. Would have blown your balls right out of the Med."

Dripping rain from his poncho, Gunny Barlow stood just inside the mess tent and caught sight of Mallory wolfing from a plate of hot sausage and potatoes. Steam rose from every other plate in front of every other Marine under the canvas. Barlow nodded in satisfaction and shouted for the man on mess duty to dish him up some chow.

"You deliver them souvenirs like I told you, Mallory? A deal's a deal."

Mallory swallowed and smiled. "Took 'em out to *Inchon* myself on the afternoon admin run, Gunny. Can't say the chief had much time for 'em, though. He was wallopin' pots like fourteen motherfuckers."

Barlow snorted, accepted a heaping plate full of hot food and sat down across from the squad leader. Mallory watched him chew and smirk for a few moments and then asked the question he'd been saving since that day in the muddy field next to the mosque.

"I admit that was one hell of a scam, Gunny, but what was the point? Enough people was bitchin' about the chow and laundry. The Old Man woulda got it fixed eventually."

Barlow stabbed his fork at a wayward potato and popped it into his mouth. He chewed with relish but his eyes were rock-steady, boring through the canvas wall of the mess tent.

"Coulda waited. Wasn't nobody around here gonna starve. Gettin' bored, I guess."

"You mean you ran that entire game down on the chief just because you were bored?"

Barlow belched resonantly and moved his face across the table slowly. When he was nearly nose-to-nose with Mallory he suddenly smiled and spoke in a hoarse whisper.

"Got to live out on the edge of the envelope, man! You wanna run with the big dogs, you gotta learn to piss on the tall trees . . ."

PFC Deeter Dale decided not to wake Private Walter Stankey just to look at a couple of Hebe APCs knocking over olive trees. He'd wait to see if they stopped fucking around out by Hooterville and came closer to the perimeter road. Stankey'd probably panic and piss himself anyway.

Fuckin' clown almost dropped a load the other day when them sand niggers started shootin' up the area out by Checkpoint 35. Reg'lar Wild West Show when the Lebs took to bustin' caps. Gawdam ragheads got their finger out of their ass in a hurry then. Shit fire! Had a ringside seat from up here in the OP. Naturally, they won't let *me* load no rounds in the gun.

Be different next week when we take over out at CP 35. Tell you what ah'm gonna do . . . ever' fuckin' time I got the watch. Pop this feed cover right here. Grab the bitter end of a little 250-round belt and slap her in there. Good firing position . . . nice and steady. Flick of the thumb . . . little squeeze on the trigger . . .

"Dale! Goddammit, man! How many times I got to tell you to stop fucking with that machine gun?" Mallory was striding across the roof of the OP and he was not happy with his watch-standers.

Dale rolled away from the gun to see Pvt. Stankey emerge from the shade without his helmet or weapon. Shit was bound to hit the fan now.

"This is an *observation post*, Dale. And you're senior man aboard it. You pass the word to the CP about those Israeli APCs?"

"Naw, Corporal Mallory. We was waitin' to see if they come any closer . . ."

"So you could do what, Dale? Open up on 'em? Stankey, what's the rule on machine guns?"

Stankey thought this might be his chance to move up from assistant gunner and he tried hard to remember the exact words. "Uh, machine guns is to be kept on safe with the bolt forward. Ammo loaded only on command of squad leader. Automatic weapons not to engage targets unless gunners is given the order by a commissioned officer . . ."

Mallory popped the feed cover of the M-60 and stripped out the belt of mixed ball and tracer ammo. "Outstanding, Stankey. Something about that you don't understand, PFC Dale?"

Deeter considered his squad leader's recently acquired penchant for assigning extra duties as punishment for minor infractions. Prob'ly a result of spendin' too much time around that lifin' Gonorrhea Sergeant Barlow. Fuck 'em both.

"Ah was just practicin' . . ."

Mallory stared out over the roof of the OP momentarily. The Israeli APCs seemed to be headed for the perimeter. They'd done that before a couple of times. He was sure they would turn off before they hit the fence.

"Practicin' for what, Dale? Don't you remember any-thing you're taught, man? LAF troops gotta be the first to

open fire. If we are directly threatened and have to return
fire to save our asses, we use minimum necessary firepower. That means rifles, Deeter. And not this fucking
machine gun. Is that clear?"

"It's raht clear, Corporal . . . but me understandin' alla
that shit don't help none. It ain't fair fer them to put us slap
in the middle of this rodeo without a horse!"

"Awright, you two assholes are gettin' on my nerves.
There's a brand-new pallet of sandbags down below. When
you get off watch, I want . . ."

The remainder of Mallory's order was lost in engine roar,
grinding tracks and the shriek of metal. He bolted for the
stairs leading to the ground as shouts for the corporal of the
guard were passed along the perimeter.

PFC Dale and Private Stankey calmly reloaded the M-60
machine gun and drew a bead on the Israeli Armored
Personnel Carrier that was just crashing through the airport
fence line.

Lance Corporal Justice was on the horn to the Combat
Operations Center on the other side of the runway when
Mallory rushed past his post. He nodded approval and
headed for the point along the perimeter where the IDF
armored vehicle, heavily sandbagged against armor-
piercing rounds and festooned with machine guns, had
smashed into the Cyclone fence.

The lead APC was sitting halfway inside the perimeter. A
second idled loudly in trace, ready to lock right track and
follow the leader into the American sector. What kept that
from happening was Private First Class William Stone of
Rochester, New York.

He stood directly in the intended path of the Israeli
vehicles, snapped the M-16 off his shoulder, came to port
arms and shouted at a bearded figure sitting behind a
.50-caliber machine gun.

"Hey, bud! This is U. S. Marine territory. Take that tin can back to Tel Aviv!"

Mallory arrived just in time to catch the next exchange. Across the runway he could see the rooster tails of two jeeps approaching at speed. That would be the colonel . . . and a good thing. It appeared the armor commander was concerned about rank.

"Do you know you are addressing an Israeli officer?"

Stone seemed seriously underwhelmed by it all and grew bolder as Justice and several other Marines arrived to back his play.

"Listen, ass-wipe. I don't give a fuck if I'm talkin' to Moses! My orders say no one comes through here . . . and if they do, they show authority and use the goddamned gate. Back this rig outa here . . . now!"

Mallory saluted as Colonel Skaggs and Lieutenant Colonel Mattson stormed out of their jeeps. Black Jack walked to a spot directly behind Stone and glared at the Israeli officer. Skaggs inquired who was corporal of the guard and then approached Mallory.

"What the hell is *this* all about, Steve?"

"Got me, Colonel. I was up on the OP when they hit the fence. First time they ever come this far the other side of Hooterville. Stone stopped 'em. I thought sure as hell someone was gonna open up."

Skaggs glanced over at the Israeli officer. The man seemed to be making a radio transmission, speaking quietly into his helmet microphone. The muscles in Skaggs's jaws bunched and Mallory knew from experience he was fighting to control his temper.

"OK . . . you run up the line and see that nobody gets trigger-happy. I don't want anybody snapping in on that guy up in the turret. I'll take it from here."

Colonel Skaggs stepped into the perimeter road and shouted over the throbbing engines.

"Sir, you are in an area jointly controlled by the Lebanese Armed Forces and the American contingent of the Multinational Force. What are you doing here?"

The bearded officer stripped off his helmet and shrugged. "It's a big city. I got lost."

Skaggs jammed his fists onto his hips and glared into the sarcastic smile on the face of the Israeli officer.

"You couldn't see my sentries? You don't have a map? You're asking me to believe a bit more than I care to, sir. What I care to believe at this point is that you are an independent agent operating outside your orders."

Skaggs pointed a stubby finger at the officer and swept his hand toward the nearby village.

"Now, you turn these vehicles around and get 'em out of my area."

The Israeli officer retained the insolent expression but he jammed his helmet back on and spoke into the radio. As a result, the second APC ground into gear and began to reverse. The officer watched it for a moment and then leaned over the side of his vehicle.

"Sorry about the fence. *Someone* has to chase the terrorists. *Shalom.*"

Skaggs stood in the road watching the departing vehicles and fighting the temptation to call out his antitank gunners. It was a hard battle and he would have lost if PFC Stone hadn't moved up beside him with a question that could not be ignored.

"You want me to shoot that bastard, sir? I fired expert on the range."

Skaggs laughed loudly and threw an arm around the startled sentry. "Naw, son. Let's not shoot that bastard just yet."

Colonel Skaggs was still chuckling on the way back to his jeep, but Stone failed to see the humor in the situation. Probably some kinda officer joke. Still . . .

"Anytime you *do* wanna shoot the sonofabitch, sir . . . will you let me know?"

In the maudlin week following the Marines' first Christmas in Beirut, incidents of incoming fire increased and there were some very near misses. Superstitious Marines put it down to the same sort of bad luck that kept Bob Hope from making it over to entertain American troops committed to a combat zone for the first time in contemporary history. Regardless, the reins were kept tight and they chafed.

On a cloudy Saturday morning out near Hotel Company, a sniper winged a few desultory rounds at an inner-perimeter sentry. In an interview with the press following the incident, the sentry told reporters he could easily have nailed the shooter if he'd been allowed to load his rifle and fire. While the Marine public affairs officer gritted his teeth in agony, the young Marine grinned at the cameras and called the situation "a damn shame, since I coulda blown a hole in the dude big enough to drive a jeep through and then he wouldn't be shootin' at no more Marines."

The next day, a bird hunter in nearby Hay es Sallom fired his shotgun at a pigeon and started a pointless firefight between the Lebanese Army unit at OP 35 and several armed villagers who presumed they were being attacked. The Marines at the outpost were forced under cover for an hour and a half, until the firing eventually petered out.

Despite the best efforts of the Marine PAO to downplay such incidents, the copy-hungry American press in Beirut had a field day with the stories and the Marines involved who were more than happy to vent their spleens.

While generals and admirals up and down the chain granted interviews and assured the press that American Marines would be given every opportunity to defend themselves, secret messages burned through the air to Beirut ordering Colonel Skaggs to review and reemphasize the Rules of Engagement.

It was about that time that the Tactical Communications Satellite downlink was installed in his CP.

The only happy camper in the Combat Operations Center after the civilian installation team left was First Lieutenant Denning, the MAU communications officer, who equated high-tech with heaven-sent.

"Basically, Colonel, it's a satellite link that puts us in direct comm with anyone in the chain of command from Frankfurt to Washington. It eliminates the lag time for message traffic and contains a shielded circuit that lets us talk in the clear with anybody who has a similar set . . . even the President!"

Skaggs raised his bushy eyebrows and motioned for Lt. Denning to have a private word with him. "Does it work the other way around?"

"You mean can the President talk directly to us? You bet, sir. It's the next best thing to being there."

Skaggs stared into a canteen cup full of black coffee and tugged at his earlobe. "So, it's very sophisticated, right? And Murphy's Law says the amount of trouble you have with a piece of gear is directly proportional to its level of technical sophistication. Ain't that what it says?"

Denning was confused. This is state-of-the-art equipment. Virtually maintenance-free. "Sir, if you're worried about downtime . . . I think I can guarantee this equipment will stay up."

Skaggs shook his head and stared directly into Denning's eyes. "That's where you're wrong, Lieutenant. We're gonna have a *lot* of trouble with this damned Batphone. In fact, I'd say it's gonna be down a lot more than it's up . . ." Skaggs put a firm hand on his communication officer's shoulder. "As an expert, what would you say?"

Lieutenant Denning finally completed the mental circuit and grinned back at his boss.

"I'd say this damn high-tech comm system is full of gremlins, sir."

In the predawn darkness—just at the hour before the sun peeks over the Anti-Lebanon Mountains and begins to chase the murky shadows out to sea—Eladar steered his taxi onto Sidon Road and began to count trees. When his headlights had illuminated eleven of the gnarled olive trees on the east edge of the road, he switched off the engine and let the vehicle roll to a stop.

Leaving the headlights on and cursing loudly in French, he walked to the front of the car and raised the squeaky hood. More loud curses, and then he switched off the lights, fetched his flashlight and tool kit and began to tinker with the engine.

Ibrahim motioned for Masra to remain in the car and unwound himself from the backseat. He moved to the side of the road to urinate and was not surprised to find himself semi-erect. It was not necessary to bring the woman, but she made it easier to travel the roads at night. The soldiers manning roadblocks were not so suspicious of men traveling with women. And she certainly was a distraction.

He shook his head slightly to clear unwelcome thoughts and searched the area around him carefully with his eyes. Eladar's reconnaissance had paid dividends. The spot was perfect. Phalangist sentries out of sight to the south, around a curve in the road. Americans asleep behind their wire at least a kilometer to the north and no Zionist patrols until dawn. Perfect.

He returned to the cab and spoke quietly to Mohammed, who was sitting next to Masra and tinkering under the soft glow of a red-lensed flashlight. "We have thirty minutes, no more. Will it be enough?"

Mohammed merely grunted and completed a wiring circuit. He had been pulled away from much more important work and he was anxious to get back to his shop.

Carrying the specially prepared antitank mine, he crawled from the cab and rolled underneath. The large pothole Eladar had spotted was full of rainwater but that did not present a problem. The mine was fully waterproof and made of plastic so it would not trip Zionist detectors.

He planted the mine carefully and booby-trapped it using a pressure-release mousetrap device rigged to a blasting cap. Even if the Zionists happen to find the mine, he told himself with satisfaction, they will not be able to remove it.

When all three Hezbollah men were back in the taxi and headed toward Beirut, Mohammed aired his complaint. "We have little time to complete work on the truck, brothers. Such harassment tactics could wait."

Ibrahim rolled down the window and sniffed at the freshening breeze. It would soon be dawn and another day would bring them closer to the final objective. "You must have faith, Mohammed. I see the larger plan and must do what is necessary."

Without taking his eyes from the roadside, Ibrahim slid a hand under Masra's leg and began to tickle the tender flesh at the back of her knee. She stiffened and Ibrahim remembered the swell and flex of her leg muscles in another time, when she walked the fields with her skirt pinned up to her waist. He would see them again . . . *feel* them. Men of destiny choose any woman they want, and those women come panting.

Eladar swung his taxi off Sidon Road, the main supply route for Zionist troops based in Beirut, and glanced at his rearview mirror. Pink fingers of sunlight probed the foothills. The Zionists would soon be on the road and he would be elsewhere, cruising along like an old married man with

Ibrahim's cousin. There were still more explosives to be brought in from the Bekaa Valley.

"Bagel Express up ahead, Gunny. Buncha trucks and a couple of APCs, it looks like . . ."

"Shit! Assholes oughta put their resupply run on some kind of reasonable schedule. See if you can find room to swing around 'em."

Mallory began searching for cutoffs he knew were not there. They'd have to sit behind the IDF convoy until they reached Golf Company's area, where the road began to skirt the eastern edge of Hay es Sallom, or Hooterville. On the way back from a scrounging mission to the Lebanese Ministry of Defense at Ba'abda, the Gunny made him drive. Barlow had made some kind of deal with a Leb officer up at MOD and he was anxious to get back to the MAU CP.

Lance Corporal Justice needed to baby-sit a cranky radio and the Gunny said Doc Grouse "drives like old people fuck." Naturally, PFC Deeter Dale couldn't be pried out from behind the pintle-mounted M-60 machine gun he kept swinging from side to side like some reject from the Rat Patrol.

Barlow turned in his seat and glared at the machine gunner. Helmet on backwards. Tanker's goggles. Jesus Christ! Everything but a white silk scarf blowing in the wind.

"Dale, for fuck's sake will you leave that gun alone, boy? It ain't loaded and the rules say you *can't* load it."

The Texan stood with his legs spread, riding the swaying jeep like a familiar old horse, and pulled the gun tightly into his shoulder.

"Them fuckers don't know that . . ."

Doc Grouse reached over and shoved at a canteen that was brushing his nose. "Who the hell are '*them fuckers*,' Dale?"

Dale let go of the machine gun long enough to sweep a hand across the foothill villages to encompass a ragged line of pedestrians on their way to business in Beirut.

"Far as ah'm concerned, them fuckers is every raghead, dune coon, sand nigger and camel jockey in this whole country. First sumbitch takes a shot at me is gonna wind up with an air-conditioned asshole."

Lance Corporal Justice was just about to inform Dale that he didn't appreciate the words "coon" or "nigger"—even if they *were* references to ragheads—when a concussive crack whipped over the jeep and caused Mallory to jam on the brakes. Unchastised for his language, PFC Dale was thrown forward over the machine gun and into the windshield, which yielded to pressure from his helmeted head. His sputtering complaints were lost in the echoing boom of a large explosion.

Mallory stood beside Barlow on the jeep seats watching a pillar of smoke and flame build at the head of the IDF convoy. Mine or RPG? Got to be a mine. We would have heard the firing signature of a rocket launcher. Troopers bailing out of the trucks. APCs barreling forward. Must be one of them hit the mine.

Barlow thumped Mallory on the shoulder and jumped to the ground. "Let's go. Leave the jeep here. Justice, get on the horn to the COC and let 'em know the Israelis have hit a mine out here. *Now* load the fucking gun, Dale!"

Mallory set off after Barlow at a dead run but he could tell it was pointless after fifty meters of dodging around excited Israeli soldiers scrambling into a defensive perimeter.

Lead APC has had the cock! Burning like a bitch. Anybody inside that shoe box is a crispy critter for damn sure. Mine musta been planted up in that big pothole. Blew off the entire left track. Two dead . . . three, four wounded. That fucker with the burns ain't gonna make it either. What are you assholes starin' at me for? I didn't do it.

Doing his best to ignore the glare of IDF troopers helping to clear the carnage around the burning vehicle, Mallory walked toward a small rise overlooking the road, where Barlow had located the convoy commander.

IDF light colonel from the shoulder boards. Black beret. Armor. Looks like a pro. A very pissed-off pro.

"Sir, I've got a jeep and a medic back there to the rear. I'd be glad to help if you need a quick medevac . . ."

"Now you decide to be an ally, Sergeant? Where were you when the bastards planted the mine? You want to help? Go tell your officers to do something about the terrorists coming through the American sector to kill my men!"

Barlow noticed Mallory and motioned for him to keep his distance. No matter. Can't miss hearing them yell at each other. Every Israeli trooper within thirty meters is in on it. Probably intentional. Light bird is definitely gettin' his licks.

"Don't give me this business about the nature of your mission, Sergeant. The nature of the mission is to stop these terrorist bastards from killing people. If the Lebanese could control them, we wouldn't be here!"

Troops look like they'd just as soon take it out on a couple of Americans. This is not the time to argue. Let's go. Leave 'em to it.

Mallory couldn't help glancing over his shoulder as he followed Barlow back toward the jeep but the Gunny just stalked along, shoving his way past shell-shocked Israeli soldiers watching medics load casualties into an ambulance. He flinched only a bit when the IDF officer fired a parting shot.

"Iwo Jima was a long time ago, Sergeant! I think the U.S. Marines have lost their balls since then!"

"That slimy cocksucker . . ."

"Shut up, Mallory! Don't mean nothin'. People get into some weird reactions when they lose troops."

Lieutenant Colonel Ravi Lundstrom smeared ointment on his flash-burned forearms and glared at the diplomat sitting on the other side of his field desk. He finally broke an uncomfortable silence by tapping the paper in front of him with a greasy fingertip.

"And how am I to interpret 'take whatever actions are necessary to protect Israeli soldiers' when the same message tells me 'not to endanger the lives or safety of the Multi-national Forces in Beirut'?"

The visiting diplomat removed his tinted glasses and rubbed at a sore spot on the bridge of his nose. He hadn't cared much for this mission into Lebanon, just as he hadn't cared for the initial incursion and the continued presence in this God-forsaken place. The pressure at home was building to fever pitch. What interest did Israel have in remaining in Lebanon now that the primary terrorist formations were gone? Jewish mothers, fathers, wives, sisters and brothers wanted the troops back on home soil. Why couldn't Tel Aviv simply order them out rather than send him up here to mince words with soldiers who only understood tanks and guns?

"It seems quite clear to me, Colonel. You do whatever is necessary and prudent to protect your troops . . . except where those actions will endanger American, French or Italian lives."

Lundstrom angrily lit a cigarette and jabbed it at his visitor. "Doesn't anyone in Tel Aviv read my reports? The Palestinians may be gone from Beirut, but other terrorists are not! They come at us through the sectors controlled by the Lebanese and the Americans. Aren't we supposed to be allies? Why don't the Americans do something about it?"

"You are being shortsighted, Ravi. If this was the only

American connection we had to worry about . . . fine, we'd cooperate. But there are other considerations. Everyone wants us out of Lebanon. Our lobby in Washington is plagued by people who say we should go home. And back home? My God, the Kinesset is inundated with pressure to bring the boys back to Israel . . ."

"This business of leaving it up to the Lebanese has always been nonsense and it remains so."

The diplomat wearily placed his hands on his knees and levered himself out of the chair. "You have your orders, Ravi. Please try to cooperate. *Shalom.*"

Leaving Lieutenant Colonel Ravi Lundstrom's command tent, the diplomat felt exactly the same as when he left Tel Aviv. These arguments between the soldiers and the policymakers went nowhere. Not here and not at home. The orders were issued. Only time would tell if the soldiers would obey them.

Captain Ron Jennings focused his field glasses on the Bagel Express and listened as Corporal Mallory relayed the count from a checkpoint out by the gate. The observers confirmed what he could see from the roof of his CP.

"They're comin' heavy this morning, sir. Oscar X-ray counts four Centurians, at least three APCs and an unknown number of trucks."

The APCs meant another frustrating hour ducking incoming fire while the IDF convoy probed the sides of Sidon Road with heavy machine guns. Recon by fire—stupid as it is with friendlies in the area—was one thing. But why the tanks? Jennings shifted his concentration to the man in the cupola of the lead tank. Lieutenant Colonel of armored troops conferring with another officer on the ground. Somewhere in the back of his brain the battle-stations bell sounded.

"Gunny Barlow! Secure the working parties. In the holes. Helmets and flak jackets."

Barlow looked up from his grid map and squinted at the idling tanks. "Dragon gunners on standby, sir?"

"Let's not ask for trouble we ain't got yet, Gunny. Just get everybody under cover and stand by for the standard recon by fire." No sense in pointing a clutch of antitank missiles at the Bagel Express. Not with the IDF and the Marines taunting each other like two scrappy kids in a schoolyard. Still, something doesn't feel right . . .

"Corporal Mallory. Go stand by the jeep. Don't make an issue of it. Just hang around down there."

Jennings followed the squad leader down the stairs from the roof of Marine Barracks Beirut to a point where he could follow the Israeli activity out on Sidon Road by radio. As a Mormon, Jennings believed in the power of prayer. He spent the next ten minutes praying that the skittish Lebanese Army troops out in the courtyard would not suffer a sudden infusion of nationalism or courage.

If they finally let the Israeli needle get under their skins and returned fire, Golf Company Marines would be caught right in the middle of a nasty firefight.

Gunny Barlow was the first man on the roof to figure out what the Israeli troops were doing. He sprinted for the stairs, bulled into the Company CP and shouted over the babble of radio traffic.

"Skipper! Two Centurions! Turnin' off the road. They're gonna come through the wire!"

Jennings bolted for the stairs leading out of the building and shouted over his shoulder. "Call Redman Six and report it. Get out there and see if you can keep the Lebs from panicking!"

Mallory had the jeep idling in gear as soon as he heard his CO's heavy boots on the stairs. He figured they'd be heading out to the front gate and onto the road but Jennings surprised him.

"Straight out there! Head for those tanks!"

Jesus Christ! Look at those bastards come. Battle speed right through the perimeter wire. What the hell are they doing? They'll run right over our ass! Lebs are at lock and load. We better head for the ditch!

Jennings reached over and flipped the jeep ignition switch just as Mallory whipped the wheel to the left in an effort to avoid the path of the oncoming tanks.

"They ain't gonna stop, Skipper!"

"Just wait here!" The Golf Company commander vaulted out of the jeep and headed for the dirt road down which the tanks were headed. Mallory thought he'd seen the last of a man he liked and respected as Jennings planted himself directly in the path of the roaring vehicles. When the tanks were only twenty-five meters away, he screamed for his captain to move before it was too late, but the warning was lost in the rattle and creak of tracks.

Only when the rounded glacis plate of the lead Centurion dipped and halted just two feet from Captain Jennings did Mallory manage to shut his mouth and take a breath. Until that time, he was certain he was about to see a man murdered; run over without the slightest hesitation. He'd seen his hardheaded captain in enough tough situations to know once planted, the man would not be uprooted.

Over his shoulder, Mallory heard several weapon bolts go home but he was afraid to take his eyes off the strange tableau of 170-pound man facing 115,000-pound tank. If that driver's foot slips off the clutch . . . If some jerk gets tense on a trigger . . .

Captain Ron Jennings sucked hard on his teeth, trying to lubricate his throat so the challenge would come in a martial tone rather than a bleat or a croak. He looked up at the grinning Israeli officer in the turret and decided he'd had just about enough foolishness.

"I want to talk to whoever's in command!"

The officer in the Centurion turret stared around him and pursed his lips. Jennings did not take his eyes off the man's face, but he could tell the Israeli was evaluating, considering the number of muzzles pointed at his tank and the one behind it.

"I'm going to go through here!"

"These are Marine lines. You better talk to your general!"

"You talk to *your* general. I'm coming through!"

When the engine of the lead tank began to accelerate upwards from a throaty idle, Jennings stepped back a pace, where he could be clearly seen by both driver and tank commander. He reached down, calmly unsnapped the flap of his holster and drew his service .45.

With a deliberate motion, he pulled the slide to the rear, jacked a round into the chamber and assumed the raise-pistol position like a target-shooter on the range. Jennings considered how ludicrous he must appear holding a pistol and facing a 105-mm tank cannon. He prayed silently that none of his men would decide to even the odds.

The Israeli interrupted the Hebrew transmission he was making on the radio and glared at the camouflage-clad figure standing in his path. Captain Jennings knew he would live or die in the next few seconds. When he finally spoke, he was surprisingly calm.

"You want another war, Colonel? You got one . . . right here."

With a sort of detached interest, Jennings watched the senior officer evaluate him. He noted the sardonic smile; the lift of the eyebrows. Taking my measure. Should put a round right past his ear. Clear up this obvious failure to communicate. Show the Israelis they aren't the only ones who can pull a trigger in Beirut.

Mallory was wondering how much difference it would make if he drove the jeep down in front of the tanks to back the Skipper up when he saw the vehicles jerk into reverse gear.

Sonofabitch! They're backing off! Can you dig it? One goddamn Marine officer with a piss-ant .45 and he faces down two Centurion tanks. Now *that* is some kinda heavy shit!

Mallory started the jeep, getting ready to drive Captain Jennings back to a hero's welcome, as every eye in the compound followed the retreat of the tanks. Suddenly, the rear Centurion rattled into a forward gear and swept around the lead tank. Making an end run! Bastards are gonna force it!

There was no slack on any trigger in Golf Company's area as Captain Jennings leaped on the leading Centurion and grabbed the officer in the cupola by the collar. He jerked the Israeli forward and screamed into his face.

"Stop that tank! Stop your damn tanks!"

The Israeli tank commander noted the similarity between the steel in the American's glare and the cold surface of the pistol aimed directly at his left ear. He slowly, carefully, thumbed a switch on the side of his helmet and spoke a Hebrew command into his microphone.

Mallory didn't know what to say on the ride back to the barracks. There didn't seem to be any appropriate words in his lexicon to congratulate a man who had just pulled off what his captain had managed. There was complete silence in the compound for several minutes after Mallory parked the jeep and Captain Jennings made no move to dismount.

And then it started. It roared across the compound and echoed off the walls of Marine Barracks Beirut. Golf

Company Marines grunted, snorted and screamed their approval.

For a full week following the incident, the American press celebrated the Marines, their discipline and courage, all personified in Captain Ron Jennings. Editorial cartoons depicted Jennings and his pistol as "America's newest secret weapon." The ironic twist of a superpower David facing down a Third World Goliath was lost somewhere between the excitement of the moment and dire predictions of worsening relations between a country committed to affairs in the Middle East and its only active ally in that area.

Masra saw him again for the first time outside her dreams on a cloudy day in Hay es Sallom as she walked out of the butcher shop near the main crossroads. It was the checkered *kefiyeh* that caught her eye when she rushed to see why the police had been summoned to an area where a noisy crowd had gathered outside the vegetable-seller's shop.

Mallory, she remembered. Steve Mallory, a tall American with startling green eyes and a crooked grin that suggested he was amused by nearly everything he saw.

Masra stood on the edge of the crowd and stared as Mallory and some other Americans watched the police arrest the vegetable-seller. All seemed fascinated; nearly shocked at the scene in the street. They could not be expected to understand.

The old woman who sold charcoal and dispensed gossip in her street said that the Americans had driven by in their jeep at the worst possible moment. Just when the vegetable-seller was forced to shoot the young Druze who had been seeing his sister, along came the Americans. Now there would be trouble, the old woman said. She had seen that kind of thing before in her life. *Ins' allah,* she said, it is the will of God; and she shuffled off with barely a glance at the dead Druze still lying in the muddy street.

Masra heard the vegetable-seller using the same phrase as he was disarmed and stuffed into the Lebanese police car. *Ins' allah!* The vegetable seller surrendered the smoking pistol and declared that he was guilty of no crime. She knew that would totally confound Steve Mallory and his American friends. Such an alien concept. To them it would seem as if a murderer had been caught in the act.

Of course, the vegetable-seller was not denying that he killed the young Druze. Yes, he killed the man . . . but there was no *crime* in that. *Ins' allah,* as God wills it, so will it be done. No man can change destiny or deny the will of God.

And God had willed that the Druze die, the vegetable-seller protested, for the crime of harboring designs on a Shi'ite woman from a respectable family. He was only the *instrument* of God's will in this case. Since God could commit no crime, no crime had been committed. *Ins' allah!*

Still, the police took the vegetable-seller away to jail as the Americans walked back to their jeep shaking their heads and talking excitedly about the killing. Steve Mallory did not seem to think it was amusing. He sat silently in the backseat of the vehicle. The alluring, captivating grin was gone but Masra still thought him the most handsome man she had ever seen.

She walked home slowly, carrying a parcel of goat meat and fresh squash; wondering what it would be like to live in a place where the will of God and the law of men did not always seem in conflict. She felt a strange blush spread from just above the swell of her breasts.

Ins' allah, she prayed.

Hooterville had been relatively quiet over the past four days since his squad was assigned to Checkpoint 54 but Mallory still didn't care for the foot patrols. The streets were narrow, constricted; bordered along many of the serpentine alleys and side streets by two-story structures that made havens for snipers. Still, he was required to show the flag at least once a day, leaving the crucial crossroads leading to BIA in the care of a Lebanese officer and his small platoon of dispirited infantrymen.

He'd gone to the chain of command about modifying the Rules of Engagement on foot patrols through Hooterville, but the platoon sergeant always came back with the same response: Don't ask for problems you ain't got. Magazine in the weapon but no rounds in the chambers. In the unlikely event you step in a bucket of shit, call the Lebs and let them handle it.

It wouldn't be so bad—Mallory mused as he gave the hand signal for his squad to close interval and move right into a twisting, curiously deserted Hooterville street—if we didn't have to keep changing routes. Never know where the hell the Lebs are and you can't modify your routes to meet them or you set a dangerous pattern.

As he turned to walk backward for a pace or two, Mallory scanned the roofs of the adjacent buildings. Nothing to see but shadows and those can fuck all over your imagination. He took a deep breath to chase away the gremlins and turned his attention to the squad. Justice humping the Prick 77; monitoring the command freq. No problem. Deeter Dale across from him with the unloaded M-60 machine gun. Probably got his pistol locked and cocked but ain't no point in sweating the small stuff with him. Where the hell is Stankey? Told that little maggot to stay within arm's length of the gun.

Mallory spun in his tracks and faced toward Rojas, who was walking point as usual. Stone at slack; Doc at drag . . . shit, there he is, ahead of the gun and got his eyes right smack down on the deck.

"Stankey! Get your head up, goddammit! And get the hell . . ."

Mallory froze. Did something move up there to his left? He craned in that direction and peered out from under the rim of his helmet. An arm flashed out of the shadow and into the sunlight briefly. He was about to shout a warning, when he saw it. Grenade!

Instinctively, he flattened into the mud and shouted the alert, hoping he wasn't ghost-dancing and about to embarrass the hell out of himself. He lifted his head and saw brown water splash as the grenade landed in a mud puddle to his left front. There were more shouts as Marines dove for their own piece of earth, but they were lost in the dirty crack of the exploding grenade.

Mallory heard shrapnel buzz over him like a swarm of angry bees and the hollow splat of a piece or two impacting his helmet. He lifted his head again and tried to swallow away the ringing in his ears. What the hell was Rojas screaming about; waving his arms like a traffic cop at rush hour?

"Get outa de street! Move right! *Dos* . . . two of de bastards!"

Mallory managed to get a knee underneath his quaking body and pull his rifle out of the mud. He was about to break for a low stone wall in the indicated direction when his vision was dimmed by gouts of mud and water. A burst of automatic fire stitched the street just a foot from his face.

Sonofabitch! Plunging fire and I'm the only sorry-ass in the beaten zone. Either move or lay here and die! Won't miss with a second burst. Up . . . up . . . go for the wall! Jesus God, don't shoot me in the back, you rotten raghead cocksucker!

As he vaulted over the wall and landed on his shoulder, Mallory heard the second AK open up in a long, chugging burst. A sound like someone cracking a bullwhip made him duck but not before a sizzling concrete chip raked his cheek and drew blood. Mallory wiped at it idly and peeked quickly over the wall to determine the disposition of his troops. He had a heartbeat to determine the street was deserted before another burst smacked into the wall of a stone house at his rear.

Trapped! Shit! Can't move up or back. Bastards must be on both sides of the street. Cross fire. All the doors and windows along here shuttered and locked. Either run it from here or wait until they burn through all their ammo.

"Rojas! Doc! You OK?"

"Yeah! Let's get the fuck outa here!"

"Mallory! I see de *puta*. Top floor to de right front. Gonna fire 'im up, man!"

"Hold it! Lemme see if Justice got through to the COC . . ."

Another burst of fire followed by a second grenade made Mallory wish he'd moved his bulky magazine pouches back toward his hips so he could get closer to the ground. If only one of these people had left their door open, I'd be inside and out of this bastard's line of fire.

"Justice! You hear me, man?"

"Yo . . . back here . . . same side of the street."

"You get through to Redman Six?"

"Yeah . . . they say Leb patrol is inbound. We're supposed to stay under cover and hold fire. Can you *believe* that shit?"

Before he could respond, Mallory felt a sting like scalding hot water poured over his hands. His M-16 snapped back at him like a bayonet fighter delivering a vicious butt stroke. He convulsed and tried to mesh himself with the rough stones of the wall. The off-side AK gunner was getting the range and moving for a better angle on the man trapped behind the wall. He retrieved the errant rifle and saw the black plastic stock was shattered. The heavy recoil spring waved at him like a broken-necked jack-in-the-box. A round had hit just forward of the rubber butt plate.

Got to move! Got to get the hell off this bull's-eye! Must have me spotted as the squad leader. Out to get himself an NCO and a commendation. Jesus! No place to hide. I'm gonna die here in this fucking Beirut! Wait! What's that? Wind? Who gives a shit? Open door on my right. My ass is gone!

Doc Grouse was screaming something over the rattle of gunfire—all incoming—but Mallory didn't listen. Nothing was as important as getting out of the gunman's increasingly accurate sights. He bolted for the dark rectangle of an open door and launched himself over a small porch into the cool interior of a low stone house. Two slugs gouged the wooden door as he rolled right and hugged a damp cement wall.

Made it! Christ! Thank you, Lord. No shit. Thanks. My ass was suckin' buttermilk out there. Another fifteen seconds and that sonofabitch woulda . . . what the fuck?

Over the ragged rasp of his own breathing, Mallory heard something rustle in the murky shadows at the back of the room. He snapped the shot-up rifle into his shoulder as best he could and hoped nothing but the stock had been damaged. Without the recoil spring, he'd only have one shot.

"Don't shoot! Don't shoot!"

That voice . . . English. Holy shit! "Hey! That you? You . . . from the street . . . with the kid?"

She shoved the door closed with a broom handle and emerged from the shadows.

It *is* her! Jesus, I finally run into this woman after three weeks of wet dreams and she's savin' my ass from gettin' blown away. What can I say? How the fuck you gonna act?

"Hey, thanks . . . really, thanks a lot. I was in big trouble out there . . ."

The woman cringed as one of the ambushers emptied a

magazine at something in the street. Mallory's ears told him all the reports were from an AK.

Hope the guys are holding tight under cover. Think I hear the cavalry coming. What's she saying?

"It is the Hezbollah . . . the Party of God. Do you know of them?"

Cavalry's inbound. Recognize the whine of one of those armored cars anywhere. Jesus, she looks great. Go figure it, man. Nearly get your ass nailed and when you don't, your crank swells up like a boa constrictor wearin' a turtleneck sweater. Edge of the envelope is a kinky place, man.

"Never heard of that outfit . . . but the bastards can shoot, I'll give 'em that. Listen, what the hell is your name anyway?"

"I am called Masra . . . I . . . I wanted . . . for saving . . . the boy." She smiled and Mallory noticed her teeth were strong and white.

Probably learned a thing or two about nutrition when she was in school. Certain smell . . . comes through the damp odor in here. Musky, hot, sweaty . . . but it doesn't stink. Shit, I got to start payin' attention here. Lebs have arrived.

A .50-caliber machine gun began to chuff and chatter out on the street. He heard Justice whistle through his teeth and Rojas shouting at the Marines to stay behind the armored car. He had an absurd thought about the amount of paperwork his broken rifle would engender. Maybe they'd let him keep it for a souvenir.

He rose and noticed his legs had gone to sleep. He stomped twice, grinned and fought off an urge to hug the voluptuous woman kneeling before him.

"Listen, uh . . . Masra, I owe you one. My squad's stationed up by the crossroads. Let me know if there's anything I can do . . ."

Another smile. Strange woman. Seems somehow . . .

anxious or maybe . . . hot for my skivvies? I should be that fucking lucky . . . just one day in my life.

"Corporal Mallory! Bad guys boogied outa here. Six callin' for you on the hook."

Mallory smiled and tried to put a little of the sexual heat he felt into the expression. The woman simply stared at him and nodded. What the hell did that mean? Yes? No? Get the fuck outa my house?

He stepped out into the gloom of an overcast day and tried to concentrate. The squad was chattering and bitching in a cluster behind the Lebanese armored car. The Leb gunner was swiveling the muzzle from side to side, aiming at all the second-story windows along the street. Mallory could see huge gouges in concrete and splintered wood where the man had walked his rounds in a devastating sweep up and down the street. Maybe he killed the . . . what the hell did she call them . . . the Hezbollah?

"Head count, Rojas. Who we missin'?"

PFC Dale peeked around the side of the armored car and reluctantly unloaded his machine gun. "Stankey ain't here. Fucker was supposed to bring me the extra ammo but I never seen him after the shit hit the fan."

"Stankey! Anybody seen him?"

PFC Stone angrily ejected the ready round from the chamber of his rifle and deftly caught it in midair. "I seen him hit the deck up there behind that road marker. Far as I know he never moved."

Mallory felt a pain somewhere deep in his guts. It was not like Stankey to be far away from the crowd.

"Move easy. Fan out. Check and see if he's laid up in one of these houses along here."

Mallory desperately wanted to stay rooted in place. He didn't want to look for Stankey. He wrestled with his conscience for a moment, cursed his own reluctance, bitched virulently about assholes who issue suicidal orders and then followed Rojas and Doc Grouse up the muddy streets of Hooterville. It seemed the only thing left to do.

They found Private Stankey of Pea Green, Colorado, mashed into the mud behind a bullet-pocked stone road marker. Before it was creamed by steel-jacketed slugs, the sign indicated the distance to Beirut in English and Arabic. Now the arrow hung lopsided, pointing down at Private Stankey like an accusing finger. Two AK-47 rounds had turned his neck into hamburger. When Doc Grouse rolled him over, the exit wounds gaped below the edge of his camouflage flak jacket. Knots of intestine bubbled up through the rents in Stankey's gut and Mallory thought there might be a chance.

There wasn't. Doc Grouse batted at the blowflies that buzzed in to suck at Stankey's useless body fluids and quietly covered the corpse with a poncho. Everyone stared, as if their collective will might change the shapeless blob back into Private Stankey.

Mallory found it hard to speak into the radio handset Lance Corporal Justice shoved at him. Finally, he depressed the transmit switch and said all that was left to say.

"Redman Six, Hotel One Alpha. Be advised we have one Kilo India Alpha. Transport will be required, over."

It was the last piece of paper in his PX letter-writing kit and Mallory hesitated to bring his pen into contact with the pale blue surface bearing the embossed Marine Corps emblem. Around the mortar ammo crate he was using as a desk lay five similar pieces of paper wadded into tight little balls of frustration with the duty he was trying to perform.

Mallory had no idea where Pea Green, Colorado, was or what people there might know about U.S. Marines in Beirut. In fact, he had no idea who Private Walter Stankey was or what he might say to the Stankey family that would give them any comfort. He'd tried lying about how well he knew Stankey and how much he liked the guy. He'd experimented with high-sounding phrases about The Corps and Ultimate Sacrifice. It all ran into rivers of shit as he stared at the words.

Only two pertinent things about the dead man came to mind as Mallory tried to concentrate on the matter at hand. Stankey had flunked every personnel inspection he ever stood and he was the only guy in the squad who ever proved you really could light a fart with a kitchen match.

Dear Mr. and Mrs. Stankey: We'll all really miss Walter, especially when times are hard and we're looking for someone to entertain us by lighting a fart . . . Jesus God, what can you say? What can you possibly say that will mean something and not sound like absolute bullshit?

Mallory stared into the yellow flame of a candle he'd stuck into an empty C-ration can and let his mind wander.

What if it had been me? Mom would be a basket case for the rest of her life. She damn near quit her job and went into mourning when I joined the Crotch. And then she plasters that phony fuckin' "My Son Is a Marine" sticker in the window of her car after I survived Parris Island.

And Dad? Christ, he hasn't been inside the VFW Post since the Vietnam thing. Tough deal for a guy who sells cars and depends on the good will of the community. I get nailed over here and he'd be running for post commander and drinking himself to death within a month. Fuckin' guy. You gotta love him. Writes one letter and asks two questions: Am I getting enough chow? And how come we don't just stick it to the Bad Guys and come on home? Chow sucks, Dad. Stick what to which Bad Guys? Can't write that letter either.

A chilly wind blew out Mallory's candle but he didn't need light to recognize the Company Gunny. Barlow ducked into the tent and held out a sweating beer can. Condensation dripped on Mallory's last sheet of letter paper. He shrugged and accepted the beer as Barlow pulled up an extra ammo box.

They drank silently through the beer and popped the two spares that appeared from the pockets of Barlow's flak jacket.

"You got it?"

"No, Gunny. I ain't got it."

Barlow nipped at his beer and held a match to the candle. He seemed more than a little drunk but it was hard to tell with the Gunny. One eye seemed unfocused; the other flashed with the flinty gleam that meant business as usual. He belched and tapped a dirty finger on the letter-writing kit.

"Hurry up and get it."

"Jesus Christ, Gunny . . . I hardly knew Stankey. How the fuck am I supposed to write his parents a letter?"

"You're his squad leader; you write the letter. It's tradition."

Mallory squeezed hard to crush his empty beer can and heaved the container at the canvas wall of his tent.

"Is it some kinda tradition to get blown away because some stupid rule says you can't shoot back at the guy who's tryin' to kill you?"

"Shut up and write, Mallory. I'll help you . . ."

"Fuck it, Gunny! I'm tired of this shit . . ."

Barlow leaned across the ammo box and Mallory could tell he'd shipped a lot more beer than he'd brought out to CP 54 with him. Barlow breathed deeply once or twice. The wavering yellow candlelight made him look like a jaundiced, sick old man.

"Let me tell you something about guys like Stankey . . . even guys like you, Mallory. It takes us about eighteen years to grow you into something useful. We take you down to San Diego or Parris Island and then we turn you into fuckin' national assets. See? Sometimes we waste those assets. It's always a crying'-ass shame when we do."

"Well, we sure as shit wasted Stankey, didn't we?"

Barlow blinked a few times and then stared around the muddy tent. He swept his eyes over the combat equipment piled on field cots and stopped when he spied the stuffed Willy Peter bag containing Stankey's personal gear. He shook his head as though the place had failed his inspection and then stood to leave.

"Maybe we did, Mallory. I don't know. But I learned one thing over the years I been wearin' this suit. Ain't no political image in the world worth wrappin' a national asset in a body bag. Write the letter. I'll pick it up in the morning."

Mallory gave up and hit the rack shortly after Barlow left CP 54. Doc Grouse finally wrote Mr. and Mrs. Stankey a nice, inconsequential note and listed all their names at the bottom.

Mallory's squad was still on duty outside the airport perimeter when Walid Jumblatt and the Druze militia decided to experiment with Syrian-supplied assertiveness training. He was checking posts around 2130 when he saw the sky over the Chouf foothills light up and heard the thunder of artillery roll toward him across the bean fields east of the crossroads.

Doc Grouse left a running cribbage game and walked out to join the squad leader as the first two rounds of 130mm artillery splashed into BIA. Justice switched the PRC-77 to the command net and they were able to follow the action like spectators in nosebleed seats at a football game, trying to match what little they could see with what they heard on portable radios.

Apparently two men were wounded and LtCol. Mattson was sending a counter-battery fire mission to the Marine artillerymen manning 155mm howitzers on a small hill north of the CP. PFC Dale stood on top of a wall of sandbags with an Instamatic camera in hand, waiting for the sky over BIA to light up enough for him to get a shot.

"Them fuckin' gun dummies are gonna *get some* in a minute, by God. I seen 'em shoot one time out at Twenty-nine Palms. They get Time on Target and they'll knock your dick stiffer'n a squeegee handle!"

Mallory's squad settled in to watch the show like anxious kids at a Monster Movie Matinee. The vampire was about to get a high-explosive stake driven through his heart. All that was missing was popcorn and jujubes.

Black Jack Mattson stood on the hood of a jeep in the parking lot outside the Battalion Landing Team CP and watched two more incoming rounds tear up the terrain out near Hotel Company. His two wounded Marines were OK; being held out in the field until the worst was over and they could be moved back to the Battalion Aid Station. Below his feet the fire support coordinator and the S-3 were working out a grid to pinpoint the Druze guns.

"C'mon, goddammit! I ain't payin' you guys to screw the pooch. Gimme a grid!"

"We got six digits, Colonel. Bein' passed up to the battery right now. FDC estimates five mikes to first shot."

Before Mattson could let all and sundry know that wasn't good enough, Colonel Skaggs roared up in his jeep and sprinted for the battalion commander.

"What have you got, Jack?"

"Two down. Priority medevacs, but we're waitin' to get choppers up. Battery's standin' by with a counter-battery mission. I figure two guns up there. Battery two oughta get it."

Skaggs nodded and motioned for his ground combat

element commander to join him some distance from the CP group.

"Jack, I've been on the horn up the chain ever since this started. We're ordered not to return fire."

Mattson breathed so hard he was wheezing when he finally found his voice.

"Goddammit, Colonel. This is a situation clearly spelled out in the Rules of Engagement. We gotta defend ourselves!"

"Jack, don't make it any harder than it already is. Keep your people under cover until I get this sorted out . . . and don't launch any helos until the air is clear."

Skaggs headed for his jeep but Mattson halted him with a hoarse whisper. When he looked back over his shoulder, the MAU commander was genuinely afraid Black Jack Mattson might explode like one of the incoming artillery rounds.

"Colonel, please . . . goddammit! What the hell am I gonna tell my people?"

For a moment, Colonel Skaggs flashed on the night in Korea when a young second lieutenant had the first of many men die in his arms. The pain was the same. It never changed.

"Let 'em crank a few up at the Chouf, Jack. Fire illumination rounds only. It won't help much but the Druze might think it's an omen or something."

PFC Dale clicked his camera anxiously as the sky over BIA flashed with the strobe effect of outgoing rounds. Doc Grouse hooted with glee and sprayed everyone with spittle as he made concussive sounds as a preview to coming attractions. PFC Stone karate-kicked a pile of wet sandbags and sparred with Justice as they waited for the first high-explosive blossoms up in the Druze-dominated Chouf. Even the normally taciturn Rojas did a little celebratory *salsa* step as rounds roared over Hooterville and Checkpoint 54.

And then the haunting whoop of illumination cannisters falling to earth followed by the erratic squeak of magnesium flares sputtering under parachutes. Doc Grouse was the first to break the stunned stillness that descended over the squad like the eerie light over the Chouf.

"Where the fuck is the HE?"

Mallory finally put it together from the scattered bits of radio traffic he'd monitored between the CP group, the artillery battery FDC and the 81mm mortars of the weapons platoon.

"There ain't gonna be any HE, Doc. Only illum. They can't get permission to fire . . ."

Stone kicked the pile of sandbags so hard he ruptured three and sprained his ankle. He hobbled up to Mallory as the nearest symbol of authority and placed his hands on his hips.

"Now, this is just too fuckin' much, man. I ain't shittin' you. I'm requestin' mast. I mean it! Fuck, fight or footrace, a motherfucker shoots at you . . . you got a right to shoot back. I wanna know how come we ain't shootin' back!"

Mallory promised to forward Stone's request to speak to the commanding officer, posted his sentries and hit the rack. Light from the flares over the Chouf leaked through the ragged canvas of the squad tent and kept him awake long enough to hear PFC Dale's final thoughts on the matter.

"Well, it's pretty clear these old boys don't want to fight no fuckin' war. And if you don't want to fight no fuckin' war, you ain't got no use for no fuckin' Marines. Ah believe we all ought to just pack our trash and go on home."

Like a smoldering ember in a bed of ashes, Colonel Skaggs generated intense heat and caused the senior officers seated nearby to lean slightly left and right of him. They'd been around enough volatile materials in their careers to recognize a potential detonation. And the commander of the American contingent of the Multinational Force was clearly about to explode.

Colonel Jean-Luis Germaine, commander of the French contingent, nervously filled an old briar pipe while Brigadier Antonio Starvotti of the Italians played with a key chain and tried to pay attention to the briefing. General Ibrahim Tannoy, Chief of Staff of the Lebanese Armed Forces rubbed the bridge of his crooked nose and motioned for Colonel Jason Cameron of the U.S. Embassy to continue.

Cameron glanced at the livid flush coloring Colonel Skaggs's bull neck and hoped for another five minutes.

"In the wake of the Israeli withdrawal, Christian Militia elements attempted to move into the Chouf and take over. Walid Jumblatt's Moslems resisted fiercely using Syrian-supplied heavy mortars, tanks and artillery. We believe the shots which impacted out at the airport were long or short rounds aimed at . . ."

The last length of fuse fizzled and Colonel Skaggs banged the polished table with his fist. All the other old soldiers gathered at the Lebanese Ministry of Defense in Ba'abda turned to see how effective the American's fire would be.

"Colonel Cameron! By God, I'll not sit here and have my intelligence insulted. Are you trying to tell me that my men were wounded unintentionally? Are you saying this is all some kind of regrettable accident?"

Colonel Cameron collapsed his retractable pointer and looked to his notes for a way out. None jumped off the page at him and Skaggs was not about to roll over on this one.

"Tom, please . . . we all regret what happened down at BIA last night. I mean, we're all old soldiers here. It's never easy, is it? The intelligence indicates your troops were not the primary Druze target."

Colonel Skaggs spluttered and tried to organize his thoughts around the rage that was boiling up in his throat. He glanced around the table for support, but all the other officers seemed to be occupied with maps or notes. Even the feisty General Tannoy, the bulldog who was supposed to be his country's version of George Patton, seemed engrossed in a hangnail problem.

"I can't speak for these other gentlemen, Colonel Cameron, but, personally, I don't give a big rat's ass whether my Marines were primary target, secondary target or target of opportunity. Those Druze gunners shot the hell out of us and I was continually denied permission to silence them with counter-battery fire. I want to know why . . . and I want to know right goddamn now!"

"It's quite simple, Tom. We denied permission to return fire up at the Chouf because of potential damage to innocent civilians . . ."

Colonel Germaine aimed a stream of sweet-smelling smoke at the ceiling and raised the stem of his pipe. He'd fought enough brush wars to know such excuses should not go unchallenged.

"Permit me, Colonel Cameron . . . but I do not think you can class these Druze Moslems as innocent civilians. Such people simply forfeit their innocence when they allow artillery pieces to fire from their backyards."

The Defense Attaché leaned forward on his knuckles and turned a placating smile on the Frenchman. He needed a break from the murderous glare of Tom Skaggs.

"Yes, well . . . thank you for your comments, Colonel Germaine . . . but this is strictly an American affair and we have some experience in dealing with this sort of thing."

The Frenchman smiled around the well-chewed pipe stem. "That experience was in Vietnam, I believe . . ."

Brigadier Starvotti rattled his keys and remembered the morning cable from Rome.

"This sets a very dangerous precedent for all of us, gentlemen. I can assure you I will not allow my men to be endangered without returning fire. Rome would be furious and there would very shortly be no more Italians in Beirut."

Colonel Skaggs felt a secondary explosion building in his chest. He was not going to be sidetracked by philosophical discussions or speculation. He needed something solid to tell his Marines.

"None of this crap answers the mail, Colonel Cameron. Civilian casualties are always regrettable . . . unfortunately, they are also inevitable."

General Tannoy gave a final, painful tug on the bothersome hangnail and rose to end further discussion. There was apparently a misunderstanding here and he intended to resolve it quickly.

"I think it's important for you all to understand the position of the Lebanese government in this. We asked you to come here and help . . . not to become sacrificial lambs."

Colonel Cameron refused to retake his seat. These were dangerous waters and he needed to keep the American oar in the power position.

"Excuse me, General Tannoy . . . but you must realize you are practically asking us to engage in open war with comments like that."

Tannoy's bushy eyebrows rose and fell once. He stuck a pudgy finger in his ear as if something was wrong with his hearing.

"Is this something you did not expect when you came to Beirut, Colonel? There has been open war in Lebanon for the past twenty years. If you did not want to get involved in it . . . why did you send your soldiers here?"

It was difficult but Masra tried to keep her eyes averted and move silently around the table. She had been taught by her mother and an older sister to serve men unobtrusively; to move around them like a butterfly on the desert wind, adding to the pleasant surroundings rather than demanding attention with her presence.

Yet she felt the eyes of the Hezbollah cell boring into her as she served sweet tea, fruit, bread and salt. Ibrahim leered as usual, doing to her with his eyes what he would not yet allow his body to do. He breathed like a camel in heat when she approached his end of the table. And Mohammed, the strange, suspicious one . . . Masra wondered whether he hated all women, or just her.

She silently finished serving and returned to the alcove, where a charcoal fire smoldered. She breathed deeply, fighting smoke and the demons that were screaming in the next room. For the past hour she had listened to a death knell and it frightened her badly.

They claim to want an end to foreign presence in Lebanon but they really mean an end to everyone who is not Moslem. They will fight . . . or cause others to fight . . . until there is no more Lebanon. Only a great Persian Empire with Ayatollah Khomeni at the head of it all.

Their plan is good. They cannot lose. Even if they are defeated, they win. When the foreigners are forced to send all their airplanes, tanks and guns to destroy the Hezbollah, they will also destroy Lebanon in the process.

And a Moslem nation will rise from the ashes. I don't want that. I don't want to be here . . . or anyplace where the madness infects even the children. I want to have my own children; to see them grow and prosper. It's my right . . . but what can I do? Is it better to die trying . . . or just to die?

Ibrahim tore bread, sprinkled salt on two pieces and handed one to the Palestinian. It was late and time for a summary.

"The plan involves three stages, Wafic. We will strike at a symbolic target in the first stage. You will be our sword for that operation and we are most grateful for your courage and commitment. In stage two, we divide the Lebanese Army between Moslem and infidels . . . and then conquer it. The third stage, as you know, will remain optional. If the foreigners do not leave this country, we will show them death on a scale they cannot withstand."

The Palestinian swallowed bread and nodded his understanding.

"My reports have been made. The last of the explosive material has been brought to Beirut and my work here is nearly complete. In return, I ask only your prayers that God will steady my hand."

Ibrahim raised his tea cup toward the glowering poster of the Hezbollah's Iranian mentor and smiled. It was nearly time for the plan to be put into action. And once started, it could not be stopped.

"You will be in our prayers until the great day, brother, and long after. The blade of *badal* has the keenest edge."

Overhead rays from a raw noonday sun signaled a change of watch for the Marines at Checkpoint 54—and siesta time for the Lebanese Army sentries who shared responsibility for the critical outpost. Mallory posted Rojas and Justice at the crossroads and noted the Leb soldier in the sentry box had fallen asleep with his stubbled chin resting on the receiver of his rifle.

What a gang of fucking weenies! Even their lieutenant is crapped out in his hammock. You guys havin' a war? Hey, no big thing. Wake me when it's my turn to fight. If the alarm don't go off, fuck it. Plenty of war to go around. You wanna fuck all over a Leb outpost? Attack at noon.

Mallory stood at the crossroads until his sentries were comfortable and remembered the story Gunny Barlow told him when he complained about the Leb soldiers not holding up their end of the mission at Checkpoint 54. He said the ARVN soldiers in Vietnam were mostly the same way. Crapped out all the time.

Should have just said, "Fuck you very much" and gone on home when we saw they weren't interested in fighting, Barlow said. Instead, America decided to do the fighting for them. Barlow ended the story with a warning and a piece of advice.

"You look like you're gonna do it for 'em, and these pukes will damn sure let you. Don't do it. Wake their slimy asses up and make 'em earn a living."

Easier said than done with this lash-up. Goddamn officer is a Christian who goes home to East Beirut every night. The rest of the maggots are Moslems of one variety or another. He don't like them and they don't like him and orders amount to doodley-squat. He does what he hopes they want him to do. And they do exactly as they fuckin' well please.

Rojas interrupted his musing and offered the first smoke from a fresh pack. "You better talk to dat *loco* Dale, man. He still fucked up over Stankey. Leb sentry went to sleep and he try to beat de shit out of him. He gonna fuck around and kill somebody out here."

Mallory walked toward the squad tent. He never made it. A rifle shot sent him and all the other Marines sprawling for cover.

Who fired? Goddammit! That was somebody here. Accidental discharge? I'll have somebody's ass. Oh Christ! The Leb sentry. Jerked the trigger in his sleep. Panicky bastard is nowhere in sight.

What *was* in sight as Mallory stepped out from behind a wall of sandbags disturbed him more than the accidental discharge of a sleeping sentry's weapon. The muzzle of the man's G-3 assault rifle had been pointing directly down

Hooterville's main drag when a spasm made him jerk on the trigger. The single steel-jacketed slug had hit someone out there. The victim was lying in the muddy street in the middle of a circle of angry villagers. If events ran true to form, some of those villagers would very soon be headed home to get their own weapons and teach the Lebanese Army a thing or two about random shootings.

"Rojas, get everyone up and in the holes! Justice, call COC and tell them we had an AD out here. I'm gonna see if the Leb lieutenant wants to go down there and explain it all before the shit hits the fan."

Before he could reach the Lebanese CP, the first burst of incoming fire drove Mallory into a bunker. Doc Grouse piled in behind him minus his shirt and medical kit.

"Doc! Get your Unit One and get up to the roadblock. See if you can tell whether that fucker out there is wounded or dead. I'm gonna get the Lebs."

Mallory sprinted for the CP, but he was already too late to avoid the shooting contest. Two Lebanese soldiers were burning through magazines from a position up on the roof of the observation point. A third was threading ammo into a machine gun.

On the other side of the Checkpoint 54 roadblock the action in downtown Hooterville was escalating. An old Arab with only one arm propped an ancient Enfield rifle on a stone wall and cranked off five quick rounds. A sixteen-year-old burned through a magazine of AK rounds as he sprinted across the street, screaming and splashing water. The man who ran the butcher shop emptied his revolver in the direction of the offending Lebanese Army contingent. Everyone else was sprinting for cover.

Mallory flinched instinctively at the sound of an M-60 spitting a long burst into the fray. He turned away from the direction of the Leb CP and saw Doc Grouse behind the barricade struggling with PFC Deeter Dale.

"Dale, you silly bastard! Hold your fire! That's it, man. Your ass is on report!"

"Then report my ass, goddammit! Them fuckers is shootin' at us. The rules say we got a right to protect ourselves!"

Doc Grouse interrupted the argument. Enough people had cleared out of the street for him to focus binoculars on the casualty.

"Steve . . . it's an old man. Hit somewhere in the upper torso looks like. Pretty bad. You want me to see if I can get to him?"

"Shit no, Doc! They'll blow away the first thing they see. Ain't no point to all this and they don't give a fuck who they shoot."

Both men peeked cautiously over the barricade when they heard a female voice shouting in Arabic. The fire was slacking off as a result of her pleas and the shouted orders of the Lebanese lieutenant, who was angrily complaining about being disturbed in the middle of his nap. Shooting slowed to the occasional high-velocity hiccup.

"Hey, ain't that your girlfriend out there?" Doc Grouse handed over the field glasses and Mallory fixed them on a female form bending over the casualty and waving her arms in supplication to her angry neighbors.

It's her. What the hell is she doing out there? She'll get nailed for sure. Still too much tension in the air. Bastards won't want to stop until somebody on this side is bleeding. Don't look like she's gonna give it up anytime soon. And that Leb asshole sure as hell ain't gonna walk out there and apologize.

Mallory felt like a drunk staggering helplessly toward a mine field as he hung his M-16 over his shoulder and stepped out from behind the barricade. His skin crawled and he could feel the muzzles traversing toward his chest.

"Doc . . . real easy. Get your Unit One and follow me. Don't do anything stupid."

He sensed the corpsman's presence and heard the whispered comment as they took a first cautious step into Hooterville.

"I can't imagine anything more stupid than this."

They reached the wounded man without incident other than some virulent curses delivered from behind shuttered windows as they walked down the muddy street. Mallory wanted to kneel next to Masra, but he remained upright. Something in an illogical recess of his mind made him stand before the hate that emanated from the shadows along the street.

He tried to conjure up alternate expressions of martial authority and genuine regret over this unfortunate incident. He suspected all that came through was blatant fear and the hint of brain damage.

"How is he, Doc?"

"Lung shot. Not as bad as it looks . . . but we gotta get him outa here."

Mallory bent to help Doc Grouse pick up the wounded man. They'd have to turn their backs and hump the guy back to the CP, where they could call a medevac. Hopefully, the angry villagers would not presume a kidnaping or a ritual execution and let them pass unharmed.

Masra turned so that her back was to the villagers' view of the rescue party and put a hand on Mallory's wrist. "Please . . . I need you help. You said you would help me."

Mallory caught the tension in her touch and the anguish in her eyes. The woman was in trouble. He had the fearful feeling that he was about to jump into dark, dangerous waters. *If only we were born without balls.*

"Look, there's an old shed back there about a hundred

meters . . . just back of that bean field. Meet me there tonight."

It was the last of a precious, dwindling supply, but Colonel Skaggs thought Harlan Barlow would need a little loosening up before the first-round bell. He emptied the bottle of Jim Beam into two canteen cups, handed one to the NCO and proposed a silent toast to better times.

Barlow glanced over the rim of his cup. He noted the distant stare. The Old Man was not in Beirut.

"Thinkin' about that log cabin again?"

Skaggs breathed whiskey fumes, let a smile spread and shook his head. Long, spatulate fingers wiped away the cobwebs and he returned to the CP.

"May not have enough money to buy the damn thing, Harlan. The way I been pissin' people off up the chain of command, they'll probably kick my ass out before I get a chance to retire."

"Still hittin' brick walls?"

"Steel shutters, Harlan. The kind of steel shutters that slam down over a man's mind when he's been too long in the rear and forgets what it's like to be out in the mud and the blood and the beer. They won't let us take the high ground, they won't let us disperse the troops, and they won't let us fortify. Funny . . . I never thought of my Marines as expendable commodities."

"Yeah, funny ain't it? I been thinkin' about it lately . . . about how I'm gonna die eventually. I mean . . . after all the shit we been through. You catch a round . . . or a bad burst of shrapnel . . . and it's OK, y'know? You signed up to do this shit, so what the hell? I mean, you hang around long enough, it's bound to happen. I guess we all accept that. But this shit in Beirut . . . I don't know. I think if I got wasted here I'd feel like I was stood up in front of a firing squad. You know what I mean, Colonel?"

"Yep. Disgraceful way to go. Shot by your own people."

Colonel Skaggs drained the last of the whiskey from his cup, closed his eyes and ran a hand through a thatch of white hair. When he opened his eyes again, Barlow had produced a pint bottle from the cargo pocket of his trousers.

"Been doin' a little horse-tradin' with a Leb officer up at MOD. Fucker's addicted to Marlboros and his cousin owns a liquor store over in East Beirut."

Skaggs lifted his cup in a toast again and smiled. "God helps those who help themselves, Harlan . . ."

"There it is . . ."

". . . which is why I want to put you out on a little special duty. Our intelligence ain't worth a shit here. We're cut off; totally reactive. We need someone out on the street listening to rumors and gossip. I'm tired of the reporters knowing more than we do about what's going on in Beirut."

"Damn, Colonel. Ain't no way a fuckin' Company Gunnery Sergeant can just waltz around the city askin' questions and expect to get anything."

"He can if he's assigned to Public Affairs. That's what those people do for a living."

"Just a minute, sir. I ain't no PAO. Christ, I'll pick my nose in public or stick my dick in the mashed potatoes."

"Bullshit, Harlan. You know most of the old-line reporters up at the Commodore Hotel from Vietnam. More importantly, you know what questions to ask and when to listen. I want you to start circulating. And I want you to bring me what you hear, private and exclusive."

Barlow knew an order when he heard one. He stood and planted the bottle of whiskey in front of his commanding officer. "I'll get on it in the morning . . . for what it'll be worth."

"Might be worth something, Harlan. I sure as hell hope so. I just got word my second lieutenant son is coming here to take over a rifle platoon."

Barlow headed for the hatch but a final word from Skaggs brought him up short.

"Harlan, one last thing. Find one of those reporters up there you know and trust. Bring him by one evening. Tell him I've got a hell of a story for him."

"Colonel, I wish you'd think that over. I mean, with retirement and all . . . hell, it ain't like you to fight a war in the newspapers."

"When supporting arms fail, Harlan, you use whatever weapons are at hand."

A silver sliver of moon peeking through a low winter cloud bank gave Mallory just enough light to find a flat spot and spread his poncho liner. With the cold concrete wall of the blast-damaged storage shed at his back and an impenetrable gloom shrouding the bean field when the moon disappeared, he felt fairly safe.

He quietly checked the chamber on his M-16. If anyone but Masra approached, he'd have surprise and a clear field of fire on his side. Tree frogs chirped and a chilly wind brought the mossy smell of well water through the musty odor of the freshly plowed bean field. He listened, sniffed and sent his mind back to the shores of a lake somewhere in southern Illinois.

She wore braces and her father was a Lutheran minister. Mallory had secretly brought her to the lake because locker room wisdom held churchmen's daughters were "hotter'n a freshly fucked fox in a forest fire." In a bathing suit, her body promised to support the premise. There were sweaty flashes, painful lip abrasions and secretions that left them both panting, but the tryst turned into a frustrating fiasco.

She let him slip his sweaty hand inside her suit several times, offering that freedom as her ante in the ultimate gamble. An engorged nipple roused him into a painful, pouty fever. She moaned, sighed and convulsed under his hands, but she folded before the final card was dealt.

Mallory spent a year after he returned from the lake—angry, frustrated, embarrassed, humiliated—critiquing his approach. Did he make the right physical moves? Was his make-out technique acceptable? Were his arguments cogent and persuasive? Did he have an unimpressive body or an ugly dick?

In the end, he decided it was her religion; what God had intended for man and woman; the long-running morality play that cast girls as virtuous and boys as villains. And *she* was a Christian! They believed in the same God and saw the same movies.

How the hell do you handle a Moslem woman? Can't feed her booze and pop it to her while she pretends to be passed out. Can't double to the drive-in with your buddy bouncing around the backseat and rely on peer pressure. What about holding hands? What about hugs, licks, nips, squeezes and breathing in the ear? Do Moslems get horny in the regular way? Do they touch and kiss and shit like that? Or is Allah in bed with Jesus Christ on the morality issue?

She was walking across the bean field toward him, her stride steady but cautious. He saw her eyes glint and a flash of moonlight off prominent cheekbones as she turned to look back toward Hooterville.

"Masra! Over here."

She flowed onto the camouflaged poncho liner, spreading the long black skirt and collapsing her ankles, knees and hips in a sensual slither. Shadows outlined the ample curve of breasts and hips despite Masra's simple, shapeless attire. Mallory was momentarily mesmerized. A woman who could move like that would never have to rely on bikinis, garter belts or sexy frills.

She smiled and he breathed in the essence from her olive skin. It was fecund; slightly unwashed, stimulating. She let him hold her right hand. It was rough; calloused from hard labor.

He moved his face closer to hers and saw the dark, sad eyes dilated in the dark. She bowed her head as she'd been taught to do in the presence of men and his lips brushed her hairline. Masra made no other move until Mallory finally sat back on the poncho liner and lit a cigarette.

Masra studied his face in the glow. He looked different from the first time she had seen him. The taunting smile was grim. There were dark, dirty lines around his pale eyes. There was a slight tremor in the grubby hand that moved the cigarette to his mouth. Some of the smooth roundness that gave Steve Mallory's face such a pleasant shape had firmed into a hard ridge of muscle around the jaw.

Did he expect lovemaking? She thought of the American films she had secretly seen with her friends from the university. The kissing had made her squirm in the dark. The girls had all touched lips afterwards to experiment with the strange ritual. It was pleasant; stimulating enough to make them giggle away the thought of ever doing it with a man.

What was she to do here? Beyond the movies, what was her experience in such matters? She had been frightened on the night she peeked into her father's bedchamber and saw him stabbing at her mother from behind. As she grew, Masra came to understand the substance of what she had seen but there was no one to tell a single girl of the intricacies.

She wanted to submit; to make Steve Mallory happy, to soothe him. But how? If she lifted her skirt; if she offered herself on elbows and knees, would that be right? Right or wrong, it would be better than Ibrahim's cold touch. He must be stopped.

"Please. This is hard for me. There is so much about you

I do not understand. I am told you are the devil . . . and I come here to make a bargain with the devil."

Mallory ground out his cigarette in the damp earth of the bean field. What the hell was there to understand?

"Masra, I'm attracted to you . . . have been since I first saw you. I'm not a devil and I don't want to make any deals."

She moved closer and searched his face. Strength and sympathy. He will understand. He will help.

"I want to leave Lebanon. I want to go to America. If you could help me . . . I know some things . . . some important things . . . about the Hezbollah."

Jesus. Trading intelligence for a ticket to the Big PX. What the hell does she think I am? And who gives a fuck about some gang of lunatic ragheads?

"Masra, I'd like to help you out . . . but you're talking about stuff that's way over my head. I'm only a corporal."

"You are an American. That is a very powerful thing to be. I need papers to go to America . . . and money."

"I got some money . . . shit, you can have it. But it's not that easy to get to America. Passports and stuff like that. You gotta know somebody high up. I could talk to my Gunny. It's the best I can do."

He will do it. He *is* strong. He is an American. They can do things . . . all sorts of great things. I will have my chance to live. This man will give it to me. I know it.

"If you try, it will happen. I have faith. This is very important. Now I am to give you something."

Mallory felt his stomach churn. Please, he prayed. Jesus Christ, Allah, Whoever. Let me love this woman. If you do, the other stuff will work out. I need this.

"I think the Hezbollah will attack the American Embassy."

Mallory's ardor washed away with a cold chill. If those

crazy fuckers would open up on a Marine patrol in Hooterville, why not attack an Embassy?

"What else? Who are these guys? When are they gonna
attack? How do you know all this stuff?"

"Please. It is a family matter . . . I mean to say, some
of my family are with the Hezbollah. I know nothing more.
If I can find out, I will make a signal. A white ribbon. I will
tie it in the olive tree by the intersection. We must be very
careful."

Mallory searched her dark eyes for insincerity. Nothing
but fear and . . . guilt? A family matter? Was she rolling
over on a brother or her father? If it's true . . . if they find
out she's talking to an American. Holy shit! They'll tear her
fucking heart out. Maybe I can do something . . . protect
her, I don't know. She . . . I . . . ah, fuck, we all ought
to know a little something about love before we die.

"I'll talk to the Gunny, Masra. I'll do what I can. Take
care of yourself. Meet me again . . . please."

She took his hand in both of hers and raised the knuckles
to her forehead. Mallory had no way of knowing it was the
Moslem way of signaling a woman's submission to a man's
will. He only knew it was the strangest, most exotic and
sensual thing he'd ever felt.

"Did she tell you this shit before you popped the pork to her
or afterwards?"

Gunny Barlow had barely looked up from the C-ration
meal he was preparing as Mallory related his intelligence.
He screwed the top back onto a bottle of Tabasco sauce and
blinked in the sunlight, waiting for a truthful answer to a
serious question.

"Wasn't nothin' like that, Gunny. I mean, yeah, I went
out there hoping I could get laid but she told me this story
and . . . well, hell, I just thought you—or *somebody* in
the chain of command—oughta know what she said."

"You gotta know there's people gonna say you're thinkin' with yer dick instead of yer brain."

"Well, fuck 'em. You hear something about an attack on an Embassy, for Christ's sake, and I figure it's your duty to report it."

"You're right, Mallory. Anything else?"

"She wants someone to help her get papers. She wants to go to the U.S."

Barlow chewed thoughtfully through a ham slice, swallowed and pointed his white plastic spoon at Mallory.

"Let's keep that part of the story quiet for right now. It don't look good credibility-wise. There's some people would sell their own kids into a whorehouse for a ticket to the States. Now, I heard about these Hezbollah fuckers. There's a file on 'em and most of the reporters up at the Commodore are scared shitless of the dudes. That gives what yer girlfriend has to say a little weight. I'll pass it along to the colonel. He can either ignore it or take it to the Embassy."

"Thanks, Gunny. What about gettin' her out of Lebanon?"

Barlow belched, swigged from his canteen and squinted up at a strange young Marine. Different. It makes 'em so different in so little time.

"Tell me a story, young Mallory. What the hell happened to that wise-ass little turd that come with us over here to Beirut? You know, the guy who said his name was Donald Duck and he didn't give a fuck?"

"Got pissed off and went home, Gunny. I'm his replacement."

"Yeah, well, his replacement has got a rifle squad to move out of Checkpoint 54 and back into the BLT CP. How about you turn to and get hot on that?"

Mallory shrugged and shoved off toward the motor pool. He could concentrate on relocating his troops now. He'd learned to read between Gunny Barlow's profane line. If Masra turned out to be telling the truth—and he knew she was—the Gunny would see her safely out of Lebanon.

Nobody can barter, scrounge, hustle, maneuver and scheme like the Gunny. The guy's got more shit than a Christmas turkey.

Barlow cornered Colonel Skaggs just after the MAU officers and staff NCOs had enjoyed a weeks-old videotape of a pro football game. The colonel's team won and he was sipping the first of several bartered beers.

"Is that all you've got, Harlan? No supposed method of attack? No date or time?"

"I know it don't sound like much, sir, but I figure we ought to mention it up at the Embassy anyway. These Hezbollah dudes are supposed to be the lead element of the Looney Tune brigade."

"You obviously—and thankfully—don't know those assholes up there. Colonel Cameron's OK for a rear-echelon pogue but the ambassador's got his head lodged firmly up his ass. Still thinks the doves of peace will come winging out of the sky and make everything OK again. They're gonna figure the Embassy is untouchable. We're gonna have to come up with details to make 'em pay any attention at all."

Barlow snagged one of the colonel's beers and headed for the hatch. "I'll stay on it, sir. Mallory's apparently locked in pretty tight with the source."

"Let's pull him off his other duties, Gunny. He's a smart kid. Best keep him on this thing full-time."

"Does that make him my full-time house mouse, sir?"

"Whatever you want, Gunny. Just don't let that young agent get in over his head."

"I'll check his SRB to make sure he's swim-qualified, sir."

*   *   *

"Jason, I'm not talking about major troop movements here. I simply want to spread out. I want to build more reinforced positions; get some of the kids out of these damned dangerous clusters. Hell, I've got nearly three hundred troops living in the Battalion Landing Team CP. It doesn't make tactical sense."

Colonel Jason Cameron scorched the end of a fine cigar and shoved the cedar box toward Skaggs. "You don't have to sell it to me, Tom. You know I'll forward any reasonable request up the chain . . ."

"Dammit, Jason, that's not the answer! I need the ambassador's endorsement. He's got to stop blindsiding me. Nobody in the chain is gonna override State on this."

"State's not the only culprit, you know. The ambassador personally approved your request to put in traffic barriers down there. It was CINCEUR and CINCNAVEUR that turned you down on the rest of it."

Skaggs rubbed wearily at his eyes. It felt like there was a pump inside his head spewing sand and grit. He supposed it was simply a lack of sound sleep. A steady parade of political and military visitors in and out of Beirut had him feeling like an overworked tour guide.

"I'm trying to keep this thing in the chain, Jason, but I'm running out of alternatives. I've got no earthly idea why CINCEUR turned down my request to take over external security from the Lebanese Army. The damn Lebs are falling apart along religious lines and everyone knows it. And this business of requiring my Marines to walk around with unloaded weapons on the basis of safety is an insult!"

"Tom, I think you're facing some inter-service rivalry here. You know damn well the Navy is pissed off at the Marines for grabbing all the headlines and excluding them. And the CINCEUR Chief of Staff as much as told me he thinks the American contingent ought to be a battalion of Army MPs."

"God save us from chairborne commandos and officers who've been in the rear so long they forget the smell of blood."

Colonel Cameron puffed on his cigar and examined the ceiling of the Defense Attaché Office for a moment. "I don't see why it's such a surprise, Tom. Hell, this is the biggest military action since Vietnam. Everyone wants a piece of the pie. It ain't much, but it's the only war we've got . . . and wars make careers."

Skaggs remained silent and morose. He took two cigars from Cameron's open box and stuffed them in his shirt. This meeting was going nowhere. He might as well come away with a cigar or two. The MAU S-2 officer had just gotten word his wife delivered a son.

Cameron shuffled papers on his desk and examined one he retrieved from a stack. "Take a look at this and you'll see what I mean. Says here three officers on CINCNAVEUR staff and five on CINCEUR staff have been decorated for outstanding performance of duty in support of the American mission in Beirut."

"And I have trouble getting the combat distinguishing device on decorations I recommend for my Marines on the ground."

"Well, there it is. You start putting combat devices on medals and then you want combat pay for the troops and then you've got people thinking fire and maneuver. You wind up talking yourself into a war."

Cameron exchanged the paper he was holding for another and glanced at it briefly. "About this rumor of an attack on the Embassy, Tom. I can't go to the ambassador with anything this thin."

Skaggs looked up at the Defense Attaché and squinted through cigar smoke. He could spend the next half hour teaching these people to react to intelligence. That might save a few lives if the story had a basis in fact. Or he could leave now and make it back to BIA in time to have chow with his troops.

Colonel Skaggs thanked Colonel Cameron for the cigars and stood to depart. The Embassy was full of petards and a damn good hoist might just be the solution to a lot of fatal problems for his Marines.

Gunny Barlow led the thick, bespectacled man up the circular, wrought-iron staircase to the MAU commander's office on the second floor of the old airport fire station and rapped reluctantly on the hatch.

"Al, I know what the fuck he's gonna say. If there's any way to protect him . . . do it."

Before the veteran reporter, one of the only civilians ever to be decorated by the Marine Corps in Vietnam for gallantry in battle, could offer reassurances, Colonel Tom Skaggs growled his permission to enter. Barlow could tell the old man had found a Jim Beam resupply somewhere. His pale eyes were red-rimmed but there was a firm, sober set to his jaw.

"Colonel Skaggs, this is Al Walters with *U.S. News* magazine. He's sorta the honcho up around the Commodore. Been in Beirut since Mohammed went on mess duty. He's a straight-shooter, believe me. I hauled his ass around the rice paddies enough to know that."

Skaggs rumbled up out of his chair to shake hands and then reached for the bottle beneath his desk. He poured generous shots into three coffee cups and they all drank quietly. There was no need for subterfuge or pleasantries. They drank like doomed men about to make a last-ditch effort.

"Colonel, I appreciate your seeing me. Harlan has

indicated you are looking for a forum. If that's really what you want, I'm here to provide it."

Skaggs glanced wistfully at the framed photographs of his wife and son. He downed his whiskey and poured more for himself and the reporter.

"Harlan, go below and keep the PAO out of our hair. You tell him this is my business and not a matter of command policy."

Outside the closed door of the colonel's office, Barlow paused a moment to listen. It was happening just as he expected it would.

"Al, everything I say you can use. Just be damn sure you quote me personally and don't make it sound like I'm speaking for the whole Marine Corps. Now . . . this mission in Beirut is getting damned flaky . . . and the lives of my Marines are being endangered by . . ."

Barlow clumped down the stairs before he could hear any more. For twenty years he'd played the game straight and true. Worried about rations and ammo rather than rationale and political ambivalence. Sheltered his people and shunned the press. Concentrated on the mission and ignored the motivations.

A different cadence was being called and he'd have to get in step.

Mohammed angrily snatched his coffee off the tray the woman was carrying and motioned for her to get away from the truck. Ibrahim's cousin was becoming like a fly, appearing everywhere and buzzing around just enough to bother men engaged in important, delicate labors. He would speak to Ibrahim soon about keeping Masra out of the garage completely. Warriors who can kill effectively with sophisticated weapons and wire delicate explosives can certainly get their own coffee and food.

A *cousin* is not a sister! Why not simply lock her up

someplace and fuck her when the urge strikes and time allows? Now that they were so close to the start of the mission, Ibrahim should forget about his penis and concentrate on military matters.

Mohammed heard Ibrahim arriving at the garage in Eladar's taxi and quickly checked the charge he had wired into the blue panel truck. Three hundred kilos of mixed hexogen, plastique and RDX. All wired for sympathetic detonation with primacord. Each charge tamped for maximum blast effect. Batteries in place and wires running freely to the cab of the truck. It's good . . . but we *should* experiment with the gas. An experiment would show us the effect and solve timing problems before we use it on the final objective.

Ibrahim and Eladar dumped a pile of photographs on the workbench which ran along one wall of the garage and accepted the coffee Masra offered. The mission was successful, if Mohammed had learned to read the smile on his leader's face.

"All is well, Mohammed. We checked the height of the portico again. The truck will pass under with three feet to spare. We will attack."

Mohammed slammed the door of the truck loudly to muffle Ibrahim's revelation. The unexpected noise in a room full of prepared explosives made both Ibrahim and Eladar jump. Masra nearly dropped her serving tray and Mohammed noted the flicker of fear that crossed her face. Was it tension around explosives . . . or was it something else?

"Send the woman away, Ibrahim. I have something important to discuss with you."

The Hezbollah leader bristled at the effrontery, but this was no time to argue with his explosives expert. Too much was at stake when the truck left the garage tomorrow morning. He casually motioned for Masra to leave and watched her supple movements as she replaced the tray and walked through the black-out curtain to the street outside the garage. She would soon see and feel his power. And Mohammed would learn that a war stallion chooses his mares carefully.

"You are happy now, Mohammed? There are no women to bring you bad luck? We left the Palestinian at his prayers. Tell us of your progress."

Mohammed reopened the door at the rear of the truck and shined a flashlight around the maze of wiring that criss-crossed the cargo compartment.

"Everything is ready for tomorrow. You can see I have tamped the charges so the force of the blast will be directed forward and upward. The shock wave should completely collapse the building. There are no technical problems."

Eladar chewed on his mustache and tried to imagine what it would be like behind the wheel of the truck at the moment of impact. Would Wafic accept his glorious martyrdom . . . or would he suddenly decide it was wiser to live and fight another day?

"What if we have made a mistake? Wafic is eager for *badal* but, when the moment of glory is at hand . . . all men have their weaknesses."

Mohammed smiled and led the party to the cab of the truck. He opened the driver's door and grabbed at a set of exposed wires on the seat. Alligator clips connected the wires to a device that looked like a small mousetrap. He bent the spring-driven trap under tension and gripped it tightly in his hand.

"This just arrived from Tehran. It *guarantees* a man's commitment to a mission. When the driver opens his hand . . ."

Mohammed demonstrated and the gate of the trap snapped shut with a loud click.

". . . the firing circuit functions and the bomb detonates."

Eladar rubbed his chin in admiration of Tehran's foresight. "So if the driver is shot, or if he loses his nerve at the last moment . . ."

Ibrahim took the firing device from Mohammed and tested it for himself. "With this a holy warrior may fight . . . even *after* he is dead."

Wafic felt his pulse beat a slow counterpoint to the steady throb of the Mercedes engine. He glanced at his left hand and increased the tension on the firing device. He was shocked when the Hezbollah brothers had showed him how it worked. He balked and pouted and demanded an apology for the insult.

Did they think him a coward? Or worse, a man who would dishonor his dead family by not seeking *badal*? Had he not volunteered and returned from Tehran specifically for this mission? If a man must sacrifice his own life in the *jihad*, then that forfeiture should be a matter of will . . . not an accident.

Ibrahim had been placating and convincing in his counterarguments. It was merely a form of insurance. What if a sentry or a passing patrol should open fire before the bomb is lodged in place? There would be no explosion. The mission would fail. The *jihad* would be a step farther from final victory.

With those excuses rendered, Wafic allowed himself to be strapped to the suicide switch. Now, in a line of slow-moving traffic on Shari Baris Street, he was glad for it. It would take concentration to steer the truck into a tight turn and shift gears using only his right hand. Time was short and so many things crowded his mind.

He glanced at the yellowed photograph of his sons which

was taped to the dashboard. How can I think of life when my sons are dead?

With the transmission wound tightly in second gear, Wafic swung the wheel and rolled under the portico of the American Embassy. The startled Lebanese security guard merely watched with an astonished expression on his face. With a final glance at the picture on the dash, Wafic jammed his foot down on the accelerator. The vehicle leaped forward until it smashed into the front doors of the Embassy.

The shuddering impact snapped Wafic's head forward and he struck it painfully on the sweaty steering wheel. By reflex, he reached for the gash in his forehead with both hands. The last sound he heard was the evil snap of the firing device.

As predicted by the Hezbollah, the force of the exploding car bomb blew the concrete roof off the portico of the American Embassy. While material from the roof was still in the air, the triple-sided facade of the building began to buckle and crumple toward the ground. Shocked spectators along the corniche said it seemed to collapse in slow motion, as though some giant hand was gradually removing the support which kept the building upright.

Inside the Embassy, people died at their desks or face-down in a late lunch at the basement snack bar. Many who somehow survived the force of the blast were trapped by falling debris. A Marine security guard on duty near the entry was razored to death by glass surrounding the booth where he stood to check credentials. Two female secretaries returning from having copies of thick documents made were bowled down a polished corridor by a blast of hot air bearing loose items from the walls that became lethal shrapnel.

Ambassador Carlton Sanders was more fortunate than

most of his Embassy employees. His office was at the rear of the building. The car-bomb blast merely knocked him off his padded chair, buckled the floor, and sent ceiling fixtures falling down around him. As he struggled to his feet, he was shocked by the shrieks, screams and moans of the injured and dying. Thick office walls did nothing to protect the ambassador from that unforgettable sound.

Colonel Jason Cameron was knocked unconscious by a blast-propelled hunk of concrete. When he woke with his face resting in a pool of sticky blood, he staggered to his outer office and tried to see through the acrid smoke and concrete dust. His secretary sat perched amid the rubble on her typing chair. She'd been cleanly decapitated by some flying object.

Using a coat tree as a lever, it took Cameron nearly forty-five minutes to pry and batter debris away from his office door and reach the corridor leading out of the Embassy. He numbly counted six bloody bodies as he staggered along looking for daylight. He met a Marine guard, in charred remnants of a once-immaculate uniform, trying to lift a slab of concrete off a moaning Lebanese woman who worked on the housekeeping staff. Cameron lent his weight to the effort and they carried the woman forward. She died from loss of blood before the Defense Attaché and the shocked Marine stumbled through a huge rent in the Embassy wall and into clean outside air.

Cameron gently dropped his end of the dead woman and stared at the chaos. Lebanese Red Cross workers trotted by bearing stretchers piled with bloody, disheveled casualties. Marines from the airport had rushed to the scene and parked their twenty-five-ton amphibian tractors around the scorched entryway. Riflemen pushed and shoved at curious gawkers. TV crews moved through the carnage inspecting the casualties and the damaged structure through zoom lenses. Shouts, orders and screams created a bedlam that made it hard for Colonel Cameron to think clearly. Only one thing seemed clear. Skaggs and his source were right. They had been bombed. Some lunatic had actually bombed the American Embassy!

Gunny Barlow and Corporal Mallory found Colonel Cameron reeling around Shari Baris Street with blood streaming from his head and a broken left shoulder. They guided him to an ambulance and watched the vehicle speed away from what was left of the Embassy.

Barlow shook his head as another ambulance full of battered casualties screamed by after the one carrying the Defense Attaché. "Can't say we didn't warn 'em."

Mallory seemed about to explode with anger and indignation. "She was right! Goddammit! Why didn't they listen?"

"Bureaucrats only listen to themselves, boy. They ain't got time for the likes of you and me."

"Well, Masra sure as hell earned her ticket out of here!"

"Hey, Mallory, take off yer pack. I'm workin' a deal with Al Walters to get her a job. OK? This ain't Disneyland. You don't just buy a ticket and get on the fuckin' ride."

"That's where you're wrong, Gunny. This *is* Disneyland. And every motherfucker in Beirut is either Mickey Mouse or Goofy."

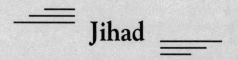

Jihad

WEARING A PRISTINE white bandage like a badge of honor on his forehead, Ambassador Carlton Sanders stormed out of his limousine and into the Marine Amphibious Unit Command Post. He was not normally an aggressive man; rarely given to fits of temper, but his self-control had been sorely tested over the past twenty-four hours.

It began with the arrival of Walters's story by photofacsimile from Washington, continued through angry phone calls from the under secretary for Middle East affairs and ended with a windy session on a direct line to the secretary himself. Dealing with the Embassy bombing was one thing. Washington had been mostly sympathetic; there had been high compliments on his coolness under fire. He'd just about gotten things back on an even keel using a spare wing of the British Embassy . . . and then this.

Sanders paused at the bottom of the stairs leading to Colonel Skaggs's office and glanced down at the sweat-stained pages in his hand. Ignorance! Sheer military ignorance of diplomatic subtleties. Accusing me of endangering American Marines through "bureaucratic intransigence." Just who in the hell does this man Skaggs think he is?

Sanders clumped his way up the iron staircase hoping the sound of his approach would disturb the Marine officer's morning ritual and put him on the defensive. He swept into the small, cluttered office to find Colonel Tom Skaggs calmly sipping coffee and poring over a bootleg copy of *U.S. News* magazine.

"Good morning, Mr. Ambassador. I was delighted to learn you survived the bombing. Can I offer you some coffee?"

Sanders took a deep breath, flared his nostrils and tossed the photocopies of the offending article on Skaggs's desk. "It appears you've seen this, Colonel. You don't mince words and neither will I. This is not a social call. I've been up all night trying to explain your baseless accusations to the State Department. Perhaps you can explain them to me!"

Skaggs rocked back in his swivel chair and fixed the diplomat with a tight grin. "What's to explain, Mr. Ambassador? Is there something in the article you find untrue?"

"Truth has a lot of definitions, Colonel Skaggs. It depends entirely on one's perspective. The issue here is perspective and yours is muddy, shortsighted and . . . damn near treasonable!"

"Oddly enough, Mr. Ambassador, the military perspective holds that the lowest form of treason is betraying the trust of the men you are assigned to lead. That's my perspective and that's what I say in that article."

"You've done an enormous amount of damage to our efforts in Lebanon, Colonel. I'm doing everything possible to have you relieved and sent home. In the meantime, I want you to call a press conference and retract or explain these remarks!"

"We have an appropriate saying in the Marine Corps, Mr. Ambassador. Want in one hand and shit in the other. See which one fills up first."

"Colonel Skaggs, I'm not without influence among your superiors. I want an explanation . . . and I want it now!"

"Call it courage of my convictions, or call it professional suicide. Whichever you prefer."

"It's obviously the latter. I'm informed that the President is sending his National Security Advisor over here immediately. I don't think it's any accident that the man chosen to represent the Administration is himself a former Marine."

"Was there anything else, Mr. Ambassador? If not, I've got some wounded Marines to visit."

Newly promoted Corporal Armando Rojas was able to scramble inside the perimeter bunker in time to save the precious can of *salsa pecante* his mother included in the last Care package from the Rio Grande Valley. As a string of 82mm mortar rounds blasted into the runway, he wiggled his hips and made room between Lance Corporal Justice and PFC Stone. The snipers would open up in a few minutes, so the day's lunch would be consumed inside the dank, cramped bunker.

Stone stuck his plastic spoon into the can of spice and heaped some on his tuna fish. "Bet Corporal Mallory's glad to be out of this shit."

Justice passed around a shaker of garlic salt and stirred his beans and franks. "Mallory ain't got no sugar-tit, man. Maybe he ain't standin' regular watches but he's still livin' up in the CP with us. If I had my way, I'd get the fuck outa that place. One of these days, them ragheads are gonna drop a round right down the center of that sonofabitch."

"Ain't nobody in dis place got no skate, amigo. Mallory workin' wit' Gunny Barlow. Dey tryin' to find out what's goin' on outside de wire."

As they had every other day for the past week, Moslem gunmen made their way to covered positions along the dirt berm around the airport and began to crank rounds at the guard bunkers. There was no return fire. The Marines had long since learned that sniper fire followed mortar attacks.

They were safely inside the bunkers, seething and bitching about being driven underground by lesser mortals.

Officially, the Marines who manned the perimeter were told the small-arms attacks were an attempt to bait them; to draw them into a firefight which radical Moslem gangs out in Hooterville could cite as provocation. The Rules of Engagement remained in force.

Unofficially, the Marines considered such rationale the most obvious crock of shit ever presented. Only tight discipline and dreams of eventual payback kept them from fixing bayonets and launching an assault over the wire and into the ville.

There was an odd, angry look on Lance Corporal Justice's ebony face when three close rounds snapped through the firing embrasure of their bunker, ruptured a sandbag and splashed muddy water and grit into his chow. He set the carefully prepared meal aside and began to sing an Aretha Franklin number in his melodious voice.

"R-E-S-P-ECT . . . tell you what it means to me . . . Hey, Corporal Rojas, you ever get pissed off when dudes call you spic or beaner?"

Rojas flinched as another close burst spanged off the metal runway matting that formed the roof support of their bunker. One or two of the gunners had obviously singled them out as an occupied position.

"Sometimes, man. Depends . . ."

"Same way I feel when some asshole calls me nigger, man. Fuckin' insult. I don't have to take that shit . . . and I shouldn't have to take *this* shit! I figger that kind of insult is personal, man. It don't make no fuckin' difference what the regulations say when a motherfucker gets personal."

Rojas chewed quietly for a moment, then set aside his ration and reached for an entrenching tool. He took off his helmet and slapped it on the handle of the shovel. "You know, man. I been thinkin' . . ."

Keeping his back to the forward wall of the bunker, Rojas slowly raised the e-tool until his helmet was showing over the lip of the sandbags. In less than ten seconds two AK rounds blew the helmet and e-tool out of his hands. He calmly picked up the misshapen steel pot and poked his fingers through the rents made by the rounds.

"De rules say we don't return fire until our lives are directly threatened . . ." He gravely passed the helmet around the bunker and watched as grins spread on black and white faces.

"Amigos . . . to me, it look like our lives been *directly* threatened."

The wall of deadly accurate fire that erupted from the three Marines in a corner bunker along the perimeter silenced the snipers for the remainder of the day and drew a spontaneous roar of approval which swept through the compound like a tidal wave. Lieutenant Colonel Mattson and everyone else in the command structure at BIA bought Rojas's story of having his helmet shot right off his head without blinking an eye. Justice and Stone never even had to testify.

Eladar swung his taxi smoothly off the main airport access road and rolled to a stop near the American sentry. As the man approached, he reached into his wallet for the security pass arranged by his cousin. Eladar could not read the English writing on the paper he handed out the window, but he'd been assured it would gain him entry to the American compound.

His cousin had sworn there would be no trouble. He ran the souvenir concession which sold trinkets to the Americans and Eladar was simply bringing in a shipment of T-shirts. The Americans searched the taxi and found nothing but cotton shirts and Eladar's Polaroid camera. This was the difficult phase. They might steal the shirts or confiscate his camera. They did neither and simply waved him into the parking lot of the Battalion Landing Team Command Post.

Eladar's cousin met him there and began sorting through the shirts, readying them for sale to the Marines who worked or played games in the parking lot. Eladar felt an attack of nerves. It was now up to him to find a reason to use his camera.

Perhaps these three men taking a break from the basketball game? The one who picks up the shirt sounds like a cowboy. A vain man perhaps?

"Hey, Stone! Check the shit out, man!"

PFC Deeter Dale snagged one of the souvenir T-shirts from the trunk of Eladar's taxi and held it up for his buddies. He turned it front and back so they could see the silk-screened Marine Corps emblem and the unofficial insignia of the Multinational Force. The accompanying inscription read: BEIRUT 82-83 and I SERVED MY TIME IN HELL.

"Heyjoe! Heyjoe, how much you want for these, man? I got to have a bunch of these fuckers for the folks back in Waco."

Eladar smiled nervously. Was the cowboy speaking to him? Then he remembered his cousin's words. The Americans called all merchants and vendors "Heyjoe." Some strange form of greeting; an impolite way of getting attention. The lines he had rehearsed so carefully did not include this situation. He smiled and held another shirt up for inspection. Where was his cousin to help with the language?

"Let's buy one of these fuckers for everybody in the squad. How about that shit, Stone?"

"Leave it alone, Dale. We don't want nothin' from this place except orders home."

"Awwww, man! I ain't goin' through all this shit and then

head back to Texas with nothin' to show for it but a Purple Heart."

Mallory tossed the basketball to Stone and examined one of the T-shirts. Marines had been waiting for the Heyjoe to get them in for weeks. He'd better pick up a couple before they hit the stands.

"Dale, I got to get up to the MAU CP and meet the Gunny. Buy me a couple of these, man. Large. I'll pay you back. And get one for Doc. His birthday is next month. October something or other. He'll dig it."

Mallory trudged up the road thinking about his errant machine gunner. Deeter Dale has gone though some heavy changes since he took that piece of mortar shrapnel in the calf last month. Started treating everybody like one of the Three Musketeers as soon as he got back off the ship. Only time he wants to fight now is when he hears somebody call Rojas or Justice spic or nigger. And Doc? Shit, Deeter would kiss Grouse's ass in the middle of the regimental parade deck. The Doc didn't know what he was buyin' into when he hauled Dale's ass out of the line of fire.

Eladar glanced around the parking lot, looking for his cousin. The souvenir vendor was nowhere in sight. There was little time left. Soon word of the T-shirts would spread and his taxi would be mobbed. He grabbed the Polaroid and delivered his lines.

"For you, please. For you. The souvenir photograph. Please, for you."

The one who spoke like a cowboy caught on first. He wrapped his arm around his friend and they both held a T-shirt up in front of them. Eladar snapped the picture and handed the developing print over with an ingenuous smile. As he'd hoped, they stood mesmerized, watching their own image appear.

Eladar walked unnoticed to the front of the taxi, where he would have a better perspective on the building and the sentry positions. He finished an entire pack of film before his cousin returned to take charge of T-shirt sales and send him out of the American compound.

Gunny Barlow sat quietly smoking in the shadow of the mosque while Mallory watched the road. It was hard to keep his mind on the mission. Barlow had explained it all to him in agonizing detail; drawing it out before he finally smiled and revealed the Big News. He'd cut a deal with Al Walters up at the Commodore.

Walters is writing an official letter promising Masra a job with his magazine. With that and a little leverage up at the Embassy, she'll have her passport and visa. She'll make it out of this fuckin' place. Tomorrow night. I'll tell her tomorrow night. There was a note with the ribbon. I know where to meet her.

Cat's-eye headlights stabbed at the dark up the road and Mallory caught the sound of a groaning diesel engine.

Here comes the Gunny's secret weapon. Probably get both of us court-martialed. Fuck it. He did me right. He stood by his word. If that silly sonofabitch wants to piss off the Pope, I'm with him . . . even if it means six, six and a kick. What's he say? War is hell, combat's a motherfucker and payback is a medevac. There it is.

Barlow stood, picked up the Willy Peter bag he'd brought along and waved the truck to a stop. The driver was a Lebanese lieutenant Mallory had seen conniving with the Gunny during trips to the MOD up at Ba'abda. Barlow handed over ten cartons of Marlboro cigarettes, two sets of camouflage utilities and a brass Marine Corps emblem pilfered from the Embassy Marines.

The Lebanese lieutenant let down the tailgate of his truck and bowed the Americans aboard. Barlow jumped up and began handing down 82mm mortar components.

"You sure this thing will do the job, Guns?"

"Soviet eighty-deuce, kid. The gooks knocked our socks off with these things in The Nam."

"Anything's better than firin' that fuckin' illum up into the Chouf. What the fuck are we tryin' to do? Ain't no such thing as death by illumination far as I know."

"I suppose you *do* know we could be court-martialed for this shit, right?"

"Gunny, I told you before . . . you got me confused with someone who gives a fuck."

Barlow unloaded the mortar tube and checked the array on the muddy ground: tube, baseplate, bipod and two crates of high-explosive rounds. He nodded at the Lebanese officer and watched as the man drove the truck out of sight.

"OK, let's go over it again. The spot I picked is down this road about seventy-five meters and to the right about a hundred meters. Check?"

"Affirmative. That puts us directly in line with the battery and on the far left flank of our own eighty-ones . . . but in defilade."

"Check. Pick up a load of this shit and follow me. Stay as quiet as you can."

Mallory struggled with the baseplate and trudged over rubble-strewn fields behind the Gunny, who was carrying the mortar tube and bipod. They stayed close to the base of the hill which served as firing point for the Marine artillery battery, walking in shadows and stopping each time a howitzer or a mortar coughed an illumination round up toward Druze artillery positions in the Chouf. Ahead, somewhere in the gloom, Mallory knew they would run across the shell of the old concrete outbuilding. Barlow had designated it as hideout for the Phantom Mortar.

At the objective, Barlow rapidly began assembling components while he sent Mallory back for the ammunition. When he returned, puffing and wheezing from exertion,

Mallory saw the Gunny hefting the bipod and checking direction over his shoulder.

"Ain't we gonna use sights and aiming stakes?"

"Forget all that shit, Mallory. Mortar's an area-fire weapon. Close counts . . . like in horseshoes and hand grenades."

"We gonna fire? You want me to break out the ammo?"

"Negative. We got time. I want 'em to be in a real pissin' contest before we crank up the Phantom Mortar. Just stow that shit over there under a poncho."

Mallory secured the ammunition while Barlow continued to fiddle with the mortar, working by feel in the dark.

"Gunny, I can't believe you're doin' this shit."

"What? This shit? I done a lot of weirder stuff in my time, believe me."

"No. Not the mortar. I mean . . . believing in me . . . and helping me out with Masra and all that. I . . . I guess I just never expected you'd do it, that's all."

Barlow chuckled softly and ran his hand over the mortar tube. When he was satisfied with the weapon's disposition, he batted Mallory on the shoulder and stepped out of the ruins. They began to walk back toward the mosque in a direction which would bypass perimeter sentries.

"Hey, Mallory . . . you remember me sayin' I knew someone like you in Vietnam?"

"Yeah, I remember."

"It was me."

"*You?*"

"Yeah, *me!* Wise-ass little motherfucker. Baddest dude on the block. Didn't give a shit for nothin' or nobody. Then something happened, see? Something squared my ass away. Came to understand this whole sonofabitch ain't so much about fightin' and winnin'. You either do or you don't and no fuckin' grunt's got much to say about it. What it's about is . . . carin' and stayin' alive and makin' things happen."

"Livin' on the edge of the envelope?"

"Yeah. And there ain't no sonofabitch in the world can balance out there without help. You hang around long enough, Mallory, and someday you might understand that."

The drill they'd doped out involved making the trips look like normal jeep patrols. Deeter Dale manned the machine gun while Stone and Justice sat as rifleman and radio operator in the back. Barlow drove slowly toward the outskirts of Hooterville, giving Mallory a chance to familiarize himself with the cut-down Remington 870 shotgun.

"Got her chopped down to room-broom size, kid. Alternating loads of double-ought buck and slugs. First one up is buckshot. You get your tit in a wringer back there in them tight quarters and you start blastin'. Clear?"

"Gunny, for Christ's sake, relax. She's got it set up. Some relative lives in the apartment building. It's covered."

Barlow swung the jeep into a quiet side street near the infamous Green Line that divides East and West Beirut. He spotted the indicated address and drove by to park half a block up the street.

"Listen, Mallory, her relatives ain't too reliable, are they? Don't be dickin' around in there. You smell something funny, pull the trigger and get the fuck outa Dodge. We're gonna play like we're inspectin' the area out here."

"Yeah, right. Gimme a half hour or forty-five minutes."

Mallory tried to appear casual, like a Marine on routine patrol, and then decided the subterfuge was silly. American Marines did not regularly patrol in this area of Beirut. If they were spotted, the visit would be marked as out of the ordinary. Mallory took a deep breath and another step closer to the edge of the envelope. The address Masra indicated was on the right side of the street.

Inside and up the rickety stairs. Smell of burned coffee and some sort of cooking spice that makes your eyes water. Crying kids; shouts in Arabic. Don't let me disturb the domestic tranquility. Beaded curtains mark the entrance to most apartments. What the hell happened to the doors? Probably removed and nailed over the windows as bullet shields. Protection much more important than privacy in this area.

Masra had apparently seen his approach. She stuck her head through a curtain and waved him in out of the corridor. Mallory could feel the tension in he arms as she grabbed his hands and performed the strange touching ritual. He decided to bring East closer to West and pulled her into an embrace. She stiffened momentarily. He felt a tremor and heard the intake of breath. And then she melted into his form. It felt wonderful and he held her until some of the tension drained.

"Are you OK? I was worried until I saw the ribbon. After the Embassy . . . I heard there was a lot of fighting in this area."

Masra led him to a low pallet near one wall of the small apartment and sat next to him. There was no other seating arrangement in the place. Everything seemed to be set up for midgets or people who crawl around on their knees. Probably a modification to keep the occupants below window level and out of the line of fire.

"I am well, but the danger is even greater, Steve. There is a man who works with my cousin in the Hezbollah . . . he is suspicious. He stops them from talking when I am around."

"That won't be much longer, Masra. There's great news! My Gunny . . . Gunny Barlow? He's worked a deal. You're gonna get a job with an American magazine. A guy is writing you a letter, and then we'll take it to the Embassy. You'll have your passport. The only thing left is a visa. The

Gunny says he can fix that with Colonel Skaggs. It's nearly all arranged."

She sobbed and tears rolled down her olive cheeks. Mallory shook her gently by the shoulders. "Didn't you hear what I just said? You're out of it now! I'm fixing everything."

"Who will fix the Hezbollah? Who will stop the killing? They must be stopped . . . or there is no chance for me . . . for you . . . for anyone."

"Masra! Forget about that stuff. They got people . . . the Lebanese police, I don't know . . . maybe CIA guys at the Embassy. They'll take care of it."

Masra dried her eyes with the hem of her skirt. Mallory caught a flash of flesh that made it difficult to concentrate on her fears . . . and his.

"It is too late for such things. The plan . . . their plan for the war has already started. Don't you see? The Embassy was just the first step. There will be more. I have heard something about turning the Christians in the Army against the Moslems . . . and other things. I must do my part. It is the way . . . does not the Christian Book say each must earn his daily bread?"

"You've done enough, dammit! What you said about the Embassy turned out to be true. Don't you see? They believe what you say. They owe you!"

"For what, Steve? The Hezbollah attacked the Embassy. Did they not? No one stopped them. More must be done and perhaps I can do it. Please understand. When I leave my country, I . . . I want to feel that I am not just escaping. I want to do something important. This is very hard for a woman."

Mallory kissed her then; tenderly at first, just the brush of his lips against hers and not like the passionate coupling she saw in the films. It was a tender thing, like the touch of a mother's lips on her baby's cheek. Not at all funny. Masra felt the tears start again and stared in wonder at the opposite wall as her American lover chased them with his tongue.

She let the surface tension of daily survival in Beirut; of walking around the razor-sharp edge of committed killers, flow from her body and into his. Masra felt Mallory's tension increase as he gently pushed her back on the sleeping mat. He touched her breast and she felt a swelling there like the rigid presence pressing against her lower belly.

Now. Now is the time for love. And if there is no other time for tenderness; if nothing else survives what we must do, then we will have this. Masra closed her eyes to everything but Steve Mallory and reached down to hike her coarse black skirt above her thrusting hips.

"So?"

"So what?"

Gunny Barlow wheeled the jeep into an intersection and stopped for traffic. Mallory slumped in the seat next to him. He seemed distant and troubled. Maybe the kid didn't have enough sense to get laid while he was at it.

"So, did you tell her we got it wired?"

"Yeah, I told her . . ."

"Jesus, Mallory, get yer head outa yer ass. Do we pick her up tomorrow? Do we get some sort of protection for her? Move her into your hooch back at the CP? What?"

"Same deal as before. She's gonna stay on it. When we see the ribbon, we make contact. Masra says these Hezbollah weenies have just started to get nasty. She figures it's her duty . . . or some such weird shit."

They drove in silence for a while, Barlow not wanting to reveal more of their affairs than was necessary in front of Justice and Stone. When they arrived at the Marine compound and checked in with the gate sentries, he sent the two guards back to duty but motioned for Mallory to stay in the jeep.

"Did you get laid while you was up there?"

"None of yer fuckin' business, Gunny!"

"Boy, listen up to me fer a minute. I know you think Lifers like me don't know shit from shinola about this kind of thing, but I been up this trail before. It ain't good to get too close. Out on the edge . . . well, it's a delicate balance."

"She's the one out on the edge, Gunny."

"Yep, and she knows the risk. Else-wise she woulda been in this jeep and gone."

"Get to the point."

Barlow lit two cigarettes and passed one to Mallory. "Remember how you felt when Stankey got blown away? You get yerself wrapped up in this thing and . . . well, just remember it's a mission. It's something we gotta do and she's gotta do. Ain't nobody at fault if . . . something happens."

"Nothin's gonna happen, Gunny, not to her. We got it dicked, don't we? She's got a job and a passport. All we got to do is come up with the visa."

"I'm workin' on it, Mallory. The Old Man is gonna put the arm on Cameron up at DAO. He owes us. Still, you oughta understand there ain't no guarantees."

"Gunny, goddammit! We owe her this. I promised . . . I mean, for Christ's sake . . . she's dependin' on me . . . on all of us . . . for her life! If I don't get her out of Beirut, she's dead."

"Listen up, young agent. Mother Corps ain't let you down yet. Has she? Go on about yer business and let me and the Old Man worry about the visa."

Mallory found his smile again and hopped out of the jeep. It was all a matter of timing. The Gunny and Colonel Skaggs would move heaven and earth to get Masra's visa.

And the heat should come off any day in Beirut. Everyone knew another MAU was headed for Beirut. There was a battleship on the way with sixteen-inch guns and fixed-wing carrier with a full complement of strike aircraft. Whatever happened; whatever the Hezbollah tried, they'd play hell standing up to that kind of firepower. And Masra would be safely out of ground zero.

Gunny Barlow was sleeping in his helmet and flak jacket. Immediately after the first 130mm artillery round crashed into the perimeter out around India Company, he was up and running through the corridors screaming for Corporal Mallory.

Between the time the third round crashed down on the scrambling Marines and the first Katyusha rocket whistled over their heads from a launcher up in the Chouf, Barlow and Mallory were outside the perimeter wire and headed for the Phantom Mortar hideout. Two rounds from a nervous sentry up near the Marine artillery battery added speed and momentum to the trip.

By the time they crashed into the pit where their secret weapon was waiting, the first outbound rounds of 155mm and 81mm illumination were on the way to the Druze redoubt. Rules of Engagement; business as usual.

As they rapidly uncovered and uncrated mortar ammo and propellant increments, they could hear the pop of illumination rounds and the eerie owl hoot of flare cannisters falling to the ground. Mallory imagined the Druze gun crews laughing and thanking the thoughtful Americans for lighting up their work spaces.

That shit will secure most ricky-tick. Gunny looks like Lou Diamond bore-sighting that tube. Some weird combination of Kentucky Windage and holding his mouth just right, I guess. Ain't like they showed us in training, but I'll bet dollars to dog turds it works. First Sergeant told me

Barlow can blow the asshole out of an earthworm with a mortar. Charge three, fusearming wire, bore-riding safety pin. It's ready.

In the glow and flutter of erupting fireflights, Mallory saw a weird grin on Barlow's face. He glanced around their position but the fact that they were about to become a beacon of muzzle flash in a sea of darkness between the Marine perimeter and the Druze position didn't seem to bother him.

"Gunny, won't they spot our tube and call some kind of counter-battery fire down on us?"

"Wise up, Mallory. Between the incoming shit and the outgoing shit and all the crap flyin' around out there in Hooterville, who's gonna notice one mortar more or less? Hang a fuckin' round up there."

Mallory slotted the tail fins of the mortar round into the muzzle of the weapon and held it at half-load. When he released his grip, the nine-pound high-explosive projectile would slide down the tube, strike a firing pin and launch up into the Chouf.

"How you gonna know how much to adjust?"

"Will you stop sweatin' the small shit? I'll watch the first one go in, throw on a handful of deflection, handful of elevation and we'll be on those bastards like stink on shit!"

Mallory tightened his grip on the round and stared up at the neon-bright sky over the Chouf, ready to call the fall of the first shot from the Phantom Mortar. He heard Barlow's exasperated sigh and glanced back into the pit.

"Kid, it don't work unless you let go of the round."

Mallory shrugged, removed his hands and ducked away from the blast of gas and burning propellant that marked the launch. As he straightened and strained to spot the impact, he heard Barlow counting softly. One thousand one . . . one thousand two . . . one thousand three . . .

The orange and black blossom of the impacting HE round

flared in stark contrast to the blue-white glow of illumination rounds. Barlow slapped Mallory on the shoulder as they heard the boom of the explosion roll down from the foothills.

"About two hundred right, drop one-fifty. Get me another round!"

Mallory scrambled to retrieve another shell as Barlow fiddled with the fire controls. He was adjusting deflection and elevation by feel, counting turns on the handwheels affixed to the mortar bipod.

By the time he had the next round ready, Mallory could hear the incoming fire staggering into an uneven rhythm. Someone up there was distracted; trying to figure out what the hell was happening. He dropped a second round and dove for a third as he counted along with the Gunny.

Barlow cackled like an oily villain when the second round burst and took a portion of a two-story building to the ground.

"Cuttin' black now, Gunny! You got the line. I'd say drop five-zero and fire for effect."

They timed the launch of three more HE rounds with outgoing illumination from the BIA perimeter. Incoming fire stopped abruptly before they could get anything more airborne. Barlow helped cover the mortar and ammunition with ponchos before the last of the ambient flare light extinguished.

"Figure it this way. They normally drop ten or a dozen rounds. They didn't get off half that many before we started shitin' in their mess kits. We saved some lives, boy."

"Yeah, and I bet we *took* some fuckin' lives too . . . up there in the Chouf. It feels good, Gunny. Real fuckin' good! You know, like revenge, man. Payback!"

Barlow wrapped his arm around Mallory and squeezed. "I've had people tell me on occasion that it's better than gettin' laid. Of course, you'd know more about that than I would. Let's get the fuck back inside the compound."

As he walked down the pristine street in East Beirut, Mohammed wished his brother-in-law would wash more often. I must speak to my sister about it, he thought, and scratched at something crawling toward his crotch under the borrowed Lebanese Army uniform. At least the uniform Eladar bought from the 8th Brigade deserter was clean.

Both men stopped to share a cigarette and adjust their loads. The objective was near and a mistake would be costly. The stolen G-3 assault rifles must be carried just so, and the knapsacks containing the bombs must look innocent and official. Staring directly into the cab driver's uncomfortable eyes, Mohammed motioned for Eladar to wipe his sweaty forehead.

The bombs are the most reliable part of the plan. I packed them personally. Two kilos of C-4 plastic explosive in each bag. The explosive studded with glass and nails for shrapnel effect and wrapped with narrow-gauge wire for compression. Percussion caps and ten-second timed fuse tied to a fuse lighter. The bombs will work. Eladar is another question.

"Once again, brother. The plan?"

Eladar drew deeply on his cigarette and kept his voice below the threshold of the Christian pedestrians who were emerging for a stroll on this sunny Sunday afternoon.

"We take your brother-in-law's place on guard outside the café. I go to the left side. You stay on the right. On signal, arm the bomb by pulling the pin and toss it in the middle of the crowd. Empty the magazines and then run west on Shari Bastur."

"Fine. Now relax. The party is for Army officers. They must suspect nothing. We are just two Moslem soldiers relieving the guard. Let's go."

Mohammed caught sight of his unwashed relative standing nervously on a street corner outside the café. He fingered an ornate *masbahah* with one hand and clutched the sling of his rifle with the other. The target was perfect. Officers and their wives at a unit party, clumped around the outdoor tables of a sidewalk café.

A casual wave indicated all was well. No duty officers to interfere or challenge unfamiliar sentries. The brother-in-law mumbled a few words to indicate he was casually briefing the oncoming watch and then walked away toward Shari Al Arz, where Ibrahim waited in the escape vehicle. He was soon to become the Hezbollah's newest recruit and this was assuredly his most useful day in the Christian-dominated Lebanese Army.

As Eladar moved to the other side of the courtyard, Mohammed examined the target. A major and three captains at one of the tables; the colonel commanding, and throngs of young Christian subalterns. Several of the officers had brought their wives to the gathering. Mostly drunk. It would be a clean sweep. Those that escaped the bombs or the bullets would report that Moslem soldiers from their *own unit* carried out the attack.

He nodded at Eladar and watched the man reach inside his knapsack to jerk on the ignition pin of the fuse lighter. Mohammed followed suit with one hand and thumbed his weapon onto full automatic with the other.

Thin tendrils of smoke streamed from the knapsacks as they arched into the middle of the Army officers' party. It took the assembled officers only seconds to realized they were under attack. Most dove for the ground. Eladar and Mohammed expected that. They aimed low and hosed steel-jacketed rounds into the swarm of terrified flesh. Male and female screams were lost in the nearly simultaneous eruption of both satchel charges.

Mohammed lost his footing momentarily when the shock wave hit him. He got up quickly and finished the magazine at anything moving in the cloud of smoke that shrouded the café courtyard. Eladar was still squeezing the trigger of an empty weapon when Mohammed ran by and grabbed him by the elbow. Both men had been bloodied by shrapnel from their own bombs, but they felt no pain.

As they ran, Eladar caught a lingering image to keep as he reflected on his role in the *jihad*. A female leg had been blown out of the courtyard to land on a nearby hedge. The bloody limb still bore a patent-leather high-heeled shoe. Mohammed saw a bigger picture. At least thirty killed or wounded! Maybe more! The Christian officers of this battalion would never again trust their Moslem soldiers.

Sirens and alarms chased them down the street to the idling van that waited for the victorious warriors of the Hezbollah.

Ibrahim waved Masra and her basket full of *shishlik* away from the greasy workbench when Eladar sounded the signal on his taxi horn and strolled into the garage. There was planning to be done. Food could wait.

The woman was attentive—as she should be now that I am commanding an important campaign—but she continues to make Mohammed nervous. And with the gas? Allah will provide for our safety and success, but he will not condone accidents due to distractions.

Eladar stopped Masra to collect a small cup of thick coffee and sipped from it as he approached the cell leader. He reached inside the pocket of his jacket and dropped a stack of photographs on the bench.

"Both targets, Ibrahim. These were taken last week. They should be sufficient for initial planning."

Ibrahim pawed through the prints and shook his head. "We must have fresh intelligence, Eladar. The fighting in the Chouf is making the foreigners nervous. They are changing dispositions; getting skittish. I want to see new pictures—especially the Americans. Tell your cousin the views taken after the second week in October, by the Christian calendar, will be very important."

Eladar finished the coffee and lit a cigarette. He had barely inhaled the first puff when Ibrahim turned from the workbench and snatched the smoke from his startled mouth.

"No smoking in here from now on! Mohammed is nervous. It is the gas. And just look at all the explosive! Never has any bomb this size been assembled. Would you have it go off in our face?"

Eladar looked toward the other side of the garage where Mohammed and two assistants were working under portable lights. The bright yellow Mercedes truck was the same type which hauled garbage all over the city of Beirut. It was packed with crates of explosive material and large cylinders that looked like the ones used by welders.

"I am sorry, Ibrahim. I am becoming nervous. It's the Americans. Each day when I drive along the corniche I can see more ships . . . big ones with many guns. When do we strike?"

"When the moment is right. That will be determined by many things. Concentrate on the photographs."

"My cousin is a poor man. He makes practically nothing from the souvenirs and trinkets now."

Fortunately, word of Hezbollah operations had spread among the dark denizens of the radical Moslem underworld. A large supply of funds in several currencies had recently been provided by a certain colonel in the Syrian Air Force who ran parallel subversive operations in Beirut. Ibrahim peeled off bills and handed them to his intelligence officer.

"Fresh photographs, Eladar, or your cousin will be a rich dead man."

Masra stayed stooped over a charcoal brazier until Eladar

departed and her cousin walked to the other side of the garage to confer with Mohammed. She pretended to be picking up dirty cups and dishes from the workbench as she glanced quickly at the photos.

Large buildings. French soldiers and Americans. She could not identify the places. In the two years she had lived in Beirut, she had never been more than a kilometer or two from her dwelling. There had been no reason.

She snatched her hand quickly away from the photographs as she heard Ibrahim's footsteps. Another time, perhaps she could steal one and show it to Mallory. He would recognize the places. She walked quickly away from the bench to avoid a confrontation with her cousin and plan another meeting with her lover.

Colonel Skaggs took the thick envelope from Colonel Cameron's desk and pawed through the pile of documents. Barlow had not lost his touch at maneuvering and deal-making. Everyone seemed to be holding up his end of the bargain. Letter of employment and work permit had more official-looking stamps and seals than the Magna Carta. Passport seemed in order. She was a pretty girl. Earthy; full of spirit. Good breeding stock. Even the blurry Polaroid photograph Barlow had taken of her couldn't hide those qualities.

"I don't find this visa here, Jason."

Colonel Cameron shook his head and blew a plume of cigar smoke at the ceiling. "That's been a tough one, Tom. I could shake it out of the bushes in a hurry if the ambassador would flex a little muscle. Unfortunately, he wouldn't give you the sweat off his balls right now."

"Jason, this woman has taken a lot of chances for us. I'm not asking for a grant of citizenship here! We manage to let every war refugee who cries the poor-ass into America whether they give a damn about the country or not. How the hell can we deny her a simple document that will save her life?"

"Tom, be reasonable. It takes time, especially when I have to cross departmental lines and sneak around the ambassador. Hell, INS and Interior have quotas and . . ."

Colonel Skaggs rose slowly to interrupt the stream of excuses. As Skaggs leaned across the desk, Colonel Cameron could feel the heat of the Marine officer's anger. He found himself staring into the end of a stubby finger pointed directly between his eyes like the muzzle of a pistol.

"Colonel, this is no longer a request. You stand and deliver on that visa . . . and you do it right goddamn quick! Understand? If you think I burned the ambassador's ass in the newspapers, wait till you see what I tell them about the Embassy bombing. If the Pentagon hears I warned you about the incident, you will wind up on a remote guard post somewhere north of Adak, Alaska."

Colonel Cameron leaned away from the threatening finger. The squeak of his swivel chair was the only sound to interrupt the ominous silence. He had no doubt Skaggs would carry out his plan if the visa wasn't forthcoming. He slowly slid his left hand toward a security phone, raised the receiver and asked the communications watch officer to dial a special number at Langley, Virginia.

In the time it took for Scaggs to leave and his connection to be made, Colonel Cameron decided he was fully and finally surrounded by lunatics.

Most of his platoon's personal gear was packed and staged as Second Lieutenant Joe Pennington roamed the sand-bagged building that guarded the eastern approach to Hay es Sallom. He wanted to insure everyone's safety and security on their last night at Checkpoint 35. As usual, the Marine watch-standers were tense and alert. The Lebanese soldiers who shared outpost duty with Pennington's platoon were mostly engaged in domestic chores.

It was the tense time of evening. Hooterville crazies were out in force. Pennington could hear the shouting and shooting that had kept everyone awake for the past ten nights. Somehow—from somewhere—organized paramilitary bands from the PLO, PFLP, Syrian PLA and a confusing menu of other groups had managed to infiltrate and find sanctuary in the ville. Despite repeated complaints, the Lebanese weren't doing much about it. Their attention was focused on a major battle in the mountains. Pennington could hear the rumble of artillery from the fighting up around Suq al Gharb.

Over the past week, Pennington's rifle platoon had tap-danced neatly around the Rules of Engagement, trading fire with any number of armed bands running between Hooterville and BIA. The most decisive incident was an hour-long exchange of grenades and small-arms fire with a reinforced squad of Mourabitoun gunmen. The outpost was hit with rocket-propelled grenades and three of his men were wounded. As a result of such escalations, LtCol. Mattson had ordered Pennington to abandon Checkpoint 35. Tomorrow, he'd pull his Marines back into the BIA perimeter.

He was headed toward his CP to transmit a regular situation report when he heard the first incoming rounds smack into the sandbags protecting sentries up on the roof. The platoon corpsman, the radio operator and Pennington fell over each other as a wicked burst rattled in an open window and sent lethal ricochets caroming around the CP. A machine gun spit measured bursts and Pennington heard the roar of an incoming RPG.

"Lieutenant! The bastards are coming up the road. Looks like fifteen or twenty of 'em. Same assholes in the cammie suits. You want me to call out the reaction force?"

Pennington scrambled past his duty NCO, headed for the room occupied by the Lebanese platoon commander. The officer was crouching behind a wall of sandbags and metal planking. As the American crouched beside his counterpart, several rounds of AK fire whined and snapped over their heads.

"Let's go, Lieutenant. Do something. Rules of Engagement say you fire first and I can support you with my people."

That had been SOP over the past two weeks. Why hesitate now? Pennington shook the man by the shoulders. He had grown heartily tired of cheap shit and his respect for the Lebanese fighting man had all but disappeared. This guy was on the edge of panic.

"They are Syrians."

"I don't give a shit if they are the California National Guard, Lieutenant! Open fire!"

"No! You . . . you must open fire!"

Pennington snatched at the cringing officer. He'd been in Lebanon for almost six months and forced to sit idly by while the Lebanese Army he was supposed to be supporting did everything *but* fight. Now he intended to force the issue.

"I'm gonna open fire all right, you maggot, but not before you at least make a pass at it. Now tell your people to open up!"

Both officers were distracted by the rumble of an armored-car engine. The Panhard clunked into gear and pulled out of its protected parking slot. Pennington presumed the driver and crew would block the road and take the marauding Moslems under fire. He roared in anger when he saw the vehicle wheel right and speed off in the opposite direction.

"Where the hell is your armored car going?"

Before the Lebanese could answer, Pennington heard angry shouts from his men. He glanced out a window and saw LAF soldiers running away from their posts, headed after the retreating armored car.

Pennington kept his hold on the officer as he ducked another burst of incoming fire that tore into a wall at their backs. "Where are your people going?"

"They are Moslem, Lieutenant. They do not want to fight other Moslems."

"Well, kiss my ass. You ain't gonna fight. Is that it? You're gonna run?"

The Lebanese officer squirmed in the vise grip of Pennington's hands. "They do not want to kill others of their faith. There has been much trouble in the Army over this. The soldiers of Lebanon . . ."

Pennington whipped his service .45 out of the holster on his hip and cocked the hammer. "Don't you ever call yourself a soldier of Lebanon, you two-bit fucking fairy! This country deserves to die. Get the fuck out of my sight!"

Second Lieutenant Joe Pennington shoved the officer into the open and watched him scamper away from Checkpoint 35, propelled by close bursts of small-arms fire. He roared a single command and the entire front wall of the outpost erupted.

The enraged Marines pressed triggers until their magazines ran dry and then jammed a loaded replacement into smoking weapons. Grenade launchers popped and machine guns chewed up the streets of Hooterville. Gradually the fire ebbed with the availability of hostile targets. Lt. Pennington went below to send his evening SitRep. Despite the Lebanese desertions, he could truthfully report the morale in his platoon had vastly improved.

Mallory swung the wheel and let the jeep roll to a stop along the corniche. The rearview mirror told him the second vehicle had followed. He ground on the starter with the master switch turned off for a minute and then walked around with Gunny Barlow to raise the hood. Machine gunners in both jeeps swung their muzzles in opposite directions.

"Note said she'd be somewhere down around Pigeon Rock."

"OK. We'll fuck around for as long as it takes. You disappear, find out what she knows and get back up here."

Mallory nodded, glanced up and down the nearly deserted avenue and stepped over the railing toward the bench. He carried the shotgun cradled like an upland bird-hunter. Barlow watched him depart and noted subtle differences in the pre-Beirut Corporal Mallory and the man walking alone toward the Mediterranean. The helmet stayed on his head these days, low over the eyebrows and adjusted to fit. The little things an infantryman always needs at hand—packet of C-ration toilet paper, can opener, matches—were tucked in the camouflage band.

Flak jacket molded to his body; gear arranged for access and comfort no matter how he stands or sits. K-bar upside down on a suspender strap. Real Old Salt for such a Boot. Damned *kefiyeh* still around his neck. Tattered, stained and torn like his uniform . . . like his spirit.

"Mallory . . . wait one . . ."

Barlow stepped over the guardrail and walked toward the younger man, boring into his eyes, offering strength, confidence, whatever was required. "Do me a favor. Tell her I said thanks, willya? And one more thing . . . all this herky-jerky bullshit aside . . . you're a pretty good Marine."

It brought a short smile; a little of the old Mallory returned and winked at the Gunny. Barlow returned to the jeeps. Some balance had been restored. He felt better.

Mallory swept his gaze across the deserted shoreline and focused on the black rock covered with pigeon and gull droppings. Most of the birds were airborne, sweeping and swooping over the rippling water in search of a meal. She squatted in the sand about fifty meters from the rock. She rose and retrieved a plastic pail. Her skirt was pinned up to reveal dimpled knees and muscular, well-rounded legs.

He maneuvered to place the rock between himself and prying eyes along the corniche and sat in the sand. She saw him but made no outward sign of recognition. Masra walked slowly in his direction, stopping once in the ankle-deep surf to stoop and pick something up from the sand. She inspected it closely and then plopped it into her pail.

"Jeez, Masra. I never noticed before. You've got great-looking legs."

She slid in behind the rock and wrapped her arms around his neck. Masra had adopted the Western custom of kissing with full vigor. "I have longed for you. I have dreamed about being with you . . . in America."

"There's news. The letter is OK. Gunny Barlow took it up to the Embassy yesterday and they've granted your passport. We're working on the visa. It won't be long."

She stroked his cheek with her rough hands. Mallory tasted sea salt. She seemed to be feeling better; more relaxed. He hoped this would be the last of it. It was time to stop playing dangerous games and get her into some sort of protection.

"Masra, come back with me to the compound. We'll arrange something. I don't want you . . ."

"No! You don't understand. The Hezbollah . . . they are like ghosts. They are everywhere. The only escape is to kill them. I have heard more. Not enough. There is another bomb."

"Just tell me what you know. I'm sure the right people will listen. They'll find these jerks and arrest them."

"Arrest? The police? You are so . . . what is the word? Not informed . . . naive?"

"Remember what you said. Americans can do great things. We're getting you out of here, aren't we? Have a little faith."

"My faith is all that keeps me alive, Steve. Now listen to me. I do not know so much just now, maybe later. But there will be another bomb . . . two bombs, I think. Very soon. The French and the Americans. I saw some picture of buildings. They have a yellow truck, a yellow Mercedes truck to haul the bombs."

Mallory tried to concentrate on Barlow's words. A mission. It's just a mission. Something that's gotta be done.

"What buildings, Masra? Did they say what buildings? What do they look like? That's very important."

"The pictures were confusing. I do not know many places. There were Americans in uniforms like yours . . . Frenchmen . . . with guns. I could see nothing else."

"Did they say when they will attack?"

"They do not talk much anymore, especially when I am around to hear."

Mallory stood and pulled Masra to her feet. He gave her a strong hug. Holding his breath and grunting softly, he tried to force strength out through his pores and into hers.

"I gotta go. Be very careful . . . for me. And think about a lake . . . in a place called Illinois. I'll show it to you. Think about that. It won't be long."

Masra watched him walk away up to the beach. Illinois. In American. A peaceful place. She would be there soon . . . with Steve Mallory. The Hezbollah—and all the ones who lived on hate and fear—could stay in Lebanon and consume each other. When she returned from Illinois, they would all be dead.

Mallory and Barlow settled side by side on Colonel Skaggs's well-worn footlocker and popped the tops on their first cold beers in a week. The Old Man had listened quietly to their report and then passed the cans. He seemed anxious to talk despite a busy schedule that got more hectic as congressional delegations breezed in and out of Beirut.

"Is that all you've got?"

Mallory squirmed under the colonel's gaze. *What did he want? We gave him everything but date and exact target. After the Embassy, that should be plenty.*

"Sir, what she's given us is straight scoop."

"I know, Corporal Mallory. Believe me, I won't have any trouble convincing Colonel Cameron of that. But the waters these days are a little muddier than they were back in April. BIA is a backwater. State Department people seem to think it's live or die for the Lebanese government up in the Chouf. General Tannoy's 8th Brigade—the guys we trained over across the street? They're up there duking it out with the Druze and the Syrians right now. It ain't going as well as they expected and Washington wants me to support the push with arty, naval gunfire and air strikes. I'm worried about security down here and everyone says forget it. Get up there and knock hell out of the Druze. It's getting hard to remain neutral."

Barlow crushed his beer can and belched. "Kiss my ass! Catch-22 again."

"There is is, Harlan. They want me to support the legitimate government of this country by helping 'em fight insurgents, and yet the orders say I'm supposed to remain absolutely neutral."

Barlow could see the anguish in Skaggs's eyes. *Bastards ought not to put a good combat commander in a bind like this.* "Sir, this is a bit above my pay grade, but it seems to me there's enough shit flyin' these days to fire 'em up and claim we was actin' in self-defense."

Skaggs raised his eyebrows and tossed two more beers across the room. Talking seemed to help and he was in no mood to end the first intelligent conversation he'd had in days.

"Sure, I could cut the ships loose on the Chouf and order up a bunch of air strikes to get the 8th Brigade unstuck. But it wouldn't be smart. S-2 says the bastards have got about five hundred tubes of mixed artillery up there. You think they've been tearin' us a new asshole lately? They turn those guns on us and we'd never see the light of day down here.

"If I commit Marine support to the Lebs we become a legitimate target. There ain't no reinforcements offshore. One battalion of Marines—even two with another MAU on the way—wouldn't last long without having to call in enough supporting players to get us involved in a full-scale war."

Mallory could see the reasoning but it was hard to tear his concentration away from the immediate threat. Yeah, OK, but what about the bombs? What the hell are we gonna do while the politicians argue? Sit here and let Hezbollah kill a bunch of people and then say: Oops, my mistake?

"Sir, what are we gonna do . . . about what Masra says?"

"Truthfully, Corporal Mallory, I don't know what we're gonna do. Officially, the President and everyone else in Washington is telling people we're not in any immediate danger. That attitude makes it mighty hard to get an attentive audience. Anyway, there's still a few cages left to rattle."

When the duty officer finally cleared the Combat Operations Center of all but the most essential watch-standers, Colonel Skaggs slipped into the chair marked with the Batman symbol and studied the red phone. The kids had been prophetic in calling it the Batphone.

All you gotta do lately is pick the damn thing up and the

commissioner or some other fuzzy-headed bureaucrat is bound to be on the line. The trick is gonna be reversing the tables and reaching the JCS chairman without getting sidetracked by some highlevel gatekeeper.

Without much hope for instant success, Skaggs picked up the phone and waited for his common officer to complete the requested circuit. The cardinal military sin was jumping the chain of command, but Skaggs was desperate. It was already October and nothing he'd been able to do or say officially had resulted in permission to fortify his positions at the airfield.

He'd been informed that the President succeeded in getting congressional authority to maintain 1,200 Marines in Beirut for at least eighteen months. If they were in Lebanon for the long haul, Skaggs wanted it to be on his own terms. He listened to the irritating electronic squeaks and beeps, rehearsing his lines.

"This is Vice Admiral Dailey. Go ahead, Beirut."

"Colonel Skaggs, Admiral. I was hoping to speak with the chairman . . ."

"I'm DCS`Ops, Colonel. The chairman sends his apologies. He was summoned to a meeting with the President just before your call was scheduled to come through."

Skaggs gripped the phone tightly and lowered his voice slightly. "Admiral, I'll be honest with you. This call is operational in nature and outside the regular chain because I need high-level help."

"Fine, Colonel. I understand. The chairman has authorized me to speak on his behalf concerning operational matters."

"I understand, sir, but I'm afraid I have some requests that will require the chairman's personal approval and support."

"As I said, Colonel Skaggs, the chairman has given me

full written authorization to act on his behalf while he's away from the Situation Room."

Shit. Stonewalled. They're not gonna let me get any higher. Telegraphed my punch and they had time to duck. Ignore the realities and they might disappear. OK, let's fold, spindle and mutilate, Admiral.

"Sir, are you familiar with our message traffic regarding airport security and increased fortifications out here?"

"Absolutely, Colonel. The chairman reviews all that traffic daily as a matter of routine. I believe your last message asked CINCNAVEUR for permission to disperse your troops, restrict airport access routes and build a series of blast-proof shelters."

"That's correct, sir. And CINCNAVEUR turned me down on everything. In fact, the situation on the other side of our wire has required me to pull most of my outlying units back into the perimeter. Incoming arty is still a very grave threat to my Marines and it's bound to get worse as the LAF continues to push up in the Chouf foothills. Add to that some information I've received concerning another potential bomb threat and I think you can see my problem, Admiral."

"Well, I can certainly hear your concern, Colonel Skaggs. It makes me wonder why CINCNAVEUR would turn down your requests. They've had observers on the ground out there, haven't they?"

"Yessir. Frankly, I've been up to my ears in observers. But I'm the commander on the deck out here, Admiral, not some junketing staff officer. My professional opinion is that we *must* dig in deeper and we *must* take control of airport security. I'm formally requesting that the chairman of the Joint Chiefs give me permission to do so."

"Colonel Skaggs, I'm afraid it's not within our purview to authorize Marine control of airport security. That's a matter for the Lebanese government to decide. And I'm not sure it's in the best interest of the mission in Lebanon to authorize further reinforcement of your position out there. General Kline, your own Commandant, was recently on the Hill and he assured Congress there as no direct and immediate danger to the Marines in Beirut. Those assurances won't hold much water if we give you permission to start circling the wagons."

Skaggs understood he was beaten. He thought of the conversation with young Mallory, and decided he'd really like to change places. Fuck a bunch of horses. My Kingdom to be Rudy in the rear rank with a rusty rifle.

"Admiral, were you in Vietnam?"

When the admiral finally responded there was a note of concern in his voice. The change-step caught him off guard.

"I was on the MACV staff in Saigon, Colonel. Why do you ask?"

"I was at Khe Sanh, Admiral. Kindly tell the chairman that. And ask him to research the casualty figures for that operation. Good-bye, sir."

Like many Administration power brokers, the President's National Security Advisor was a former Marine. When he left active duty after four undistinguished years, he had considerably less rank than the officers sitting across from him in a borrowed Embassy Office.

Cameron was still quaking over the close call in the Embassy bombing. Skaggs? Well, Skaggs was just being a pussy and he didn't care to take orders from a former first lieutenant.

Wiley Fairborn propped his feet up on a government-issue desk and reviewed the slim file compiled by the MAU commander and the Defense Attaché. Jesus, didn't these guys have any sense of perspective? Gemayel's best troops bogged down in a stalemate at Suq al Gharb, the rest of the Army coming apart at fictional seams, and they're pissing themselves over vague rumors about a possible car-bomb attack.

"So this information comes from some Moslem refugee woman who claims to have a relative that's the local Hezbollah cell leader?"

Colonel Skaggs tore at the Velcro fastening of his flak jacket. It was hot in the Embassy office spaces and Fairborn's condescending attitude was making it worse. Before he could answer the rhetorical question, Colonel Camerson put a restraining hand on his arm.

"As we explained before, Wiley, this source is the same one who warned us about the Embassy bombing. She was sure as hell right about that."

Fairborn flopped his feet back onto the floor and shut the file folder with a snap. He'd heard enough excuses.

"And what was the ultimate value of that information? Nil. She didn't know the when or the how of the attack and we were unable to do anything valuable with her revelations. It seems to me she's trying to put us back in the same boat here. In fact, it sounds to me like propaganda. Scare tactics. There are people who would like us to hunker down in Beirut even more than we already are, Colonel Skaggs."

"Wiley, listen for a minute. We've got more this time. She says it will be a car bomb directed at us and the French. We know they may use a yellow Mercedes truck to carry the explosives."

"Has anyone ever considered how many yellow Mercedes trucks there are on the streets of Beirut, gentlemen?" Fairborn rose and stalked over to a wall map displaying MNF positions in Beirut. He examined it briefly, with his chin pinched between a thumb and forefinger.

"Which building, Colonel? This one . . . this one here? How about the university? Which road will they use? There are at least four with direct access to the compound. That's assuming they want to hit you at the airport. Why not try for the Embassy again? You don't have details on a potential attack, gentlemen. You've got rumors, and, if you ask me, a bad case of nerves."

"Wiley, I shouldn't have to remind a former Marine that my mandate is to do everything in my power to insure the safety of my men."

Fairborn crossed his arms and leaned against the wall. The nut-cutting cometh. He smiled and shrugged.

"Then I'd suggest you start worrying about getting some artillery and naval gunfire missions going up into the Chouf. Seems to me that's the real threat to your Marines. I have General Tannoy's personal assurances that the LAF will move on the troublemakers out in Hay es Sallom."

Colonel Cameron got to his feet and adjusted the sling that still supported his broken left shoulder. He shivered slightly as he remembered the chaos of the Embassy bombing. Another try at logic seemed worth the effort.

"Wiley, let's be honest and rational for a moment. General Tannoy lost any hint of effectiveness when his troops got stopped up at Suq al Gharb. He's got his hands full just trying to stem the tide of Moslem deserters from the ranks. He'll never be able to move into Hooterville, much less provide adequate security for the Marines. Colonel Skaggs is right. We need to shut down access to the airport."

"Thanks for your opinion, Jason. Now I'd like a private word with Colonel Skaggs . . . if you don't mind."

When the Defense Attaché had disappeared, Wiley Fairborn moved across the room closer to Skaggs and sat on the edge of the metal desk.

"Let me tell you something . . . Marine to Marine . . . Tom. You've stirred up some hornets back at Headquarters Marine Corps. I'm afraid it's terminal unless you get with the program in your press interviews and start doing something effective with the available supporting arms."

"All you've got to do is tell me I'm no longer neutral over here, Wiley. You take the lid off officially, provide the necessary long-range support, and I'll let 'er rip, believe me. Until then, I'm not gonna willfully turn my Marines into defenseless targets."

"I can't believe I'm having to sit here and *beg* a Marine officer to use air and naval gunfire. A couple of months ago you were bugging hell out of people to cut you loose and let you fight. Now, you want to sit in a corner and pout. Don't you know there are colonels all over the area panting to take a shot at this?"

"You want to relieve me of my command? Take your best shot. But before you do, let me point out something that's being ignored in this rush to pull Gemayel's fat out of the fire. From the git-go, my mandate has been to remain officially neutral in Lebanon. I am forcefully reminded of that every time I request permission to take active measures in defense of my Marines."

"Now who's talking like a mealymouthed politician? Mandates don't mean a damn thing in a situation like this. A pro does what needs to be done. Listen to reason, will you? Gemayel is stuck up there at Suq al Gharb and you're refusing to support him! If the Lebanese Army is defeated, the government will not survive."

"And my Marines will not survive if we take sides in this thing! The situation has changed since I was asking for a few counter-battery missions to punish random shooters. Wake up, Wiley! This is not some rash of factional fighting. The war has started again.

"I can't hold off Moslem fanatics, the Syrian Army, the Druze and the Iranians with one battalion! If I start shooting up there, I become a legitimate target, just like any other unit of the Leb Army. They'll turn every one of those arty tubes on us, and they'll follow it with a full-scale ground attack. Boom, bang! I call in the Navy with air and naval guns. They escalate in return. Now you've got us in a genuine war and my troops will be ground into dog meat before help can arrive. You want to bring in a couple of infantry divisions, tanks, air, arty—the whole shooting match—fine! Until then, I'm not gonna make a stupid call."

"The decision is no longer yours, Tom. I'm carrying the President's personal authority in this matter. If you won't give the orders, I will."

Colonel Skaggs slapped his helmet on his head and snorted through his nose as he headed for the door.

"Nothin' new there, Wiley. Seems like I'm the only one in the chain of command who isn't allowed to give orders these days."

Colonel Skaggs was fuming as his jeep swung away from the Embassy leading a convoy of two five-ton trucks and two other jeeps back toward the airport. He'd had a long talk with the officer commanding the security detachment at the new American Embassy. There were still some orders he could give.

From this point on, the Marines on duty at the Embassy would double their security watches and discreetly reinforce bunkers and guard posts. Engineers and supplies would begin arriving tomorrow.

A yellow Mercedes truck ground by the convoy heading in the opposite direction. Skaggs turned his head and saw a load of used furniture strapped into the cargo bed. The damned things were everywhere! Practically every vehicle you saw on the streets in Beirut was a Mercedes. And a bomb could be hidden under anything a truck could carry as camouflage. Why was that so damned difficult for everyone to realize?

Two twenty-five-ton armored amphibians joined the convoy as it swung along the beach road and the entourage slowed to stay with the escort. Skaggs was still fuming and fretting over his unsuccessful meeting with the National Security Advisor. He was trying to think of a way he could quietly post his Marines along the main access routes to the airport compound and the university complex. Even if he could get away with it, the snarl would be monumental. As long as Gemayel kept the airport open, people would need to approach it.

Colonel Skaggs's driver shifted gears on the other side of the Italian sector and started up the long slope which marked the last straight to run down to BIA. The sergeant had been on duty in Beirut for the past five months and he'd developed a combat veteran's extrasensory perception about imminent danger. Something felt wrong about the slow crawl uphill and the white Mercedes sedan along the side of the road. He could not remember seeing the vehicle there on the trip up to the Embassy. He swung hard around the amtrac he was following and stomped on the jeep accelerator.

As the five-ton truck immediately behind Skaggs's jeep also accelerated and drew abreast of the parked car, the bomb was triggered. The truck slewed sideways under the force of the blast and a second jeep smashed into it from behind. The colonel's driver hunched his shoulders and refused to stop until they were safely atop the rise and behind an amtrac.

Colonel Skaggs stood up in his jeep seat, surveyed the damage and radioed for his rapid reaction force. Of course, there would be nothing for them to fight by the time they arrived, but it seemed like the right thing to do. It did not help to dwell on the obvious fact that someone had been trying very deliberately to kill him.

A senior corpsman reported that no one had been killed in the blast and Skaggs spent some time determining on his own that the wounded men were not seriously hurt. When the reaction force arrived and the damaged vehicles were hooked to a heavy wrecker, he ordered the convoy back on the road.

Skaggs walked silently into his CP and up the stairs to begin writing his driver up for a commendation. It would be difficult. There were other things on his mind.

Maybe that was the bomb the woman was talking about. Maybe that's the best shot the Hezbollah has to take. Maybe they've shot their wad and missed the target. Maybe there's no need to panic. Maybe.

Gunny Barlow slid into the jeep seat and grinned at Corporal Mallory. They silently lit smokes and got as comfortable as they could to watch the supporting arms show just beginning up on the lower slopes of the Anti-Lebanon Mountains. The Gunny was fresh from an ass-chewing by the MAU public affairs officer, who was more than a little upset with Barlow's quote in a wire service story out of Beirut.

An enterprising reporter at the Commodore Hotel bar unlimbered his expense account and asked Barlow for an opinion of the Rules of Engagement now that violent encounters between Marines and various extremist groups were escalating.

"You gotta look at it from the Moslem standpoint," he was quoted as saying. "If we meet an attack with anything less than an equal attack, it's the same as no response at all. A weak response to an attack is a sign of weakness, and the ragheads figger weak people were put on this earth to be screwed over. So, in answer to your question, the Rules of Engagement have a lot in common with a jet engine: They suck and blow!"

If he wasn't in such a shitty mood over the continuing lack of contact with Masra, Mallory would have been delighted with the incident. Like most of the other beleaguered Marines at BIA, he was fed up to a mind-numbing fatalism over their worsening situation. Black humor abounded throughout the compound. Even the promise of payback by the three ships steaming on the gun line off the coast and the carrier aircraft hovering just over the horizon didn't help morale much.

Mallory poked the Gunny in the ribs with his elbow and pointed at a newly created sign that marked a shot-up guard post at the southern access to the perimeter. A pissed-off PFC with an artistic flair and access to felt-tip pens had gotten it all down on the sleeve of a C-ration box.

The eagle was a glowering buzzard, the globe was a black eight ball, and the anchor was a rusty fishhook with a grubby worm impaled on it. Under the symbol were the letters *USMC* and the newly accepted definition: Uncle Sam's Misguided Children.

Barlow looked, nodded and shrugged his shoulders. "There it is, kid." The first rounds of naval gunfire screaming up into the Chouf foothills promoted a feeble cheer along the BIA perimeter and ended further conversation.

The five-inch rounds from destroyer main batteries had been a long, agonizing time coming. No one who understood their significance was very happy about the situation. The American-trained Lebanese 8th Brigade was wallowing in blood outside the market town of Suq al Gharb. After an auspicious initial assault on the entrenched Druze and Syrian troops, the LAF steamroller stalled.

They were pounded incessantly by Druze artillery and subjected to flanking attacks by fanatical PLA formations. When General Tannoy's supporting artillery batteries ran out of ammo, Colonel Skaggs supervised emergency resupply through the port of Junieh. The offensive sputtered briefly and then fizzled.

Over Skaggs's repeated objections, the cavalry—in the form of three destroyers authorized to expend some three hundred rounds and a few carrier-based air strikes—was called to the rescue. The battleship *New Jersey* uncorked her sixteen-inch naval rifles and the mission of the Marines in Beirut suddenly, irrevocably changed.

More and more ground attacks were directed at the perimeter by marauding gangs in Hooterville, where it had become a popular form of recreation to harass the Marines. The new U.S. Embassy and the ambassador's residence were shelled. The main Italian contingent ammo dump was destroyed by a Druze rocket round and several French contingent soldiers were killed in a grenade attack.

Through it all, Colonel Skaggs continued to press Barlow and Mallory for information on the suggested car-bomb attack. They drove through Hooterville daily in an amtrac with a heavily armed escort, hoping to see a bit of ribbon in a certain olive tree.

"Christ, Gunny. It's the third week in October already. Did something happen to her?"

"Relax, Mallory. She's OK. She'll contact us when she's got something. When that happens we pull her out for good. The papers are all set. The Old Man said you can put her on the first plane out. Watch the show up there."

Mallory reluctantly turned his attention to an air strike going on up around the Chouf. Navy A-6 Intruders and F-14 Tomcats. Pretty and powerful; enough to make you think things might be OK.

"At least the squids are finally kickin' ass. Maybe they'll get us all outa here now."

"You still got a lot to learn about campaignin' boy. Like the man said: It ain't over until it's over."

"Ain't no buncha ragheads in the world can stand up to shit like that."

"Too little, too late, Steve. Won't change shit. I seen it before . . . but I never thought I'd see it again."

* * *

Ibrahim was in a foul mood. A setback sent the Hezbollah war plan into high gear before the Beirut cell leader felt it was time. Ibrahim wanted to wait for Christmas—to crucify the Americans like their own false god—but an interim battle had been lost.

Had fate not intervened; had the jeep stayed in line, the American officer would be dead. This final attack could be delayed; prepared properly for maximum political impact. He covered his dismay by scheduling a celebration. It would not do for the others to lose heart over a minor scheduling problem.

He watched his staff officers celebrate the start of the final action against the foreigners as Masra moved silently around the low table serving pita bread, dates, fruit, cheese and goat meat. The woman had done well with the money provided. Such things were hard to get in Beirut these days. She should be rewarded.

Her hips twisted through a sensual arc as she knelt to offer Mohammed bread and cheese. Ibrahim reached casually beneath the table and fondled himself. Adhering to the rigid discipline and dedication of a holy warrior was difficult. Denying yourself even the slightest pleasure; seeking the exquisite pain of denial and sacrifice, these were the things that made a fighter vicious, unstoppable.

He watched her rise, undulating to her feet, straightening her broad shoulders against the weight of the serving tray. The breasts were made for many babies . . . and for a man to enjoy. Ibrahim struggled against his own body, squeezing painfully on his testicles. Tonight. I will show her my power tonight.

Ibrahim blinked, sipped coffee and refocused his attention. "I have chosen the time, brothers. Three days from now. Early on the morning of the Christian holy day. They stay late in their beds on that day. Will the weapon be ready?"

Mohammed cut a hateful glance at Masra but she was already moving out of the room to the alcove, where a charcoal fire smoldered. He lowered his voice anyway and leaned across the table to impress the cell leader with his preparation.

"All of the gas cannisters have arrived. We have more than six thousand kilos of plastique. With the gas, the blast effect will be multiplied four times. It will be much like a small nuclear device. The critical issue will be timing. We must select the man to drive the truck very carefully."

Ibrahim frowned. He presumed Mohammed, the designer of the ultimate weapon, would want to employ it. Another problem, and no spare Palestinians around to solve it. Perhaps one of the young ones recently returned from Tehran? Most of them were granted a personal audience with the Ayatollah. There could be no question of their commitment. Or perhaps . . . no! I will be needed to lead the struggle after the foreigners are driven out of Lebanon. I must live . . . to consolidate our victory.

"We will discuss this matter later, Mohammed. You will help me select the man, and you will train him. Now, the intelligence Eladar, what changes?"

The taxi driver reached into a brown envelope for a large stack of pictures and searched the cluttered table for a place to display them. He placed the photos on the floor at his side and began to remove dishes, cups and bowls. Ibrahim grunted at the sight and roared for Masra.

She appeared from the alcove carrying a large metal tray. Placing it on her knees as she slid into place near Eladar, Masra began to remove dishes quickly and quietly. The men paid no attention as they grabbed for final helpings before the delicacies disappeared. While she stacked dishes with her right hand, she felt around on the floor beneath the tray with her left. When she rose to depart with the heavy load of dirty dishes and leftovers, Masra had the top photograph from Eladar's stack pressed firmly between her palm and the bottom of the tray.

Back in the alcove, she glanced at the photo briefly and slipped it inside her skirt. She did not recognize much about the scene except for the Americans standing around in front of a large building. No matter. Mallory would know where it was . . . and the Hezbollah would be stopped.

Ibrahim lingered over sweet tea after the other Hezbollah cell members left the apartment. Yellow light from a smoky oil lamp played on the large photograph of the Ayatollah Khomeni that occupied nearly all of one wall. Eladar had assembled the revered poster from enlarged sections of a photograph. Now the Holy Man was a silent, inspirational presence in all that the Hezbollah did or said in this place.

Bowing his head respectfully, Ibrahim spotted a bulky quilt spread on the floor beneath the photo. There. I will take her there. The Ayatollah will watch the union of a Moslem woman and a hero of the *jihad*.

She tried to slip quietly out the door, but Ibrahim rose quickly and held it shut with his hand. He smiled into her dark eyes and felt the stirring in his groin as she whimpered. She fears me. That is good. She had reason to fear a man of my power. When I unsheath this sword, she will feel as though she has been split in two. She will feel as if someone has rammed a hot poker into her guts.

Breath whistled through Ibrahim's bent nose as he moved closer to the woman and pinned her against the wall of the apartment. There would be time to spread her out like a prayer rug and kneel between her legs. First she should tremble. Her flesh should feel like a plucked goose. She should fear and respect the power that is about to enter her.

Ibrahim reached for her breasts and squeezed hard as he

pulled Masra off the wall and into him. He mashed her breasts together and worked his hands back and forth while she moaned in pain. At just the right moment—before any significant damage was done—he slid his hands around her body and clutched where the backs of her thighs joined the buttocks. Squeezing hard, he lifted her onto her toes and arched his back so she could feel the power prodding at her belly. Tears leaked from her eyes and Ibrahim knew it was time.

"Take off your clothes! Over there . . . on the quilt. Quickly! I have waited too long."

Masra's voice was a hoarse croak as she pleaded and struggled in his iron grip. "Please, Ibrahim. We are family. I do not want this. It is not according to the teachings . . ."

He slapped her viciously across the face and then brushed tenderly at the trickle of blood from the corner of her mouth. "Do not speak of teachings to me! There are new teachings for men of destiny. Take the pain to your heart, woman. It makes us strong."

Masra saw the yellow glow reflected from somewhere deep in Ibrahim's skull. This is no passing whim. He will kill me if I do not allow him to take me. But I cannot. I must not. He would spawn another killer inside me. And he would surely find the stolen photograph.

"I . . . I must clean myself for you, Ibrahim. It will take only a moment."

With a grunt of approval at her foresight, he released his grip and stepped backward. "Hurry. Do it now!"

Masra ducked into the alcove and beat her forehead with an open palm. Think, think. Is there no way to stop him? She remembered the cruel light in his eyes. Nothing will keep him from . . . unless . . . of course, the Koran!

Stripping her underclothes from beneath her long skirt, Masra stood straddle-legged in the dark alcove and reached into her own crotch. She inserted a finger deep into herself and bit off a cry of pain. She probed the cervix and dragged a ragged fingernail along the inner wall of her vagina. In moments she was rewarded by a warm splash of blood into her hand.

When Ibrahim called out in frustration, she stepped from the alcove with her head hanging, hands behind her back.

"Why are you not naked? Hurry, woman! I am ready."

She slowly brought her hands around to the front of her body, keeping her head bowed to show mortification at the weakness of her flesh. Blood was caked on her palms and fingers. She could feel a trickle running down the inside of her thigh, but that did not matter now.

"We cannot do this, cousin. It is my time. I am unclean."

Ibrahim's eyes flew open and his jaw dropped as he moved across the room to stare at the evidence. He confirmed it was indeed blood and backed away two steps. The tight, pulsing pressure in his crotch made his knees tremble. Still, he would have to wait. The Koran was very clear about such things. Ibrahim reached carefully around her bloody hands and dug his fingers into Masra's neck.

"Stay out of my presence for the full term, woman. And when you are clean again, come to me on your knees. Do not make me search for you."

Mohammed stepped gingerly away from the warming fire and back into the shadows when he heard her footsteps. He gave his place near the blaze burning outside the butcher's shop at the main crossroads of Hay es Sallom to another man. If she spotted him, the evening would be wasted.

She passed quickly and quietly through the firelight, waddling slightly as if there was something painful between her legs. Mohammed smiled in the dark. Perhaps not now, but very recently she did have something painful between her legs: Ibrahim's cock! He stepped out of the shadows and followed her down the street.

The woman was moving toward her house. Perhaps he was making too much of all this. She might simply be nervous around so many strong men. Maybe it was the weakness born into a woman's soul. But there was fear in this one's eyes that was motivated by something deep in her guts. Mohammed had seen it many times in men who worked with explosives. Like a poorly made bomb, she is delicate and dangerous.

His instincts told him the woman was acting in a highly suspicious manner. The *jihad* had taught him one thing well: If you do not trust your instincts; if you do not act on your suspicions, you do not live to do battle.

He followed her for another kilometer, nearly deciding he was wrong about Ibrahim's cousin, when he saw her stop by a gnarled olive tree near the road that led toward the airport. What is she doing? The tree bears no fruit at this time of year. A white ribbon? Why would anyone tie such a thing in an olive tree in the middle of the night? Perhaps a signal?

Mohammed decided to continue watching the woman. Maybe tomorrow he would discover her secret. He nearly walked away into the dark after the woman disappeared in the direction of her house, but his instincts were screaming. He stared again at the bit of white cloth fluttering in the night wind. As he walked past the olive tree Mohammed reached up into the branches, removed the white ribbon and stuffed it into his pocket.

Gunny Barlow had grudgingly volunteered to help with preparations for Doc Grouse's twenty-first birthday party in the BLT CP. He had to miss an inviting poker game in which Al Walters typically lost a lot of money to him, but, what the hell? Anything to get Mallory's mind off Masra.

And even a squid shouldn't turn twenty-one in a place like Beirut without some kind of benchmark.

He gave his pet project a final squint and carried it across the CP toward an area where Mallory and the Marines from his old squad were wrapping birthday gifts.

"Look here, troops. Learned to make these fuckers in The Nam." Rojas, Justice, Dale, Stone and Mallory gathered around the senior NCO and began to chuckle. Damned if he didn't do it. In the midst of all this shit, the fucking Gunny comes up with a birthday cake.

"Nothin' to it. You just take a coupla cans of pound cake from C-rations, mash 'em up with fruit juice until you can mold it into shape, then add the fruit. Put that fucker into a canteen cup, heat it over a stove and add the candles. There you go . . . field expedient birthday cake."

The troops went back to wrapping gifts. Doc Grouse would be returning from the Battalion Aid Station anytime now. Barlow watched them with a scowl that effectively hid his real feelings. Troops hanging on to each other when times are hard. They don't know it yet, but that's what *Semper Fi* is all about.

The Marines had scrounged for two weeks, picking up small things that symbolized Beirut and adding them to a plaque they made for their medical corpsman. There was the doe-eyed "goat-meat girl" from Palestinian ration cans; a hammer-and-sickle origin plate from a Soviet artillery piece; strange-shaped hunks of shrapnel; patches and pins with Arabic words inscribed; and a belt of AK ammo framing a souvenir shot of all the guys standing in front of the building they were forced to call home.

And there were personal things to make the Doc's twenty-first birthday more memorable. Mallory bought the souvenir T-shirt and scrounged a stencil to put Grouse's name, rank and unit on the back. Deeter Dale braided a sturdy dog-tag chain out of rawhide his daddy had sent.

Rojas added a Mexican silver coin to the necklace. Stone wrapped two new pairs of the sweat socks Doc Grouse always admired. In a corner of the CP, Justice rehearsed the Soul Brothers a capella group to do a few of the corpsman's favorite tunes, including "Happy Birthday, Baby."

Barlow tapped Mallory on the shoulder and smiled. "This is good shit, Mallory. It'll do wonders for morale, which happens to be somewhere down below snake shit these days."

Mallory nodded distractedly and checked his watch. "Gunny, is there any chance of checking the tree one more time?"

"Steve, we been by there twice today and no signal. She ain't dropped off the face of the earth, man. She's got too much to live for. I figger she's just waitin' to be completely safe. There could have been some heat after that car bomb missed the Old Man. Give it some slack. She'll show up out at the gate with her shit packed."

Mallory was about to tell the Gunny how much he hoped that would happen. He was about to confide in the older man just how much he had come to love the strange woman who had crossed his trail and confused his heart in such a strange way here in Beirut, but Doc Grouse ducked in the door and the party started.

Masra had been walking up and down the beach below the corniche for two solid hours. Her bare feet were nearly frozen by the frigid water and there was a painful thump each time her heart beat, marking the delay in Steve Mallory's arrival.

He is never late. Has something happened? Is he hurt? Did they send him away someplace? He must have gotten the signal! He passes the tree each day. I see him there and long to catch his eyes. Please, God! I must see him. The time is so short!

Masra set a silk scarf containing all her personal belongings up on dry sand while she pretended to comb the beach for mussels. The tide controlling the waves that lapped at the beach had nearly reached her bundle. She closed her eyes tightly and prayed with such a concentration of energy she thought for a moment she would lift off the sand and follow the prayer to heaven.

When she opened her eyes and blinked away the tears, Masra saw the water had soaked her things. Mallory was nowhere in sight. *He will not come. Something has gone wrong. I must go to him.*

She dried her eyes, picked up the bundle and reached into the pocket of her skirt. Thirty Lebanese pounds, saved from the money Ibrahim had given her for food. *It would be enough.* If only she could find a taxi or someone willing to give her a ride to the airport.

Mohammed watched Masra flag down a taxi slowly cruising the nearly deserted avenue. There was a brief haggle over the fare, then the driver wheeled onto the coast road and headed south. Mohammed angrily pounded the steering wheel with his fist and loudly cursed everyone born into the female gender. When the fire in his belly was slightly banked, he started the car, cranked the wheel hard and roared away to find Ibrahim.

It is his blood; his kin. Let him bear the responsibility and extract badal for this betrayal. Along the reckless route to the garage, where Ibrahim waited for him, Mohammed had a flash of inspiration. His problem was solved. He knew who would drive the truck against the Americans.

The attack was scheduled for the day after tomorrow and the thorny question of who should drive the truck had still not been answered. Ibrahim paced the garage and hoped Mohammed would come up with a satisfactory suggestion. The bomb expert was supposed to be through interviewing three young Hezbollah volunteers by noon.

It was half-past one and the final wiring for the bomb had been completed. All that remained was for Mohammed to check the charges and circuits. It was not like him to dawdle during such a delicate time.

Ibrahim heard breaks squeal and tires skid in the alley outside the garage. *Mohammed should drive more carefully. We cannot afford to lose him now in some stupid accident.*

The garage door flew open with a disturbing crash and Ibrahim knew immediately something serious was wrong. *Had the Americans suddenly pulled out of Beirut? Had they abandoned the building?* He walked quickly toward Mohammed, noting the enraged snarl on the man's normally placid face.

"Quickly, Ibrahim! Come with me. It is the woman . . . your cousin! I told you she would betray us."

During his five months in Beirut Lance Corporal Hawkins had seen enough Lebanese to last him a lifetime. Still, he wouldn't mind seeing a little more of the foxy lady rushing down the MAU CP access road toward his sentry post.

He spat a stream of tobacco juice into the small fire started to keep gate guards warm on these wet, chilly winter days and focused on the woman's face. *Looks like she's runnin' from the devil himself. Probably pissed her old man off and he come after her with a big-ass knife.*

When the woman made no move to slow her hurried pace. Hawkins remembered the special orders emphasized by the OD when he came on post. *Be especially watchful for unauthorized vehicles or unidentified civilians. Allow nothing to pass without calling the sergeant of the guard.*

Hawkins shouted down the line for assistance at his post, then stripped the M-16 off his shoulder and came to port arms. "That's far enough, lady. Just hold it right there. Halt! Understand?"

Masra slowed her pace and tried to control her breathing. "Please . . . I am here to see Mallory . . . Corporal Steve Mallory."

"Take a walk, lady. My orders say no Leb civilians beyond this point. That means you."

"Please! It is very important. I must see Corporal Mallory or Sergeant Barlow. Just for a moment, please! They will vouch for me."

Hawkins decided he'd like to vouch her right over into that bean field and cut loose the terrible one-eyed trouser worm. But he'd get his ass burned for it. Everybody was so fucking paranoid these days. Including this broad.

"Lady, you ain't gettin' in here and I ain't runnin' no errands for you. You wanna leave a note or somethin', here's a pen. Otherwise, get the hell away from my post."

Masra stared into the man's hard face. It was tight and mean and the eyes were dull, lifeless like the haunted, homeless ones who wandered the streets of Beirut in search of lost dreams. Except for the uniform, he looked like one of the Hezbollah.

She reached for the pen and then drew her hand back. She reached into the pocket of her skirt and withdrew the picture. "Please give this to Corporal Mallory or Sergeant Barlow. It is most urgent. They will understand. Please, please help me . . . and tell them I will wait out by the street."

Lance Corporal Hawkins took the photo and glanced at it briefly. He squinted at the woman, shrugged his shoulders and stuck the photo in a pocket of his flak jacket. Right, lady. And you'll be waitin' out there until Christ makes corporal for all I care. There's the fuckin' sergeant of the guard. Best get the civilian off my post or I'll be fillin' sandbags for a week.

"Take off, lady. I got no more time for you."

Masra walked back toward the main airport access road praying as hard as she knew how. It was up to Allah now, and she believed he would be merciful. She would sit outside the airport fence until her prayers were answered and Steve Mallory came to take her away from this place that turned nearly everyone to stone.

Lance Corporal Hawkins reported the incident briefly to the sergeant of the guard and was delighted to see the NCO did not intend to make a big deal over it. He glanced at the Polaroid picture, shrugged and walked away. It was certainly nothing to waste time recording in his logbook.

"Fuckin' Lebs are nuts anyway. Probably just some souvenir shot she wants to sell. Anything for a fuckin' buck, y'know?"

Hawkins took one more look at the photo. He had plenty of better views of the BLT CP in his scrapbook. He checked his watch, hoped there was still some cold soda left from the corpsman's birthday bash and threw the picture into the fire.

Ibrahim told a Lebanese Moslem soldier on duty at a guard post along the airport access road that he had come to pick up a wayward wife he suspected of sleeping with an American.

The man shrugged and allowed Mohammed to drive the car very close to the airport perimeter. "*Ins' allah,*" he said. "If you wish to kill her, take her someplace else."

The sentry and two of his cronies watched with unmuted admiration as Ibrahim and Mohammed chased Masra nearly to the access road before grabbing handfuls of her long hair and jerking her to a painful halt. They paid no attention to her screams as the woman was hustled into the car and pounded senseless by the tall one who claimed to be her husband.

A few curious Marines who rushed to the intersection to see about the shouting caught only a fleeting glimpse of a black car speeding away from the airport through the Lebanese Army checkpoint. Most of them had seen stranger things in Beirut, and if the Lebs didn't give a fuck, why should they?

Masra lay bleeding on the quilt under the glowering presence of Ayatollah Khomeni. Ibrahim stood over her, breathing hard and cursing under his breath.

"The bitch! My own cousin. I will kill her for this!"

Mohammed kicked at the woman as she began to struggle back toward consciousness. "Of course, she must be killed . . . but not before we find out what she told the Americans."

Ibrahim stalked toward the alcove and returned with a plastic bottle of distilled water. He poured it over Masra's swollen face and watched some of the caked blood drain away from the purple cuts above her eyes. Blood streamed from one ear. She would not live long.

When her eyes finally opened, they propped her up against the wall-size photo and ripped away her blouse. Ibrahim drew a razor-sharp knife from his belt and poked it under her chin until the glazed eyes began to focus.

"You will die very slowly, Masra. Tell us what you told the Americans and I will be merciful."

She ran her swollen tongue over broken teeth and tried not to look in his evil eyes. She must not show fear or weakness.

"I told him nothing, Ibrahim. I swear it! I went to see a man . . . an American . . . but he was not there. Nothing more . . . I swear it!"

While Mohammed held her against the wall, Ibrahim clenched his fist and drove a calloused knuckle into her temple. She moaned and he pressed harder with the sharp blade. A trickle of blood ran across the back of his hand.

"No more lies, whore! What did you tell them?"

Masra mumbled only some foreign-sounding name and then slipped into a black void. She was beyond pain and Ibrahim spit at her in frustration. When she did not respond, he dropped her like a sack of wet sand.

Mohammed pondered for a moment and then led Ibrahim to a seat and poured water for them. "I do not think she could have told the Americans anything useful. If they believed she knew something important, she would be inside their compound right now. Still, this is a very grave insult, Ibrahim, and she is of your blood."

Ibrahim blinked away tears of shame. She had ruined it all for him. There was no other way out of the predicament.

"Then my blood will be shed to atone for the insult. I will drive the truck. I will reinstate the name of my family on the list of heroes of the *jihad!*"

Mohammed smiled to indicate his approval and then helped Ibrahim desecrate the body of his treacherous cousin.

When Colonel Skaggs answered the urgent call from the MAU Service Support Group officer of the day, he got a feeling in the pit of his stomach like he'd just swallowed lead. He sent a runner for Gunny Barlow and Corporal Mallory and then trotted through the front gate toward the wire on the northwestern side of the compound.

A group of MSSG medical officers were gathered around a shapeless form wrapped in a poncho. The officer of the day looked sick and upset as he waved his soft cover over the shape, dislodging a black blanket of flies. A cordon of armed MPs was keeping Marine gawkers out of the area, but no one had any doubt about what was being protected.

They'd seen enough bodies by now to get the picture without further visual cues.

Skaggs shouldered his way through the medical officers and lifted the edge of the poncho. It was the woman he'd admired in the fuzzy passport photo . . . or what's left of her. He sent the OD to head off Barlow and Mallory and then turned to his senior surgeon.

"This the way you found her, Doc?"

"Yessir. Don't know who the hell she is, but whoever did this is one sick sonofabitch. That's all we know about it so far. Sentry saw the flies this morning and then, well, we had to put him in the rack to prevent shock. Who the hell is gonna kill a woman, then cut her head clean off her neck, open up her belly and then put the head inside? Jesus Christ!"

Skaggs rose and heard the OD talking to Barlow and Mallory; telling them to wait for instructions. There were no answers to the Doc's questions, and none to the ones young Mallory was bound to ask. He motioned for the OD to let the two worried NCOs pass.

Skaggs grabbed at Mallory's shoulders, holding him away from the corpse until Barlow had a chance to confirm her identity. When Barlow had looked long enough, he spat into the dust, stood and walked back toward the younger man. Mallory suspected the worst. There was no sense prolonging it.

"It's her, Steve. Let's go back to the CP. Believe me, you don't want to see this."

Mallory broke away from the men holding him and slowly approached the corpse. Flies left their meal and investigated his mouth and nose. He didn't bother to brush at them. Slowly, he lifted the edge of the poncho. One of her dead eyes was closed; the other nearly swollen shut. The agonized face was turned slightly toward him and buried up to the ears in her stomach cavity. He tried to bite off the sob and swatted angrily at the puzzled doctor, who put a comforting hand on his shoulder.

He rose on trembling legs and walked toward Gunny Barlow and Colonel Skaggs. They stood there like cement soldiers, grim expressions carved onto their faces. Why, Gunny? Why, sir? Why, why, why?

Barlow motioned with his head for Doc Grouse. There were no answers. Hell, he wasn't even sure he understood the questions. This kid . . . all these kids . . . have suffered enough. It ain't even a war and they got to see shit like this.

"Give him some pills or a shot, Doc. Whatever it takes. I want him unconscious for twenty-four hours."

The Doc waved his hand and Mallory's former squad members came forward to help evacuate the casualty. They all locked arms with Mallory in the middle and staggered away toward the CP.

Barlow watched them sadly until Colonel Skaggs got his attention.

"Any idea what happened?"

"Wasn't no fuckin' accident. Makin' a guess, I'd say the badasses saw her with Mallory during one of our contacts and decided to kill her."

"You guys get anything more out of her?"

"Nossir. Just that one last contact up by the corniche. She was supposed to be findin' out some more specific information. If she got it, she died with it."

"Anything we can do for young Mallory? You want to send him out to one of the ships for a few days?"

"Yessir. He's a good kid. Probably bounce back . . . but he's had enough. Talked to him some yesterday and he's . . . well, you know how it is when all the incoming seems to be aimed directly at you. He's takin' it personal. A lot of 'em are these days. Seems like this goddamn

Beirut . . . well, tomorrow's Sunday. He can fly out with
the Admin run right after chow."

Colonel Skaggs took a deep breath and massaged at the
dull ache that had been haunting his barrel chest for the past
few weeks. He knew the signs but he supposed Mallory's
heart was in worse shape just now.

"You know, I knew this is what we'd find when I got the
call. Jesus! So senseless . . . makes me feel like hell
about all this."

Colonel Skaggs reached inside his uniform pocket and
unfolded Masra's visa for the United States. An Embassy
driver had delivered it last night with Colonel Cameron's
compliments.

"Give it to Mallory, Harlan. At least he'll know we did
our best for her . . . for him."

Barlow glanced at the official document briefly and then
slowly tore it to shreds. A chilly evening wind scattered the
pieces like confetti across the Marine compound.

"Let him focus on the bastards who did this, sir. Might
help . . . a little. Won't do him any good to know how
close we came to getting her out. Mallory was . . . well,
he loved her . . . something like that."

When Barlow made his way back to the BLT CP, Doc
Grouse met him in the open-air foyer. Mallory was sedated.
The squad members were taking turns watching him.

"OK, Doc. Thanks. Watch him close and let me know if
there's any trouble. I'll be up at the Commodore tonight.
You guys have him up at zero-dark-thirty and ready to
leave. He goes out of The Root for good tomorrow."

Despite exorbitant bribes and the best efforts of a virtually
unflappable staff, the Commodore Hotel was finally suc-
cumbing to the increasingly brutal battle for Beirut. Most of
the American and British reporters Barlow knew at
the unofficial press center were already gone to Cyprus,

Jerusalem, Athens or Damascus to await developments in a more moderate climate. Lebanese stringers were left with enough money to bribe their way into the phone system.

A monotonous menu of violence and vitriolic rhetoric from a confusing plethora of radical factions was the standard report from Beirut these days. Brief "situationers" were the only stories likely to make network newscasts or national headlines. The first team could be employed elsewhere on more difficult stories.

Barlow lurched slightly under the load he'd taken on before leaving the compound. He stepped over the staged suitcases and equipment crates in the lobby and saw evidence of the reporters' black humor. A hand-lettered sign hung on the entrance to the shuttered bar where much of the real investigative work in Beirut was done in better times.

CARAVELLE HOTEL—SAIGON '75
COMMODORE HOTEL—BEIRUT '83
DÉJÀ VU?

Bloodshot roadmaps had been drawn into the CBS eye logo. Beneath it, a crew member had marked a question: "Was it something we said?" As he walked down the dank corridor toward Al Walters's room, Barlow noted several other signs stapled on doors to rooms vacated by various correspondents. The wit and wisdom of the Western Press. Barlow shifted the whiskey bottles he was carrying and tried to read in the dim light from the sole surviving generator.

"Gone to Damascus. This is no joke! I'm very Syrian about the situation in the Middle East." "Desperately seeking safety . . . in El Salvador." "See you at the next shattering performance by Begin and the Jets." "Finally found reverse gear! Wire Washington ASAP."

Walters's door was open and his well-traveled baggage

was ready on the rumpled bed in his room. The reporter was out on the balcony overlooking the corniche, where he could watch the stroboscopic light show that made Beirut look like New York Harbor on the Fourth of July. Barlow slid into a seat next to Walters and handed over a bottle.

"Can't beat it, can you? Watchin' the war from a box seat."

Walters swallowed whiskey and grimaced. "Heard about the girl. How's Mallory taking it?"

"Over the edge, Al. Burn-out case. I'm sendin' him out to the ships tomorrow. If I can work my bolt, they'll send him all the way back Stateside. He don't need no more Beirut."

"You know what really pisses me off? We coulda done something for that girl. She . . . Christ, I don't know. She only wanted the killing to stop, y'know? Lots of Lebs feel the same way, but what the hell you gonna do when your government's a mess and all your neighbors want to turn your country into a parking lot?"

The whiskey made Barlow talkative. No need to pose or posture with Al Walters. Much of what they felt could go unsaid among men who had seen similar situations around the world.

"Guess we pushed her into something she couldn't handle. It ain't important now. Get involved in shit like this and you're gonna lose people all along the route. Way the game is played, Al. Sometimes the loss adds; sometimes it subtracts. I guess you just keep on keepin' on and hope the bottom line is plus instead of minus."

"Tell that to Mallory." Walters broke the seal on a second bottle of booze and passed it to Barlow.

"I did. He can't see it just now. But he will, eventually. We do what the Marine Corp wants us to do: Fuck, fight or go for your gun. In the end you just gonna hope it's the right thing. Get to thinkin' about it too much and you are surely fucked."

"Spoken like a true professional soldier."

"No more, Al. This is it for me. End of a long line. A country that won't fight don't deserve no professional soldiers."

Walters craned unsteadily over the wrought-iron balcony and watched the orange night-blossoms of incoming artillery around the airport. Big Time Saturday night in Beirut. The Marines of 24 MAU were being pounded again and their relief was delayed by yet another brush-fire war.

"You know what really frosted my ass, Harlan?"

Barlow slugged from the bottle and let the whiskey erode some of the painful weight in his chest. He shrugged and passed the drink to Walters.

"Today, when I took that wire service story out to the compound. Those kids were actually pissed because they had to be here instead of on Grenada with the 82d Airborne and the other Marines."

"Typical. Kid ships out for the action, and it always happens someplace else. They ain't in this to learn a trade or take advantage of the GI Bill. At least on Grenada they got to shoot back."

Walters polished off the whiskey Barlow brought and then exhausted his own supply. He offered Barlow a spare bed for the night. When the lights were out in the room, neither man could sleep despite the anesthetic.

"Jesus . . . after Vietnam, you'd think we'd learn to stop backing losers."

"It ain't a question of who we back, Al. Hang around with assholes; you're bound to get shit on. But that ain't important for a country like America, see? What's important is to shit once you're down on the pot. Can't walk into no war at half step. You either fix bayonets and go for the throat . . . or you don't walk onto the battlefield."

"Yeah, you'd have thought we'd learned that in Vietnam."

"You'd have thought so . . ."

Gripping the suicide switch tightly between his teeth, Ibrahim maneuvered the yellow garbage truck out of the tight alleys and onto the major thoroughfares of West Beirut. He would make a wide swing around the hotel district and onto the broad street that led south toward Kaldeh. At the intersection near Chatilla, he would swing left and begin his run along the main airport access road. He had the route completely memorized. It was the only detail he allowed to remain on his mind during an all-night prayer vigil.

When the truck was stabilized and running in a modest third gear past the headquarters of United Nations Forces in Lebanon, Ibrahim carefully took the firing switch in his left hand and glanced over his shoulder to watch the first pale, pink fingers of dawn stretch toward Beirut. The tears came and he was glad that none of his staid Hezbollah fellows could see him. There had been enough embarrassment over the woman.

Ibrahim had planned on becoming a very powerful man in the great Persian Empire that would rise from the ashes when the *jihad* was won and the infidels driven from this land. Now he would have to accept his reward in heaven.

A lone American Marine was drinking from a steaming cup outside the Commodore Hotel as Ibrahim wheeled his truck along an intersecting street. The man glanced at the garbage truck only briefly before climbing into his jeep. Ibrahim shifted gears cautiously and continued to drive sedately to avoid suspicion.

That one will escape. If Allah is kind on this glorious morning, he will be the only one. *Ins'allah.*

* * *

Barlow spilled hot coffee in his lap as he swung the jeep onto the airport access road. His watch said 0615. If he didn't run into traffic, he'd make it back in time for hot chow. And he'd be able to have a last word with Steve Mallory before the young Marine left Beirut.

Dawn light illuminated the overnight agony of the city. A smoking hulk along the right side of the road had run into the blast and shrapnel pattern of a rocket from the foothills. An old Soviet T-34 tank had been quickly called to active service, and just as quickly destroyed by an RPG. Local nationalists had quickly taken advantage of a fresh easel and painted their sentiments where the Marines were sure to see them. "American . . . out Beirut!"

Not to fret, fellas. Won't be long now unless I miss my guess. In fact, I'll pass along your druthers, soon as I can get around that yellow garbage truck up there. Holy fuckin' Christ! The girl . . . what did she say? They're gonna use a yellow Mercedes truck.

Gunny Barlow jammed the jeep into a lower gear and roared up the slope overlooking BIA. The yellow truck was accelerating now and swinging wide right for a left turn. He knew from the angle the target must be the BLT CP, where more than two hundred men—Steve Mallory among them— were just beginning to stir out of sleep.

Corporal Rojas carried Mallory's seabag down the broad stone stairs that led into the central area of the barracks. Deeter Dale had his former squad leader's pack and other equipment. Doc Grouse left the group to let the duty NCO know they would be taking Mallory down to the LZ. Stone was outside on guard duty. He'd say his farewells as the group walked through the gate and escorted a departing buddy toward the first outbound helicopter.

There was not much to say. Even the whispered attempts at humor echoed around the silent corridors like voices from a tomb. Mallory smiled weakly at his friends. There was a great deal he wanted to express, but the words would not form in his mind or his mouth. Steve Mallory was numb from the Darvon Doc Grouse had pressed into his hands with a steaming canteen cup of black coffee.

"Be back in a coupla days," he mumbled. "Soon as I get my shit together. You guys take care . . ." It was all he could manage.

Doc Grouse put an arm around his shoulder, motioned to the escort party and headed for the double doors leading out of the CP.

Stone waved to the men he could see heading out of the barracks toward his post. He was about to yell a greeting, when the whine of a tightly wound transmission and the roar of a laboring engine caused him to spin toward the approach road.

What the hell? Mallory's departure was forgotten in a rush of paranoia. He's headed right for us! What's he doin'?

Stone and his fellow sentry simultaneously decided it didn't make any difference what the lunatic at the wheel of the oncoming garbage truck was doing. They grabbed M-16s off their shoulders and fumbled to jack a round into the chambers.

Stone heard shouts of alarm from observers on the roof of the building. He had time for just one quick shot as the grill of the Mercedes filled his sights.

Gunny Barlow screamed in utter rage and frustration. His jeep was careening at top speed down the hill toward the compound, but he could see he would be too late. He hadn't prayed since that dark day in 1968 outside An Hoa. Maybe his account was still good. It was 0620.

Please, God. I never asked for much . . . but I need this one. Let him be gone. Let the kid live. Please.

Ibrahim strained against the accelerator pedal until he was nearly rigid and diagnoal in the seat. A shot shattered the passenger side windshield but he knew the mission would succeed. He was jarred violently as the truck crashed and bounded over several lengths of pipe that had been placed across the main access route into the parking lot.

As the truck plowed through rows of sandbags and an open entryway rushed toward him filling his field of vison, Ibrahim saw five Americans standing with their arms linked. He roared and laughed wildly. Did the fools suppose a wall of weak flesh would stop a warrior of the Hezbollah?

Ibrahim heard the meaty smack of muscle and bone being crushed by his bumper just as the truck crashed into the barracks interior and unclenched his left hand.

As predicted, the revered hero of the *jihad* went to his God in a bloody spray of glory.

Nearly blinded by the shock wave of the huge explosion that rolled over him, Gunnery Sergeant Barlow jammed on the brakes and squinted at the mushroom cloud that rose boiling from the ruins of the Battalion Landing Team Command Post. It looked like one of the low-yield tactical nuclear explosions he'd seen in countless training films.

A cold wind was sucked into the explosive vacuum from somewhere out in the Mediterranean and he knew without having to check that Steve Mallory had perished in the blast. In a rage, Barlow grabbed the shotgun from the seat of the jeep and emptied the magazine at nothing. There was nothing worth killing left in Beirut and—for the first time in his long military career—the solid jolt of a recoiling weapon was no comfort.

They'd been dammed up for a long time, so the tears

came easily and freely. He let them spill . . . for Steve Mallory; for Masra; for the Marines and sailors who died with the last vestiges of hope for peace in Lebanon.

Later, when the recriminations and accusations began, there would be no time for tears. The dead would be forgotten in the rush to find a scapegoat among the living. It would never be as great as the one made by the men who died in the bombing, but a sacrifice would be required to curb the nation's outrage.

Epilogue

_____ DESPITE THE UPBEAT messages of hope carried by the churchmen, politicians and generals who attended the memorial services at Camp Lejeune, it was a maudlin affair. Gunnery Sergeant Barlow attended only to insure the color detail and the squad firing the traditional rifle salute to the dead didn't screw it up. It was the least he could do in his last few days of active service.

Colonel Skaggs stood quietly beside him in the last row of the survivors' section. He was odds-on favorite for the chopping block now that Congress was sharpening the axe and officially asking everyone with an opinion just what the hell happened in Beirut. The Old Man would take it stoically—telling the truth as he knew it and trusting the system—even though he knew it would gut him in the final analysis.

Beirut was a strange situation, but odd missions had never altered the ultimate military reality. Like all field commanders throughout the history of warfare, he would be held accountable for the destiny of his men. All other considerations were eyewash and they'd be blinked away before the final note of Echo Taps faded in the muggy air over Camp Lejeune.

Ahead of Skaggs and Barlow—many in bandages, leaning on crutches or seated in wheelchairs—were the men who survived the bombing. A tight, terrible anger showed in their faces. For these men, nothing else in life would seem significant. All events—happy or sad—would be measured against the emotional yardstick of their service in Beirut. They were the new generation of stone soldiers. Barlow had seen it before. He knew the symptoms.

Arrayed in black or somber colors on either side of the survivors were the widows, orphans and grieving parents. Nothing in their lives would ever be the same either but the outward indicators were different among the civilians. They were shocked and confused. If God was up there, somewhere above this gathering of True Believers seeking solace, He'd be deafened by a resounding chorus of voices asking only one question.

Why?

Barlow didn't have an answer. All the souvenirs, trappings and trinkets that had brought him solace from past campaigns were stored. He kept little more than the uniform on his back and a bus ticket to Illinois, where he planned to spend a few days with Mallory's parents. It seemed like the right thing to do and for once in his life—despite orders to the contrary or implications of personal remorse—Gunnery Sergeant Harlan Barlow intended to do the right thing.

Giving Colonel Skaggs's elbow a firm squeeze, he faded into the background with the last bugle notes, chased by sobs and moans from the crowd. He had nearly made it to the bus stop when he was ambushed by a TV news crew. The reporter wielding the microphone did his best to be somber and respectful.

"Sergeant, can you give us your thoughts? What did the Marines accomplish with their service in Beirut?"

Barlow stared into the polished lens and let the truth come up from his guts.

"Not a motherfucking thing!"

"SHATTERING." —*Newsweek*

PLATOON

They were the men of Bravo Company. Officers and grunts. Black and white. All of them Americans. It was war that brought them together—and it was war that would tear them apart.

A novel by Dale A. Dye
based on a screenplay by Oliver Stone

___Platoon 1-55773-092-9/$3.50

290

Tom Clancy's

#1 NEW YORK TIMES BESTSELLERS

___ **THE HUNT FOR RED OCTOBER**   0-425-08383-7/$5.50
"The Perfect Yarn."—President Ronald Reagan
"A fine thriller... flawless authenticity, frighteningly
genuine."—*The Wall Street Journal*

___ **RED STORM RISING**   0-425-10107-X/$5.95
"Brilliant...staccato suspense."—*Newsweek*
"Exciting...fast and furious."—*USA Today*

___ **PATRIOT GAMES**   0-425-10972-0/$5.95
"Elegant...A novel that crackles."—*New York Times*
"Marvelously tense...He is a master of the genre he seems to
have created."—*Publishers Weekly*

___ **THE CARDINAL OF THE KREMLIN** 0-425-11684-0/$5.95
"The best of the Jack Ryan series!"—*New York Times*
"Fast and fascinating!"—*Chicago Tribune*